"I spent this whole morning thinking I was going to be stuck with a bunch of, like, mindless Catholic sheep people for the next two years," I say. "I'm so glad I'm not the only one."

"Not the only what?" Lucy asks.

"You know," I say, taking a bite out of my grilled cheese. "The only atheist."

Lucy and Avi look at each other. Avi laughs. Lucy doesn't.

"I'm not an atheist," she says.

"Agnostic, then," I say. "Whatever."

"No," Lucy says. "I'm Catholic."

A bite of grilled cheese sticks in my throat. "What?" I cough. "But all the stuff you said in class—"

"I said those things because I'm Catholic. Sister Joseph Marie was diminishing the bravery of women who died for their God." She pauses. "And my God, too."

Oh, shit.

I have few talents, but I am indisputably a world champion in destroying a friendship before it ever starts. I try to catalog how many ways I insulted her religion. At least three.

HERETICS ANONYMOUS

KATIE HENRY

KATHERINE TEGEN BOOKS

An Imprint of HarperCollins Publishers

Katherine Tegen Books is an imprint of HarperCollins Publishers.

Heretics Anonymous

Copyright © 2018 by Catherine Henry

www.epicreads.com

Library of Congress Cataloging-in-Publication Data
Names: Henry, Katie, author.
Title: Heretics Anonymous / Katie Henry.
Description: First edition. | New York, NY : Katherine Tegen Books, an imprint of HarperCollins Publishers, [2018] | Summary: When nonbeliever Michael transfers to a Catholic school in eleventh grade, he quickly connects with a secret support group intent on exposing the school's hypocrisies one stunt at a time.
Identifiers: LCCN 2017034682 | ISBN 978-0-06-269888-9
Subjects: | CYAC: Conduct of life—Fiction. | Catholic schools—Fiction. | Schools—Fiction. | Faith—Fiction. | Self-help groups—Fiction. | Family problems—Fiction.
Classification: LCC PZ7.1H4646 Her 2018 | DC [Fic]—dc23 LC record available at https://lccn.loc.gov/2017034682

Typography by David Curtis
19 20 21 22 23   PC/LSCH   10 9 8 7 6 5 4 3 2 1
❖
First paperback edition, 2019

For my grandmother, who taught me how to read,

how to pray the Rosary, and how to think for myself

THE ANONYMOUS CREED

We believe in one God, and many gods, and the possibility of none,
And also that the existence of the almighty is largely irrelevant,
Because regardless of who is maker of heaven and earth,
It is our duty to care for all of creation, both visible and invisible.

We believe in one fundamental truth:
That all people, regardless of what they worship, who they love, and
what they think
Have a right to exist, and a right to be heard.
We strive to make faith consubstantial with reason and compassion,
Through which all good things are made.

We believe in the goodness of humankind (with a few notable exceptions),
The worth of listening to our friends and understanding our enemies,
The power of a single voice in a silent room,
And the practicality of cloaks and other assorted historical outerwear.
We do not all believe in one holy, catholic, and apostolic church
But are nonetheless grateful that it brought us together.

We strive to remember that high school will not last forever
And look forward to graduation day
And the life of that world to come.

Amen.

1

THERE IS SOMETHING truly evil about plaid.

It might look like just a crisscrossed grid of colors, but in my experience, much like comets and black cats, plaid is a harbinger of doom. The amateur bagpiper who played at my grandpa's funeral wore plaid. The scratchy suit I was stuffed into three Christmases in a row was plaid. Dad's boss, who promoted Dad and is therefore ultimately responsible for the disaster my life has become, probably wears plaid boxer shorts. The evil has to be hiding somewhere.

And eviler than all other plaid things is the monstrosity I'm staring at from across my bedroom like it's a tartan rattlesnake.

"It's a *tie*, Michael," Mom said after I opened the package from the school uniform supplier last week and threatened to test out how flame-retardant the polyester fabric really was. "You've worn them before."

Yeah, to funerals and dinners with grandparents at stuffy,

boring country clubs. Not to school. I've been to four different schools—two public, one private, and one "experimental learning community"—and none of them required ties.

There are lots of things Mom promised would be no big deal. Like moving for the fourth time in ten years. Or changing schools a month and a half into eleventh grade. Or switching from a public school that observes "winter" break to a school whose motto is *Deus Meus et Omnia*—My God and My All. So far, she's been epically wrong about all those things, so there's no real reason to trust her about the tie.

In fifteen minutes, I have to leave for what should be the second Monday in October but is instead my first day at a school I've never even seen. The plaid tie sits on top of a box of books I still haven't unpacked. It's mocking me.

I grab the tie and loop it around my neck, under the collar of the Mandatory Required white button-up shirt that's only half tucked into the Mandatory Required stiff navy pants. I can't remember exactly how to put the tie on.

Attempt #1: I go under instead of over, and it twists and curls into itself like a birthday party noisemaker.

Attempt #2: I measure wrong, and the skinny half sticks out three inches from behind the fat half.

Attempt #3: It's inside out. I put it on inside out.

This must be what someone about to be hanged feels like, how the noose feels so limp and harmless even though it's going to slowly, painfully suck the life out of him.

I should have asked Dad to give me a refresher course in Basic Man Skills before he got on the red-eye for Brussels last night, but that would have interfered with my record-breaking six days of not talking to him. It would be one thing if we moved all the time because we had to, if Dad was a soldier or a diplomat or an escaped convict. But in reality, Dad's job has something to do with sales and the importation of plastic pool covers, and we move each time he reaches for that next rung on the corporate ladder.

I give up on getting the tie straight and pick up the final piece of my uniform, a navy blazer with a patch over the left breast that reads ST. CLARE'S PREPARATORY SCHOOL. They could have called it HELL and saved on the embroidery costs.

Some people are cut out to follow a higher being, like God or the hosts of the Home Shopping Network, but there are other people, people like me, who find it harder to follow the whims of parents or teachers or two-thousand-year-old undead Jewish mystics with strong opinions on divorce.

I didn't lose my faith or anything. I never had it in the first place. I never believed in any kind of God, just like I never believed in werewolves, or ghosts, or that mixing Pop Rocks and soda would make your stomach explode. Okay, I did believe that last one, but only until A. J. Rubin pushed a can of Coke and a bag of rock candy across our kindergarten lunch table and dared me to try. So I did, and my stomach didn't explode. And as I gulped down the rest of the soda, I had my first epiphany: just because a person says something is true doesn't mean it is, and anyone who tells you otherwise is probably trying to keep you from doing something fun.

The next year, when I was seven, I gave a presentation on the unlikelihood of Santa Claus for show-and-tell, but Amy Buckley burst into tears two sentences in and ruined the whole thing. In middle school, I put together a list ranking religions from most plausible to least plausible and shared my findings at Christmas dinner, which caused my great-grandmother to reroute my Christmas money to her church collection plate.

And now, at sixteen, older and wiser and dressed like a middle-aged investment banker, I'm preparing to face the greatest challenge of my nonbelieving life:

Catholic school.

2

FOR THE FIRST priest I've seen in real life, Father Peter is disappointing. I was half hoping to meet one straight out of *The Exorcist*, black robes and giant crucifixes, or maybe a medieval friar with the top of his head shaved, but Father Peter looks like every principal I've ever had: middle-aged, glasses, joyless. If I didn't know he'd devoted his life to indoctrinating impressionable children and never getting laid, he'd almost look normal.

He scans some papers in a manila folder and then glances across his desk at me. "Michael Ausman," he says, and I nod even though it isn't a question. "I see you've come to us very highly recommended by our board member Craig Collins."

It wasn't enough for Dad's boss to uproot my family last minute, oh no, he also had to arrange my acceptance at the area's best private school. I would have preferred the local public school. It's huge. The bigger the school, the easier it is to blend in.

"It's unusual for a student to enter after the semester's already begun—"

Maybe for him. I've done it before.

"—but your grades from your previous school show you're a competent student, so I can't imagine you'll struggle to catch up, will you?"

"No," I say.

Father Peter raises an eyebrow. "No, what?"

My left leg is cramping. "No, I won't struggle to catch up?"

Father Peter shakes his head. "No, *Father*," he supplies.

My throat goes dry. I am not going to call this man with bitten-down nails and dandruff flakes on his sweater *Father*. I already have a father, even if I'm this close to filing for emancipation.

Father Peter drums his fingers on his desk in a way that tells me I'm not getting out of this office with my dignity intact.

"No, Father," I say, with more breath than words.

He sighs and gets up from his desk. "Ms. Edison will give you your schedule. First period starts in ten minutes."

I start for the door, but Father Peter's voice jerks me back. "I haven't dismissed you yet, Mr. Ausman," he says. "Before you go, I want you to understand something—my job at St. Clare's is to mold young men and women into leaders in their church and their community. Whether or not you enjoy that process is irrelevant." His face softens. "But I've been at this school for two decades, so I can tell you from experience: being here is only a punishment if you make it one. You're dismissed."

No one under the age of forty has talked to me yet. A boy sharing my lab table gives me a quick once-over as he sits down, but then turns away. I have three classes before lunch, which means I have three hours to forcibly insert myself into someone's friend group. That's all you need—one person to eat lunch with on the first day. Understanding any complex social hierarchies can come later.

There's static from the loudspeaker, and the class quiets down.

"Gooood morning, St. Clare's!" The kid on the intercom is so cheerful I instantly hate him. "Let's give thanks for another beautiful day, in the name of the Father, the Son, and the Holy Spirit."

As if connected by strings, the entire class crosses themselves, perfectly synchronized. I swipe clumsily up, down, then across my body, finishing at least two seconds behind everyone else. The loudspeaker voice has already moved on.

"It's October ninth, the feast day of Saint Denis, patron saint of Paris, France, and rabies victims. Here are today's announcements—"

Standard reminders for SAT sign-ups, chamber choir auditions, and volleyball games follow, and for a second I feel like I'm in my old school again, wondering if we'll get to blow anything up during lab.

"Please bow your heads for morning prayer."

So much for that.

After an uncomfortably long prayer I barely understand, my chem teacher starts to write lab procedures on the board. Someone taps my shoulder, and I turn around to see a girl with wheat-colored hair, a gold cross around her neck, and a uniform shirt buttoned all the way up to the top. She's sort of cute, in an Amish kind of way, and I'm willing to look past the cross necklace if it means someone will treat me like I'm not invisible.

"Hi," I say. "I'm—"

"You did it backward," she says with a seriousness usually reserved for presidential funerals.

I look back at her, confused, and her mouth twists.

"You crossed yourself backward," she clarifies.

"Oh," I say. "Yeah, I haven't had tons of practice, so—"

"It's up, down, left, right." She mimes it slowly, like I'm a stupid golden retriever.

"What," I joke. "Does it summon Satan if I do it backward?"

"No," she says, narrowing her eyes, "but it's wrong."

I suddenly get the feeling she's not telling me this because she cares if I get it right next time. She's telling me because it makes her feel smarter for already knowing.

"That's too bad," I say. "I was hoping for a Lucifer sighting."

"That's not funny," she says. My brain agrees with her. My mouth does not give a shit.

"I'm not joking." I put on my best earnest face. "Do you know how I could do it? Is there a spell? Ritual sacrifice?" I lean closer. "Do you think Satan prefers goats or sheep? I've had the hardest time finding a baby."

The girl stares at me, then spins back around, probably plotting her own personal American Inquisition.

It's first period and only one person definitely wants me dead. Things are going better than expected.

By third period, I'm exhausted, and the three-floor climb to my next class doesn't help. I'm so sick of getting lost in hallways. Dad promised I wouldn't have to do this again, he promised I could stay in one place for high school. But the second he got a better offer, the moving boxes came out, just like always. I don't know what I expected.

As I struggle up the steep, narrow staircase, I look at my schedule.

PERIOD 3: HISTORY—SR. JOSEPH

What the hell does that mean, SR. JOSEPH? The only thing I can think of "SR" standing for is "Sir." Sir Joseph. Maybe he's a knight.

I reach the classroom as the bell rings, panting from the climb, but I'm not greeted by a man with a lance and a full suit of armor. Instead, it's a stout, dour woman in a calf-length gray dress, her hair and ears hidden under a black head covering. My teacher isn't a knight. She's a nun.

"You're the new one?" she asks.

"Yes," I say. "Michael."

"I'm Sister Joseph Marie. You can call me Sister."

Sister. Father. It's like getting a whole other family I don't want to spend time with.

She points to an empty chair near the back. "Have a seat there. The class is presenting reports on American historical figures today, so you'll observe for now."

I sit. If I want any chance of making it out of this place alive, I'm going to have to find a friend. Not a best friend or anything sappy like that—just close enough to eat with. Close enough to get invited to parties. But not too close. A surface-level friend, the kind of person you can leave behind if you have to.

Sister Joseph Marie selects her first victim, a girl named Jenny Okoye. She seems terrified of everyone in the room, so I dismiss her as a potential friend almost immediately.

"My presentation is on civil rights activist Diane Nash," she begins, tucking a few of her long black braids behind her ear.

"Louder, please," Sister Joseph Marie says. "They can't hear you in the back. Or the front."

Jenny looks helplessly at her stone-faced classmates and tries again. "DianeNashledthefirstsuccessfulcampaign—"

Sister Joseph Marie pinches the bridge of her nose. "Miss Okoye, it's not a race."

Jenny holds her pink notecards in a death grip. "Diane Nash," she forces out, "was only twenty-two years old when she led the first successful campaign to integrate lunch counters in

Nashville, Tennessee. She was arrested dozens of times during her decades of activism, which only goes to show that well-behaved women rarely make history."

Sister Joseph Marie rises from her desk, holding up her hand for Jenny to stop. "I would like to make a brief historical correction here. Well-behaved women often make history. They're called saints."

Before Jenny can faint, die of embarrassment, or both, a clear voice pipes up from directly in front of me.

"Sister, you can't be serious."

I didn't even glance at the girl in the seat in front of mine before I sat down, and now all I can see is the back of a starched uniform blouse, a lint-free sweater vest, and a tumble of dark brown hair tied back with a red ribbon.

Sister Joseph Marie raises her eyes to the heavens. "If I wasn't serious, I wouldn't have said it."

"But that's not true," Red Ribbon says. "Well-behaved women *don't* make history. Saints included."

I've been at this school for exactly 122 minutes and 46 seconds—not that I'm timing—and even I know this penguin lady with a dude's name is not a person to cross. But none of my classmates look surprised.

Sister Joseph Marie clears her throat. "Miss Peña, I'm sure you're not suggesting any of the saints recognized by the Holy Roman Catholic Church behaved in any way unsuited to their status, are you?"

Red Ribbon tilts her head to the side, considering. "No."

13

"Good. Now, Miss Okoye, if you'll—"

"Joan of Arc," Red Ribbon cuts in, "was sentenced to burn at the stake by a church court because she wouldn't wear a skirt."

"Saint Joan's trial was a bit more complicated than that."

"Saint Mary MacKillop was excommunicated for insubordination."

"That was lifted," snaps Sister Joseph Marie as Jenny edges back to her seat.

"Saint Catherine was martyred because she wouldn't marry who she was supposed to; so were Saint Agnes and Saint Agatha and Saint Lucy."

"They were martyred because they were committed to chastity," Sister Joseph Marie says. "That's different."

"What about Saint Clare?" Red Ribbon gestures at the school banner hanging above the whiteboard. "The saint this school is named for ran away from her parents when she was eighteen because she didn't want to get married, and then decided to live in the woods with Francis of Assisi, who was basically a giant weirdo who really liked animals. Do you actually think *she* would have been considered *well behaved*?"

Sister Joseph Marie waves the question away. "Take it up with your theology teacher," she says, "because you're getting very close to blasphemy." The girl in front of me takes a long, deep breath in, shoulders hitching and ribbon quivering.

"Well, if you're going to ignore the fact that most of those women chose to *die* rather than do what other people told them to, then I think *you're* pretty close to blasphemy."

There's something about Red Ribbon's voice, I think, as I watch Sister Joseph Marie cycle through several shades of red. It's clear and steady and urgent, like she's used to being interrupted. It sounds like the flute my sister plays, the way it can soar into the highest notes without sounding squeaky, how it can sound like an instrument three times its size.

As Sister Joseph Marie, now a color closest to eggplant, writes furiously on a pink detention slip, I decide I know two things to be true:

1. The girl with the red ribbon is out of her mind.

2. She's going to be my new best friend.

I learn a third absolute truth as I dart through the hallways after history ends: tailing someone is a lot harder when everyone's wearing the same outfit.

I have to talk to this girl. She's got to be a nonbeliever like me, or Sister Joseph Marie wouldn't have accused her of blasphemy. That's what they tell people right before they burn them at the stake. I saw it on the History Channel. At worst, she's an agnostic, and that isn't a deal breaker.

I push through the crowd, following brief flashes of red as the girl moves at a rapid clip. I could catch up with her, but I have no idea what I'd say if I did. *Hi, my name's Michael, are you also a depraved sinner? Hey, I'm Michael, want to have lunch and discuss the obvious absence of a loving God?* She turns at the end of the hall, past a statue of a sad-eyed Virgin Mary.

I skid around the corner, desperate not to lose sight of her in the sea of plaid, and suddenly find myself face-to-face with a dark-haired girl whose brown eyes are looking at me suspiciously. The tail end of a red ribbon peeks out from behind her ear.

"Hi," I say.

"Hi," she says. "Why are you following me?"

"I'm Michael." I stick out my hand, and immediately wish I'd wiped it on my pants first. She ignores it.

"Okay. Why are you following me, *Michael*?"

"I'm in your history class."

"You're also really bad at answering questions."

I put my hand down, my face prickling.

"I just—" I scramble for something to say that doesn't make me sound like an unhinged stalker. "I wanted to tell you I thought it was really cool what you did in class. How you stood up to her."

Red Ribbon's face softens for a split second, then tightens right back up. She hugs her book bag to her chest. "I didn't do it to be *cool*. I said it because I really believe it."

"I can tell," I say.

"Oh." She relaxes her grip on the book bag.

"So . . . I wanted to tell you that."

"Why?"

Because your voice sounds like the flute my sister has. Creepy. *Because I know we're the same.* Doubly creepy. *Because it's lunch*

16

and I don't know where to go. Creepy, desperate, and sad.

"I didn't want you to feel like you were alone, in thinking what you said," I tell her. "That sucks, and I feel like it probably sucks more here than other places."

She looks me up and down carefully. "I've never seen you before."

"I'm new."

"I'm Lucy." She swings her book bag onto her shoulder. "Do you want a tour?"

3

AS LUCY AND I wend our way down spiral staircases and in and out of corridors that occasionally lead to nowhere, I wish I had a map. And I wish Lucy, who walks as fast as she talks, would slow down.

"The school nurse is around that corner, to the left, but seriously, don't bother, she's not even allowed to give you Advil unless you have a note, and the teachers' lounge is that room to the left of the Saint Francis statue, though I can't think of why you'd need to go *there*."

She finally takes a breath and I wonder if I should have been recording her. Lucy showed me the whole school, top to bottom, but now that we're on the ground floor, I can barely remember my own name.

"And to conclude our tour," Lucy says, pushing open a heavy oak door, "this is the dining hall."

"You mean the cafeteria?"

She shrugs. "I've never heard anyone call it that."

As soon as I step inside, I decide "dining hall" is the more appropriate word. Cafeterias have metal tables and tubs of limp vegetables. They smell like burnt pizza and grease. This place has dark wood tables and smells like freshly squeezed lemons. I grab a grilled cheese sandwich and sweet potato fries before meeting up with Lucy in the salad bar line.

"Hey, Lucy," says the boy ahead of her in line, who I recognize from history. He has his arm wrapped all the way around a pretty girl's waist, looking like a possessive toddler with a teddy bear. "Are we ever going to have a class where you don't go off on some feminist rant?" The girl beside him giggles.

"I don't know, Connor," Lucy says, examining a bottle of salad dressing. "Are we ever going to have an assembly where you don't try to fingerbang your girlfriend in the back of the auditorium?"

The girl goes pink. Connor quickly steers his girlfriend out of the food line, glaring at Lucy over his shoulder.

"During an assembly?" I ask Lucy.

"That's what Jason Everett said, and he was sitting right behind them." I must look shocked, because she nods at the crowd of uniformed students sitting down to lunch. "Don't let the kilts fool you. This is still high school."

Lucy leads me to a table where a tall boy with glasses sits reading a book, alternating between turning pages and shoveling spoonfuls of pudding into his mouth.

19

He doesn't look up as we sit down, still frowning at the book.

"What the hell does *mirabile dictu* mean?" he asks.

"You're still on that section of the *Aeneid*?" Lucy says. "It was due like last week."

"I'm aware. Does *mirabile dictu* mean 'strange to say' or does it mean 'wonderful to say'?"

"It means both," Lucy says. "Strange and wonderful. Miraculous."

"It can't be both, that doesn't make any sense," the boy says.

"I think it does. Aren't most wonderful things a little bit strange?"

"Whatever." He closes the book and notices me for the first time. "Who's this?"

"A stray," Lucy says before I can answer myself. The back of my neck gets hot. A stray?

"I'm Michael," I say. "It's my first day."

"I'm Avi," he says, "and normally I'd try to get to know you better, but I'm right in the middle of failing Latin."

"I'll write out the translation for you," Lucy offers.

"Yes, please," he says, sliding the book toward her.

"If," she continues, "you sign my detention slip." She holds out the crumpled, salmon-colored notice between two fingers. Avi's face falls.

"What did you do?" he says, managing to sound both reproachful and bored.

20

"Sister Joseph Marie and I had a minor theological disagreement. Sign it?"

He shakes his head. "You're going to get caught."

"I have orchestra practice after school, I can't miss it," she says. "Mr. Mead is on detention duty today, I checked. You're great at his signature. Please?"

Avi looks too straitlaced to commit forgery in a crowded cafeteria, and I expect him to refuse, but he sighs and accepts the detention slip, looking warily over his shoulder.

"You could always stop arguing with teachers," he says as he signs the slip. "Then we wouldn't have to do this."

"This time it was necessary." She glances over at me. "Michael thought it was cool."

Avi looks up at me. His eyes narrow. "Did he?"

"Yeah," I say. "It was awesome."

"See?" Lucy says to Avi, and flashes me a smile.

"Especially all the stuff about the saints," I say. "I mean, I have no idea who any of those people are, but it was so smart, you found a way to use her own religious bullshit against her."

Lucy stops smiling, but I can't stop talking. "I spent this whole morning thinking I was going to be stuck with a bunch of, like, mindless Catholic sheep people for the next two years," I say. "I'm so glad I'm not the only one."

"Not the only what?" Lucy asks.

"You know," I say, taking a bite out of my grilled cheese. "The only atheist."

Lucy and Avi look at each other. Avi laughs. Lucy doesn't.

21

"I'm not an atheist," she says.

"Agnostic, then," I say. "Whatever."

"No," Lucy says. "I'm Catholic."

A bite of grilled cheese sticks in my throat. "What?" I cough. "But all the stuff you said in class—"

"I said those things because I'm Catholic. Sister Joseph Marie was diminishing the bravery of women who died for their God." She pauses. "And my God, too."

Oh, shit.

I have few talents, but I am indisputably a world champion in destroying a friendship before it ever starts. I try to catalog how many ways I insulted her religion. At least three.

"But don't worry," Lucy continues. "You won't be surrounded by—what was it? *Sheep* people?"

Well, when she says it like that, I sound like an unbelievable asshole. Probably because I am an unbelievable asshole.

"Believing in something doesn't make me a sheep, and it doesn't make me stupid," Lucy says. "I mean, there are awful people at this school, there totally are, but they aren't mindless. Except maybe Connor." She glances over to where Connor sits, pouring hot sauce into his mouth as his friends laugh hysterically. "But I don't think that has much to do with his religion."

I want to tell her I'm sorry, I didn't mean what I'd said. But I did mean it, and that makes it worse.

"I'm—I didn't—"

"It's fine," she says, waving it off. "It's your first day. Twenty-four-hour grace period."

"Really?" I say.

"We sheep people are big believers in grace," Lucy says.

Avi leans in. "If it makes you feel better, the first time I had lunch with Lucy, I asked her if she blamed my people for killing Jesus."

"Which, to be clear, I don't," Lucy says.

"But to be fair, it has historical precedent," Avi points out.

"You're Jewish?" I ask. He nods. "But like—*how* Jewish?"

"It's not a math equation," Lucy says.

"I light candles on Chanukah," Avi says. "I eat my body weight in hamantaschen on Purim and sat shiva when my grandma died." He puts his finished bowl of pudding back on his tray. "But tomorrow, I'm going to have a carnitas taco for lunch, because I don't think pork is unclean. I think the ancient Israelites were smart to avoid it, because it goes bad fast and it can make you sick, but I'm not an ancient Israelite. And I trust the lunch ladies."

"But still, you have a religion," I say. "You both do."

"What do you think this is?" Lucy asks me. "The Albigensian Crusade?"

"I have no idea what that means."

"It means no one cares you're an atheist. Actually—" She pauses, and there's a glint in her eye. "That might be really great," she says, but weirdly, she's looking at Avi when she says it.

"Why?" I say, feeling like I've missed something.

"You know, for some fresh blood," she says, still looking at Avi, not me. He gives the smallest shake of his head, and she shrugs but looks disappointed.

"What do you have after lunch?" Lucy asks. I dig my schedule out of my backpack.

"Theology," I tell her. "With . . . seriously? Another nun?"

She leans over my shoulder to look, and her red ribbon brushes against my chin. Her hair smells like vanilla extract and what I think might be incense.

"Oh, but it's Sister Helen," she says. "She's sweet, you'll like her. Avi and I are both in that class, we'll take you."

We go to bus our trays, and at the trash cans is the blond girl from chemistry. Lunch doesn't seem to have improved her mood. When she sees us, she glances from me to Lucy and Avi, then heaves a long-suffering sigh. "Typical," she mutters as she pushes past us.

"That's Theresa," Avi says. "Lovely girl. Really personable."

"Yeah, we met," I say. "I don't think she likes me very much."

"You're in excellent company," Lucy says.

When we reach Sister Helen's classroom, Lucy lets Avi go in first, then turns around, smiling like she's about to lead me into a surprise party. Like she knows something I haven't figured out yet. Something strange and wonderful.

"Don't worry," she tells me. "There's room at this school for people like us."

Us?

As I follow her through the door, I hold on to that word like it's a life preserver.

WHEN THE BELL rings at the end of sixth period and all of St. Clare's streams out the front doors, I expect to feel better, like a weight's been lifted off me, but I just feel fuzzy and lost.

I start off for what Mom calls "home" but I call "an explosion of moving boxes." The new house is still a disaster zone, I notice as I walk in the front door. I unpacked most of my things the first night. I always try to arrange my room exactly the same—books on the same desk shelf, posters in the same locations, nightstand lamp positioned so the crack on the base faces out. And next to the lamp, this old astronaut figurine I've had forever. I don't even know where I got it. Dad used to hide it around the house, as sort of a game. You never knew where the astronaut might show up. In the fruit bowl, his arm wrapped around a banana. In the sandbox, staged like he was sunbathing. In the bathtub, riding a rubber duck. Dad stopped doing that a long time ago, but the astronaut has a permanent spot in my room. It's the one place where nothing changes.

There are even more boxes in the kitchen, and stacks of pots and pans cover the kitchen table. Mom must finally feel up to cooking again, which is a huge relief—there's only so much pizza and mediocre suburban Chinese takeout a person can eat.

Sophia, my little sister, is already home from school. She sits at the breakfast bar, staring into a bowl of alphabet soup. Mom has her back to the door, busy dusting off and putting away dishes.

"Welcome home, Michael!" Mom says without turning around. "How was your first day?"

"Fine," I mumble, and sit down next to Sophia. She stays focused on her bowl.

"Mom," Sophia says, rearranging letters with the end of her spoon. "Can I have another bowl of soup?"

"What, honey?"

"I'm trying to spell 'gelastic,' but I need an *l*."

Normal ten-year-olds use their alphabet soup to spell "fart" and then eat it before their moms can see. Sophia uses it to show off her SAT word of the day.

"If you have another bowl, you won't be hungry for dinner," Mom says, straining for the top shelf. "Gelastic—that's a pretty big word."

"Eight letters isn't big." Sophia gives up on her vocab project and starts eating her words, one by one. "I know words with twenty letters."

Sophia also knows all the capitals in Europe and how to say hello and good-bye in twelve languages. I can't wait until she gets her first Nobel Prize and I can tell everyone at the celebratory dinner about how she stuck peas up her nose as a toddler.

"What does it mean?" Mom asks.

"'Gelastic.' Adjective," Sophia recites in her special two-time-district-spelling-bee-winner voice. "Laugh-provoking in look, conduct, or speech."

Mom pushes herself up farther on the counter, balancing precariously on one knee. I should help her, or at least offer. I *am* taller than her, though not by much. She's my mom, and it isn't her fault we're here, and I should help her. Dad would say the same thing, if he were home. But he isn't, so his opinion doesn't matter.

There's a lump in my throat that feels like peanut butter but tastes bitter. I swallow it down and don't get up.

Mom manages to shove the dishes onto the top shelf. "Can you use it in a sentence?"

Sophia shoots me a glance. "Michael looks very *gelastic* today."

"Hey!"

"Sophia!" Mom slides down off the counter and turns to face me, taking in my uniform in all its dorky glory. "Oh, look at you! You ran out so fast this morning, I didn't get to see you before you left."

"That was intentional," I say as she adjusts my tie.

"I think you look very nice," she says.

"I look like a Scottish undertaker."

"They aren't called undertakers anymore," Sophia says. "They're called *funeral directors*."

She takes her bowl of soup to the sink and flounces upstairs.

Mom sits down at the table next to me. "Dad called while you were at school. Do you want to call him back?"

I shake my head.

"Michael," she groans. "Don't you think you've made your point?"

"He lied to me."

"He didn't mean to. It was a very unexpected offer."

"He lied to you, too."

Mom closes her eyes. "A very *good* unexpected offer that's opened up lots of opportunities for him. Should I have forced him to turn that down?"

I hope my silence speaks for itself.

Mom puts her hand on mine. "I know this isn't ideal."

"This is about the furthest thing from—"

"Because it isn't ideal for me either," she says sharply. "Your dad traveling so much is not ideal. Having to start over is not ideal. But I'm trying, and Sophia's trying, and you need to try, too."

This is the moment I'm supposed to tell her about Lucy, Avi, and how good the dining hall food was and how "there's

28

room for people like us," so I can show her I am trying. That there's the slightest of possibilities that this year won't be as big a disaster as I thought. I could tell her, and the new crease in her forehead would disappear and her eyes would look less worried. But if I tell her that, she might start to think what she and Dad did to me is okay, and it's not, and won't be no matter how many friends I make.

"I'll try," I say. "But if Dad calls tonight, tell him I don't speak Belgian."

Mom stands up and gently strokes the back of my head the way she used to when I was a kid. "Oh, honey," she sighs. "Belgian isn't a language."

5

THE WEIRDEST THING about Catholic school is that despite all the statues of saints and a real overabundance of prayer, it's still school. There might be a crucifix in my chemistry classroom, but I still have pages of problem sets on catalysts and molar mass. The first weeks slip by in a blur of homework, putting names to faces, and getting lost in hallways.

I sit with Avi and Lucy at lunch, and she sticks close by me in theology, too, whispering definitions of words I've never heard of, like "magisterium" and "transubstantiation," spelling them out in my notebook in perfect, loopy letters. One day at lunch, I do an impression of Theresa the Ultra-Pious that makes Lucy laugh so hard she cries a little, and I'm so happy that when Dad calls later that night, I manage to say forty-eight words to him.

Avi seems less sure about being friends with me. Once, Lucy mentioned a study group they have, saying maybe I could come, but Avi cut her off, reminding her I'm in a different English class. But I think he doesn't want me getting as close to her as he is. Maybe he has a crush on her—she's pretty, I guess. Pretty like a painting behind glass, though, something you're not supposed to touch. I decide Avi and I are going to get along, even if I have to knock him down and beat the friendship out of him.

On second thought, maybe not. He's a lot taller than me.

The day after Halloween, Coach Kent tells us that today in PE we'll be walking the track all period, because he has a raging headache and paperwork to fill out, and so help him God if any of us start complaining.

I catch up to Avi, who's leisurely walking on the outside of the track. He looks instantly tired when I start walking next to him. I have that effect on people.

"I think Lucy wants us to be friends," I say.

"Lucy wants a lot of things." He blows on his hands. "But Lucy also tends to barrel into things without thinking them through. As I'm sure you've noticed."

I'm put off by the implication that I'm a *thing* Lucy hasn't thought through, but I keep the conversation going.

"How did you and Lucy meet?" I ask.

Avi shrugs. "I sat next to her in algebra freshman year, and she was nice to me." He looks at me warily before continuing. "We ate lunch together sometimes, but I was mostly hanging out with other people. And then I told her something important about me, and she wasn't weird about it. Other people were, but she wasn't, so. That was that."

"People were weird about the Jewish thing?"

"No," he says, staring straight ahead. "More about the gay thing."

I stop walking. "You're *gay*?" Avi doesn't wait for me, so I jog to catch up.

"You're surprised?" he says.

"Sort of—I actually thought you had a crush on Lucy."

"I think that's called projecting."

"What?"

"Lucy is not my type," Avi says. "And neither are you, in case you're worried."

I wasn't worried, but now I'm just offended.

"Well . . . why not?" I ask.

"Why not what?"

"Why aren't I your type?"

Avi stares at me. "You want me to be attracted to you?"

"No," I say. "But you don't have to act like it's such a given. I'm not a mountain troll."

"Yeah," Avi agrees. "Mountain trolls have more tact." But he's smiling as we round the bend.

His smile disappears as he glances to the left of the track, near the tennis courts, where a stocky boy is tying what looks like a wizard's cape around his neck, over his PE shirt and sweatpants.

"Who is that?" I ask.

"Max Kim," he says, and starts off toward him. "Come on."

"What's he got around his neck? He looks ridiculous."

Avi whirls around. "No, he doesn't," he snaps. "He looks like himself. Don't be a jerk."

I'm stung he assumes my default mode is "jerk," but I follow him over. Max nods at Avi but then goes back to fastening his cape.

"Max," Avi says, "you have to take it off."

"Take what off?" Max asks, as if he's not wearing a giant purple cape around his neck.

"Coach Kent said he'd take it away if you wore it in PE again."

"No, he didn't."

"I heard him say it."

"No," Max says. "He said he'd throw it in the ceramics kiln in the art room. That's different. It's worse." He looks over at me. "I don't know who you are."

"I'm Michael," I tell him. "I think your cape's cool."

Avi glares at me, but Max grins. "It's actually a cloak, not a cape, but you're right. It is cool. Cloaks are the best. Everybody used to wear cloaks, a long time ago, but now everyone thinks cloaks are only for wizards and vampires and Darth Vader, which ignores the entire history of cloak-wearing."

"Oh my God," Avi groans, but Max is on a roll.

"Cloaks have many practical purposes. They keep you warm, they keep you dry, you can use them as pillows or blankets or a really small tent, you could probably use them to kill somebody too, I don't know, I've never tried, but you could for sure suffocate someone, or strangle them . . ."

I like this kid. He might look like a knockoff Dracula out for a jog, but anyone who knows how to turn their clothing into murder weapons is a good person to have on your side.

"It's a dress code thing," Avi says. "Wear it after school."

"There's nothing about cloaks in the student handbook," Max argues. "I looked. Besides, how could a cloak be against the dress code when the pope wears one all the time?"

"The pope doesn't go to St. Clare's, he doesn't have to follow our dress code."

"What if you wore a sweatshirt instead?" I suggest. "If you tied the sleeves around your neck it would look sort of like a cloak. And no one could take it away from you, if it's uniform."

Max considers this for a moment. "But I didn't bring a sweatshirt today," he says, looking down at his long-sleeved PE shirt.

"Wear mine," I say, taking off my hoodie and handing it to him. He ties the sleeves around his neck. He's shorter than me, so the sweatshirt hangs all the way down his back. He twists around, trying to get a look.

"Does it look okay? Like a real cloak?" he asks. Avi and I both agree it does, so Max stashes his actual cloak in the bushes and takes off running, the improvised cape trailing behind him. Avi stares at me the way you look at an optical illusion, surprised to see anything real pop out of that mess of shapes and colors, but happy you saw it. I'm not sure if meeting Max was a test, but if it was, I think I passed.

"You're going to be cold without your hoodie," Avi says.

"Then we should probably start running."

So we do.

We get out of last period early, because it's November 1—All Saints' Day—and there's going to be an all-school Mass. I'm happy to skip Spanish conjugation drills but less psyched about sitting through my first-ever Mass. The last time I was in a church was for Sophia's orchestra concert last year, and that was painful enough. Adding Jesus to the experience can't possibly improve things.

"All Saints' Day," Lucy explains as we walk toward the chapel, "is the day we honor the lives of all the saints—and really, all the Christians—who have died."

"And it's just a super-weird coincidence that a holiday about spirits and dead people comes right after Halloween?" I ask. Between this and the Old Testament, Catholics seem like history's biggest plagiarists.

Lucy leads me into the chapel, stopping to dip her pointer finger in a bowl of holy water by the door and cross herself with it. I dip my finger in it, too, cautiously, but it feels like regular water. I resist the urge to taste it. She does a funny little half-kneel toward the altar and slides into a pew. I don't try and copy her weird bow but slide in next to her. Avi takes a seat next to us. The chapel fills up quickly. Max sits in one of the back pews next to a girl with the longest, reddest hair I've ever seen.

Suddenly, from up above, an organ plays, sounding like a dying cow, and everyone gets to their feet. Father Peter enters the chapel, wearing white robes with a green sash and flanked on both sides by young men, one holding a cross aloft.

"May the Lord be with you," Father Peter says, standing at the altar.

"And with your spirit," the congregation replies as one.

"Don't worry," Lucy whispers. "You'll pick it up."

But I don't want to pick any of it up, so I tune out all the words and the Mass becomes an endless sequence of sitting, standing, and kneeling. The sitting's the best, though I get antsy halfway through Father Peter's endless speech. The kneeling parts are by far the worst.

"This is going to give me nerve damage," I tell Lucy as we kneel on uncomfortable, though blessedly padded, pieces of wood attached to the pews.

She rolls her eyes. Father Peter holds up the Communion wafer, a little brown disc. As he prays over it, one of the altar boys rings a little bell, and, according to Lucy, the bit of bread and the goblet of wine somehow become the literal (yes, *literal*) body and blood of Jesus Christ, a man who has been dead for two thousand years.

I tell her that sounds a lot like black magic. She tells me to shut up.

The people in the front rows are standing now, forming a line in front of Father Peter. I watch as he places a wafer in their hands, which they pop in their mouths and continue on.

This is calmest cannibalization ritual I've ever seen.

"Come on," Lucy says, grabbing the fabric of my blazer sleeve and hauling me up. "It's time for Communion."

We get in the slow-moving line with most everyone else in the chapel, though a handful of people, Avi included, stay in the pews. As we shuffle toward the front, I panic.

"Lucy," I hiss at her back.

"What?" she says without turning all the way around.

"I don't want to eat the wafer."

"You don't *get* to eat the wafer, Michael. You're not Catholic."

"Then why did you drag me up here?"

She turns around to face me. "Put your arms up like this." She folds her arms across her chest like a corpse in a coffin. "That's how they know not to give you Communion. Then follow me back to the pew."

Moments later, Father Peter holds the circular wafer up in front of Lucy, then places it gently in her cupped hands. She puts the wafer in her mouth, crosses herself, and continues back toward our seats. I step forward to follow her, arms still crossed in front of me, but there's suddenly a hand on my forehead. I stare up at Father Peter, totally confused. He looks surprised to see me, too, but quickly swipes two fingers down and then across my forehead.

It takes me a second to realize it. He made the sign of the cross. On *me*. I stumble back to my pew, my skin prickling and itching where a priest just marked me for Jesus. I squeeze in next to Lucy, who is kneeling with her head bowed, a perfect image of piety.

"Did *you*," I ask her, "trick me into *getting blessed*?"

"Shhh," she says, but she's smirking beneath her folded hands.

After more mumbling and another off-key song, Father Peter commands us to "go in peace," and the chapel erupts with chatter and the sound of uniform shoes squeaking on the waxed floor.

"I can't believe you did that to me," I mutter to Lucy as we all leave the chapel.

"If you don't believe in any of it, then what's the harm?" She turns to Avi, grinning. "You should have seen his face."

She makes a sharp right, away from the crowd of students heading toward the main doors, and Avi follows her.

"Avi thinks you should join our study group," Lucy says.

"But I'm not in your English class."

"Yeah," Avi says, "but we think you'll get something out of it anyway."

I follow them down the hallway, expecting to be led to the library, or maybe the English classrooms on the third floor, but we don't go to either of them.

"Um, guys, where are we going?"

"You shall know even as you are known," Lucy says. "As the Apostle Paul would say."

"I don't think he'd like being quoted in this situation," Avi says as we stop at the end of the hall.

Lucy pulls open the door to what looks like a janitor's closet, with brooms and buckets of cleaning supplies, but also contains a set of rickety-looking stairs leading down into the bowels of the school.

"You guys study in the basement?" I say, peering down into the darkness below.

"Well," Lucy says, "not exactly."

And when I'm about to explode and demand someone tell me what the hell is going on, Lucy grabs me by the hand and pulls me down the stairs. A surge of electricity goes through my hand as she grips it, but that could easily be the basement's faulty wiring. She holds her cell phone in front of her for light as we stumble down and down until we're on level ground again, facing an unmarked door. Lucy knocks on it three times, and I nearly collapse when Max, his cloak around his neck again, pokes his head out.

"Oh, hey, Michael," he says. "Are you one of us now?"

When I was six, an irresponsible teenage babysitter let me watch a horror movie on cable, where this cult slowly gained the trust of local townspeople, only to kidnap them and sacrifice their entrails to a horned god. This feels a lot like the scene before the town doctor got his spleen ripped out.

"I'm . . ." I say. "I think I'm joining your study group."

Max frowns. "This isn't a study group."

I'm definitely ten seconds away from getting my organs burned on a pyre for some vengeful pagan deity.

"Max!" Lucy scolds. "You ruined the surprise. I had this whole speech planned!"

She pushes open the door to a dim but cozy-looking room filled with a mismatched set of chairs and a faded floral couch. Max stands by the door, and on the couch is his redheaded friend I saw at Mass. Camping lanterns light up the room, and a large sheet of butcher paper is tacked up against the far wall, though I can't read it from so far away. Lucy guides me into the room and Avi follows, closing the door behind him.

"Welcome," Lucy says, "to Heretics Anonymous."

6

ON MY FIRST day at St. Clare's, as I stood outside the main doors, I remember being surprised at how normal it looked. Sure, it had a better-manicured lawn than my old school, but otherwise, didn't look much different than most high schools. It was only once I stepped inside that I started to notice the weird statues, confusing twistbacks in the halls, and winding staircases. Apparently, it also has secret underground rooms where students gather for something that isn't a study group, but thankfully isn't a homicidal sex cult, either.

"It's more like a support group," Lucy explains as we sit on the couch, looking at the club manifesto she's pulled down from the back wall. "This school has a billion and one clubs."

"Key Club, Drama Club, Model UN," Max says, ticking them off on his fingers.

"Yeah, like those, so—"

"Junior Statesmen of America, Assassins Guild, Knitters for Christ—"

"You're making them up now," Avi says.

"But," Lucy continues, shooting a look at both of them, "there's no club for people like us, who . . . think a little differently. So we made one."

"And you hold this club at school?" I ask, my eyes adjusting to the dim light and my brain adjusting to the existence of a secret society in a building crawling with clergy.

"St. Clare's would shut it down in two seconds if they knew, obviously," says Eden, Max's redheaded friend. She's wearing a necklace with a bunch of symbols I don't recognize. Her uniform's wrinkled and her hair's unkempt, and I get the feeling it's on purpose. "But it's more fun to do it right under their noses. Don't you think?"

"I guess," I say. "What's with the name? Heretics Anonymous?"

"A heretic is someone who has belief, but not the right kind," Lucy explains. "At least according to the Catholic Church. A heretic might believe in God, but some of the other things she believes don't match up with the party line, you know?"

"Not really."

Lucy gestures to Avi. "Jewish people believe in God but don't believe Christ *is* God." She gestures to Eden next. "Wiccans believe in multiple deities."

"So do Celtic Reconstructionist Polytheists," Eden says. "Which is what I actually am, *Lucy*."

"Sorry," Lucy says. "And Max—"

"I'm a Unitarian!" he cuts in.

"What do they believe?" I ask.

"Hard to tell," he says. "But the church on Lawson Road let me have a bunch of their old computers to take apart, so I decided I am one."

"It's a free religious community," Lucy says. "No set doctrine. People decide what they do and don't believe in."

"When I went last week, someone told me a joke," Max says. "What do you get if you put two Unitarian Universalists together?"

"What?" Eden says.

"Three opinions."

Lucy laughs. "But Unitarians don't believe in the authority of the Catholic Church. So they're heretics, too."

"And I guess that makes me a triple heretic," I say, "because I don't believe in anything."

"You're not a heretic at all."

My heart drops into my stomach. What did she bring me down here for, if I'm not one of them? Maybe I have to go through some kind of initiation, like turning all the crucifixes in the school upside down, or drinking holy water to see if I burst into flames.

"You're an apostate, not a heretic," Lucy continues, "because apostates choose to reject the whole system."

"But we're not changing the group's name," Avi says. "So you'll have to deal with being mislabeled."

"Don't worry," Eden says. "Nobody gets my label right, either." She looks meaningfully at Lucy, who throws up her hands.

"It's really long, sometimes I forget it!"

"Please, you can list all the popes. In order."

"Focus," Avi says. "We haven't even asked Michael if he wants to join."

Join any club that wants you as a member, one half of my brain says. *Don't get too close,* says the other half. But what I actually feel is relief. Relief I have somewhere to go, and relief other people think I belong there.

So all I say is, "Yes." Everybody cheers, and Lucy has me sign the club charter at the bottom, with the date.

"Now you have to stand up and introduce yourself," Max says. "Do you want my cloak? You'll look cooler."

I shake my head and get to my feet. "I'm Michael," I mumble, suddenly embarrassed by all the attention, and start to sit back down.

"No," Lucy says, stopping me. "Introduce yourself properly. 'My name's Michael, and . . .'"

"My name's Michael—" I try again.

"Hi, Michael!" they chorus.

"—and I'm a heretic."

7

AFTER ALL THAT secrecy, I half expect the rest of the meeting to revolve around plots to infiltrate the Vatican or bloodlessly depose Father Peter, but everyone just goes around sharing their greatest grievances with St. Clare's. Lucy's worried about the sex ed seminar coming up in December, doubting the accuracy of the information we'll be given. Eden and Max both take issue with the rigid dress code, and Avi wants to know why Latin has to have so many goddamn declensions.

After an hour, Lucy calls the end of the meeting, and the five of us quietly emerge from the basement. We split up at the front gate, and when Lucy figures out she and I are going in the same direction, we walk together. It's nice to be alone with her, but my brain feels like it's tied in knots. After five minutes of walking, the only thing I can think to ask is: "What street's your house on?"

"Rockwell," she says, pointing over her shoulder.

"I thought you said this was on your way."

"It is. I have to pick up my brothers from after-school care," she says. "My stepdad works late shifts, so I do it."

"What about your mom?"

Lucy stares ahead. "She's in New Mexico. Or, she was a while ago. She's probably not still." She's trying to sound casual, but it's not working. "She's traveling."

I think about Dad and all his "traveling." At least Lucy's mom is probably having fun, not just working.

"When's she getting back?" I ask.

"I don't—" Lucy stops, swallows. "Soon."

"Oh," I say, because I don't know what else I could say. "I'm—"

"I totally support her," she blazes through, as if I'm barely there. "Everybody should have a chance to see the world, and she didn't get to before. So she's doing it now, and that's great. She'll by back by Christmas, for sure."

"Yeah, of course," I say, and the words sound like they belong to someone else. Lucy's shoulders relax, though, so maybe they sound real enough to her.

"How many times have you moved?" she asks.

"This one makes four."

"What's it like to pack up and leave a place? I've never been anywhere but here."

"Scary," I say. "Disorienting. It's like you have to figure out what kind of person you are, all over again. I don't know, maybe it's different if you choose it."

"Do you miss your old friends? The people you left behind?"

I miss places more. The rosebushes and rosemary stalks in House #2's front yard. The chain-link fence by my first elementary school, the one that made my hands smell like pennies. The city swimming pool where I kissed Rebecca Blanchard when I was fourteen. "It's easier not to think about it," I tell Lucy, and she looks away.

We're quiet for a block but for the sound of Lucy's patent leather shoes slapping the sidewalk.

"Did something happen?" Lucy blurts out. "To make you not believe in God anymore, did someone you knew die, or—?"

I don't know why people assume shit like that. Like being an atheist requires some sort of tragic backstory.

"Did something happen to make *you* believe in God?"

"No, I just always did."

"Yeah," I say. "And I just never did." Lucy looks skeptical. "My family's not religious. I never believed in the tooth fairy or monsters under my bed, either."

"That's not the same thing."

"All I mean is, for good or bad, there's nothing but us."

Lucy's quiet. I wonder if I'm as confusing to her as she is to me.

"You never said why you're a heretic," I say, and her eyebrows rise in surprise. "Avi's Jewish, Eden's pagan, Max is . . . Max. But you're Catholic. Why are you there?"

"I am Catholic," she says. "But I also think what it means to be Catholic should be able to change. That it should change."

That's it? "Nobody believes in it all. Except maybe priests. And who would actually want to be a priest?"

"I would," Lucy says, looking at me out of the corner of her eye.

"You can't," I tell her, shrugging. "You're a girl."

She stares at me. "I know that," she says with a hint of hurt. "Obviously, I know that."

I feel myself shrink, embarrassed for throwing that in her face so offhandedly.

"You could do other things, though," I say, trying to recover. "You could be a nun, right?"

"Nuns are great," Lucy says. "But nuns aren't priests. Nuns can't celebrate Mass. They can't hear confession or consecrate the Eucharist. They can't become bishops or cardinals or popes, they can't become the people who make the big decisions. How do you change a church that doesn't listen to you?"

Her shoulder brushes mine as she adjusts her book bag, and I wish humans could tell each other things through touch the way we can through words. *I'm not used to my friends caring about things like this,* I try to tell her as our shoulders touch for a brief instant. *I'm not used to caring about them, either.* At the crosswalk, as we wait for the light to change, Lucy clears her throat.

"Heretics are usually true believers," she says. "Martin Luther was a priest. Galileo was very devout. The only thing more dangerous than someone who doesn't care about the rules is someone who does—and wants to break them anyway."

If I didn't already know her, it would be hard to imagine Lucy, with her hair ribbons and perfectly ironed skirts, as some rebel mastermind. But now I'm certain it was Lucy, not Avi or Eden or Max, who came up with the idea for Heretics Anonymous.

We're at my house now, and for a second, I consider pretending it's farther up the block, or past the highway, or in the next county over, just to keep walking with her.

"This is me," I say, gesturing at the house.

"Oh," she says. "It's really nice."

"Yeah." It is a nice house, with its brown shingles and slightly overgrown purple wisteria snaking around the windows. "I liked my last house better, though."

She steps closer to the house and to me, peering at it over my shoulder.

"Are you still sad you had to move?" she asks, pushing a stray bit of hair behind her ear.

I could tell her the truth, which is I'm not so sure anymore. I could tell her that the closer she stands to me, the more I get exponentially less sad about moving and my palms get exponentially sweatier. I could tell her a lot of things, if my throat didn't feel so dry and my tongue didn't feel so swollen. I shrug.

"Selfishly?" she says, then drops her eyes. "I'm glad you did."

Without waiting for a response, she spins on her heel and starts up the block. I watch her, red ribbon rippling in the breeze, until she turns the corner.

8

THE BEST FEELING in the world is popping bubble wrap. The second-best feeling in the world is waking up at seven thirty a.m. as usual, realizing it's Saturday, and diving back under the covers. The worst feeling in the world is sleeping through alarms, barking dogs, and possibly earthquakes to wake up at eight a.m.—and it's Tuesday.

I spend at least five minutes looking for my tie before finding it under my U.S. history textbook. I skip a shower in favor of breakfast. I'd skip most things in favor of breakfast.

"Mom," I say as I push open the kitchen door, rubbing sleep from my eyes, "do we have any more blueberry muffins, because I'm—"

But then I stop, and not because there's a plate of muffins on the kitchen counter.

Dad's sitting at the breakfast bar.

"Look who got in last night!" Mom says as she carries Dad's

breakfast plate to the sink. It looks like she made spinach and cheese omelets, his favorite. "You and Sophia were already asleep, so I decided not to wake you."

Sophia, sitting at the kitchen table thumbing through *A Brief History of Time*, glances up when she hears her name. Dad looks at me, but I concentrate on the plate of muffins.

"Hey, buddy," he says.

I hate it when he calls me that. I hate it more than snakes, or Catholic school, or anything else, because I'm not five and we're definitely not *buddies*. We are the opposite of buddies. We're anti-buddies.

"Hey," I say. Not *I've missed you*, because I haven't, and not *welcome home*, because he isn't. I grab a muffin and stuff it in my face so I don't have to say anything else.

Dad looks tired. There are bags under his eyes and lines in his forehead that I don't think were there when I saw him a month ago. His hair is the same sandy color as mine, but his is starting to thin at the back. When I was younger and people told me I looked like my dad, I'd puff up with pride, excited for the day I would be as tall, strong, and smart as he was. If someone told me that now, I might punch him.

"How's school going?" he asks.

"Fine," I mumble, mouth full of muffin. "It's fine."

"Just fine?"

What does he want? Tears of gratitude? "Yeah."

"Good." He smiles in a satisfied way. "I know it's different than your other schools were, but I bet it's a really interesting experience, right?" He doesn't wait for me to answer. "You know, there are people who never see the world outside of a tiny bubble. The experiences you kids have had—it's pretty amazing."

Mom nods. This is my parents' favorite shared delusion: that the way we live is a great adventure. That living out of boxes is a blessing—not even one in disguise.

"So amazing," I agree. "Why doesn't everyone move four times in ten years? The *experiences* they're missing out on—"

"Enough," Dad says, then turns to Sophia. "How do you like your school, peanut?"

She doesn't look up from her book. "It's good. My science teacher has lots of weird stuff preserved in jars, like leaves and bugs and a tiny baby pig fetus, and she lets you hold the jar if you're careful with it."

Mom scrunches her nose. "There you go," Dad says. "New experiences."

Catholic school and pig fetuses. We're really aiming for the stars.

"And you're making friends?" Dad asks Sophia.

"Sure," she says. "It's not like it's hard."

"It is for some people," I say. And, okay, I have made friends, but no need to give my parents the satisfaction of knowing that.

"You will," Mom says.

"You've got to put yourself out there," Dad says, because

there's nothing he likes more than blaming me for problems *he* created. "Make an effort."

"I am, but it's—"

He's already rolling over me. "Resilience, that's what's key here."

The speech is coming on.

"In life, you have to adapt and adjust, and learning how to do that is so important, Michael. It's a life skill—"

Like swimming.

"Like swimming. If someone throws you in the deep end, you've got to figure out how to stay afloat."

The swimming metaphor is my least favorite of Dad's metaphors, mostly because he never acknowledges he's the one throwing you in the deep end.

"I know it's been hard, and I know you've been unhappy, but I really think this move, and this new school, is a great thing for you."

Oh, okay. *He* thinks it, and if *he* thinks it, there's no room for anyone else's opinion. So I won't bother. "Sure." I glance at the clock on the microwave. "I should go, since I'm walking. Don't want to be late."

"In the rain?" Mom says, turning around. "You'll get sick!"

"I'll drive you," Dad says. "Sit down for a minute."

That's the last thing I want to do. "No, really, I can walk—"

"Michael," he says in his no-argument tone. "Sit down."

I sit. I figure Dad's going to continue pontificating about

adaptation and deep water, but he opens the newspaper and starts to read. Somehow, this makes me even madder. Why did he make me sit down, if he's going to ignore me?

With Mom at the sink, Dad reading the newspaper, Sophia off in her own genius world, I feel like an unnecessary prop in some diorama of family togetherness. We used to actually do this, sit all together, before he started working as much. And he wasn't always this person, lecturing everyone about resilience and telling them how to feel. He used to be *fun*. One time, in fourth grade, he showed up at my classroom on the hottest day of the year. He told my teacher I had a dentist appointment but took me to the water park instead.

That's who he used to be. There's a tightness in my chest, and it's because I know that person's gone.

And when Dad finally looks up from the business section and says, "So, how are your grades?" the tightness bursts, and what flows through my veins is unbridled rage.

"What do you care?" I snap back, even though I know it's the wrong thing to say.

"Excuse me?" Dad says quietly. The quieter he is, the worse things are.

"If you'd been here at all, you'd know," I say. "But you haven't, so I don't see why I should have to fill you in."

Mom drops the scrub brush with a clatter. "Michael—"

"I don't like being away this much," Dad says. "But that's part of my job."

"Right. That's your job." I gesture around at me, and Mom, and Sophia, who has closed her book. "And this isn't, I guess?"

"You need to cool it," he says. "Now."

He's using his no-argument tone again, but I'm past the point of caring. My personal motto has always been if you've already dug yourself a hole too deep to climb out of, you may as well keep digging.

"Maybe Sophia doesn't get that you chose a promotion over us, but I'm not ten," I tell him, getting up from my chair. "So *I* know you can't really be a good dad if you're only here seven days in a month."

It's silent now. Dad is as angry as I expected him to be, but there's hurt flickering in his eyes, too. I feel a surge of grim triumph.

"You're grounded," he says, as if that solves the whole issue. "One week."

"Yeah, okay," I say, grabbing my backpack and blazer. "When are you leaving, Thursday? How exactly are you going to enforce that?"

Dad gets to his feet, the chair's legs scraping on the floor, and I take that as my cue to get out of there. As I leave the kitchen, Mom speaks to him in quiet, soothing tones, and I feel bad about dragging her and Sophia into this, but that's the only thing I feel bad about. I half expect Dad to follow me out the front door and into what has turned from a light drizzle to real rain, but he doesn't.

I forgot an umbrella, so by the time I get to school I'm soaked through, and my shoes have filled up with water. The school's heated, but I still shiver all through chemistry and pre-calc. To make matters worse, we have a group pop quiz, and I'm assigned to a group with Theresa and two other girls I don't know. I'm not great at math, but Theresa's worse. She insists on doing the entire quiz by herself, and after she messes up the third problem in a row, I tell her someone who believes in an imaginary God should be better at using imaginary numbers. She glares daggers at me but allows the rest of us to fix her work.

After class, Theresa pushes past me in the hall to catch up with Father Peter. I can't hear what she's saying to him over the hallway noise, but she points back over her shoulder at me.

"Mr. Ausman." Father Peter beckons me over.

Fantastic. I start off toward him, passing by Theresa, who is headed back in my direction. "You told on me," I say.

"You mocked my Lord," she replies, and flounces away.

I'm not sure what Father Peter's going to do first: yell at me for calling God imaginary, or comment on the water still dripping from my pant legs. What he actually says is "Where's your belt?"

I look down past my half-tucked shirt, and yep, I'm not wearing a belt. I must have forgotten it in my rush to get dressed this morning.

"It's at home," I say. "I forgot it."

"The belt is part of the dress code. Without it, you're out of uniform."

I take a deep breath in, trying really hard not to lose my shit. I'm wet and cold and I told my dad he's a bad father, but clearly what's crucial here is my lack of a belt.

"I'm sorry," I say. "I didn't do it on purpose."

"I'll still have to write you up. If you receive two more uniform infractions, it's a detention."

"That's ridiculous," I say, too loudly, and people walking by stop to look at me. One of them is a girl wearing pants instead of a skirt, and I point her out to Father Peter as she passes by. "What about her? She's wearing pants without a belt."

"Her trousers don't have belt loops," Father Peter says. "Yours do, so you need a belt. Please go see Ms. Edison, she'll give you one to wear for today."

"So you're saying if I took a knife and cut the belt loops off," I say, "I wouldn't have to wear a belt?"

Father Peter looks worried. "Do you have a knife?"

"No," I say, gritting my teeth, "but it's a stupid rule—"

"At some point, you'll have to learn to follow the rules, whether or not you like them."

"Why?" I ask, and I'm instantly embarrassed at how childish I sound.

"Because, trust me," he says, looking at me with what might be pity or might be understanding, "your life will be so much harder if you don't."

+ + +

Sister Helen's lecture in theology is about the Annunciation, where the Angel Gabriel appeared to the teenage, engaged Virgin Mary and was basically like, "Hey, little girl. You're going to get pregnant with a god-baby, and everyone's going to think you're a cheating slut and your fiancé will try to divorce you, and then you'll go into labor in a stable and flee to Egypt later that week because everyone in power wants to murder you and your god-baby. But don't worry, you'll get some sweet frankincense and myrrh out of it."

At least that's what I hear, as I sit next to Avi and Lucy, who keeps glancing at me. I know she's worried because I didn't say a word at lunch. What I'm really getting out of Sister Helen's lecture is that Jesus's childhood royally sucked. Having to move around all the time, knowing more than other people but being ignored, and going through all this shit even though God, his father, is literally omnipotent and could make everything easier with a snap of His giant, godly fingers. So when Sister Helen won't stop talking about God leaving His son in the loving step-care of elderly carpenter Saint Joseph so Jesus could live among the humans he would later die for, I can't take it anymore.

"What a *dick*," I say, in what was supposed to be a mutter but turned out a lot louder. There are suddenly forty eyes on me, and none are wider than Lucy's.

"I—what?" Sister Helen says, leaning on her desk for support.

"He's a dick," I repeat, and this time I do mutter it. "God. For doing that."

"For . . . sending His son to die for your sins?"

"No," I say, trying to clarify, "not for— So he knocks Mary up, right?"

"She *becomes* pregnant *miraculously*," Sister Helen says, clearly uncomfortable with my choice of words.

"Technically, the Holy Spirit did the impregnating," Lucy whispers to me.

"Whatever, she gets pregnant however she gets pregnant, and Jesus is born, and God sits up on His cloud throne and doesn't even talk to Jesus for the next thirty years. What kind of dad does that? What kind of father makes his kid the absolute lowest priority on his list, and I know, I know, he's busy running the entire world, but it's still shitty and he's still a dick for doing it!"

I'm definitely not talking about Jesus anymore. I know it, and from the look on Lucy's face, she knows it, too. Everyone else is watching me like I'm a train wreck of a reality show, too entertaining to be disturbing. Sister Helen takes a moment to process what I suspect is the least reverent speech she's ever heard.

"Michael," she says, and doesn't sound mad, only deeply, deeply confused. "I think it might be good for you to take a break. Outside."

That's the best idea I've heard all day.

Lucy comes to visit fifteen minutes later, carrying the bathroom pass. She sits down next to me.

"Are you okay?"

"Sure." I squeak my shoes against the linoleum.

"No, you're not." I start to protest, but she cuts me off. "You don't have to talk about it. But you also don't have to pretend you're fine when you're not."

"How do you know I'm not?"

"You threw a tantrum in theology. You called God a dick. You're not fine."

"Says the girl on Sister Joseph Marie's personal hit list."

"Wildly unfair comparison," she says, picking herself up off the floor. "Don't forget we have study group today, okay?"

"Okay," I say, wishing she'd leave me alone already. The longer she stays, the more I want to tell her about what's bothering me, and the more I want to tell her, the more uncomfortable I get.

"You know, that rant you went on—for a minute, it almost sounded like you were comparing yourself to Jesus. But *you'd* definitely never do *that*."

She gives me the smallest, slyest smile, and heads back to class.

By the time I get down to the basement that afternoon, the group's already embroiled in the favored Heretics Anonymous discussion topic: how much this school sucks.

"Sister Joseph Marie made me take my earrings off today," Eden's telling everyone as I sit down in the circle. "Because they have these Celtic spirals on them, and she said that was a pagan symbol so I couldn't wear it, which is—ugh. Just because it isn't a cross doesn't mean it's evil."

"You know what I'm really sick of?" Avi says. "The constant plug in the morning announcements about helping the elementary school kids down the block prepare for their First Communions."

"What's wrong with that?" Lucy says. "They're cute. It's fun."

"They keep using the word 'choice.' Like, help support these kids in their choice to receive the Lord's body," Avi says. "What choice? They're eight."

"Okay," Lucy agrees. "But so? When they're older, they can choose not to be Catholic, if that's what they want."

"I said no to getting confirmed," Eden points out. "It turned into a huge awful fight with my mom, but every religion agrees people have free will, right?"

"Not Calvinists," Lucy says, and I'm glad to see no one else knows what she's talking about, either.

Avi shakes his head. "I could become a Buddhist or a Mormon or a Republican and I'd still be a Jew, too. My mom's Jewish. And her mom is. I didn't get a choice in that."

"You don't want to be Jewish?" Max asks. "You get to ride around on chairs and stomp on glasses."

"No, I do," Avi says. "But not because of chairs or glasses. It's a community, we take care of each other. Even if you don't keep kosher or even believe in God, you're still Jewish and you still belong to this huge line of people who fought to survive, over and over, so you could exist. I like being Jewish, but it's not something I chose. And I don't think most Christian people had a choice, either." Avi pushes his glasses up farther on his nose. "Because of colonialism."

"Wait. What?" Eden says. Lucy groans.

"I'm serious. All of you were born Catholic because some-one conquered and colonized your ancestors. Ireland, Korea, Mexico." Avi gestures to Eden, Max, and Lucy in turn.

"The Irish were Catholic before they were colonized," Eden says.

"Um, Korea was a colony of *Japan*," Max points out. "They weren't Catholic."

"Okay," Avi concedes. "But—"

"And I'm Colombian, but obviously don't let that stop you," Lucy says.

"Same thing."

"They're not even on the same continent."

"Same idea!" he says. "I'm Jewish because everyone before me was, and you're Catholic because Spanish assholes forcibly converted your ancestors. How's that a choice?"

Lucy sighs. She looks over at me, probably realizing I've been quiet all meeting. Not because I'm feeling ignored, but because I don't have a single thing to add to this conversation.

"What do you think, Michael?" she asks, like I'm the weird kid in the corner at recess.

"I think this is stupid," I mutter.

Lucy frowns. "Colonialism?"

"Modern history would agree," Avi says.

"*This* is stupid," I say. "Sitting down here and doing nothing but complaining is stupid."

Lucy blinks at me. She looks around at the rest of the group. "This is what we do. We listen to each other, we try to help. What do you want us to do instead?" she asks. "What else can we do?"

Hearing Lucy say that, with such a half-hearted, defeatist shrug, makes my blood turn cold, then way too hot.

"Anything!" I yell. Lucy shushes me, but I wave her off. "You can do anything other than sit in this room and bitch about how terrible this school is. You can do anything else."

"Don't talk to her like that," Avi snaps.

"It's a support group," Eden says. "That's what support groups do. They talk."

"We can't change this school," Lucy says. "All we can do is be there for each other."

"But what about everybody else?" I ask. "The people who aren't in this room—why don't they get a support group?"

"Because they wouldn't all fit down here," Max says.

"Look, if this school hurts us, it's probably hurting other

people too," I say. "Maybe we just don't know about it. And they should know they aren't alone." I look at Lucy. "Because it's worse feeling alone here than other places." There's an idea that's been churning in my head for the last half hour, but I'm not sure how to put it into words. "I think we should go public."

The four of them explode into a chorus of *no*s, and I raise my voice.

"I mean Heretics Anonymous should go public. The rest of the school should know about us, even if they don't know exactly who we are."

"You've lost it," Avi says. "First you told a nun God was a dick, and now you want to lead a revolution."

I glare at him. "All we do is talk. Talk about how much St. Clare's sucks, and how it's so unfair, but we don't try to make it better. I think we can make it better. And not just for us."

Lucy's mouth is twisted into a worried line, but there's a light in her eyes, and I can tell she's already thinking up ways to make St. Clare's livable, while also evaluating every potential obstacle in doing so.

"Okay," she says. "How?"

"What?" Avi yelps. "Lucy, no. Do you want to go to college? Because I want to go to college, and if we get caught—"

"What about the sex ed assembly?" I say to Lucy. "The one you were talking about the other day. Why do you hate it so much?"

"Everyone hates it," she says.

"Theresa doesn't hate it," Eden says.

"Theresa's in love with the chastity speaker," Lucy says. "Too bad he's married."

"Too bad he's closeted," Avi mumbles.

"Okay, but *why* does everyone hate it?" I ask.

"So there's this guy—" Max says.

"Purity Paul," Avi interjects.

"—and he comes every year and talks to us about how sex is evil and gross and bad, except when you're married. Then it's holy and special," Max says. "And after he's done, they show us this video that basically says the same thing but also has super-bad production values."

"Production values? Half the stuff in the video isn't even true," Lucy says. "That's why I hate that assembly. They lie to us and think it's justified."

"What do they say?" I ask. "Condoms are Satan's party balloons?"

"More like, condoms fail one in six times. Or masturbation turns all your love inward, so it's harder to love another person. Or birth control will make you infertile."

"So we find a way to tell the truth," I say. "Maybe we high-jack Purity Paul's talk."

"In my experience, he's very possessive with his micro-phone," Max says.

"What if we made our own video?" Eden says. "To replace the other one. What if we made one that was true?"

"What, and then pop it in the DVD player?" Avi says. "How long would that last, ten seconds?"

Lucy nods. "I think it's better if we use the original video. And every time that video says something untrue, we correct it. Like, annotate it, with the right information."

"It wouldn't be that hard to re-edit the video, if we could get the DVD," Eden says. "And last year, I think only Father Peter and Sister Helen supervised the movie. We might be able to get through a few minutes before they notice."

"Sister Helen has the DVD in her classroom, on the bookshelf," Max says. "I saw it once when she confiscated my cloak."

They all turn to Avi. He sighs. "I guess robbing a nun is one for the bucket list."

Lucy looks at me. "So you want to do this?"

For a second, I wonder why she's asking me. And then I realize. She's handing over the reins. Definitely not forever, probably not even until the end of this meeting, but she's giving me permission to make a plan. The last time I was responsible for something, it was a beta fish, and it died after I overfed it. Hopefully, this will be more successful.

"Let's do it."

9

EVERY DAY, EXACTLY four minutes after the lunch bell, Sister Helen exits her theology classroom on the second floor, leaving the door closed but unlocked. She takes the stairs down to the first floor, turns left, and stops at the vending machine by the front entrance. She buys a small bag of gummy bears, makes a detour at the teachers' lounge to get the rest of her lunch, then returns upstairs to her classroom, taking the staff elevator back up.

This, Lucy calculates, gives us approximately five minutes to enter her classroom, find the DVD, and get out before anyone sees.

"Maybe less," she says, as I stand by her locker, a few feet away from the theology classroom. "If the elevator doesn't take forever to come. But it usually does."

Lucy is pretending to reorganize her locker and I'm pretending to watch. Her locker is already intensely organized, without a single piece of lined paper crumpled at the bottom or an assignment sheet sticking out of a book. Our plan is not nearly as well organized as Lucy's locker. The assembly's only a week away, and with all the work we have to do on the annotation, today is the best day to pull off the DVD heist. Lucy spent a few days tracking Sister Helen's lunchtime routine, since she's the one who's going to steal the DVD. I still don't think she should be the one to do it, but Lucy *is* the one with the most plausible alibi, if she gets caught. Anyone would buy sweet, pious Lucy picking through a nun's bookshelf for some weird Catholic book. Me, not so much.

"Are you nervous?" I ask her. Because I am, so I can only imagine what she's feeling.

"About my first attempt at breaking and entering?" Lucy says.

"It's not breaking and entering if the door's unlocked. It's just entering."

Lucy shuts her locker and turns to me, hugging her book bag to her chest. "I need you to take this seriously," she says, her voice low. "You're my lookout. I'm counting on you."

Something swells in my chest, and I can't tell if it's pride that Lucy needs me for something, or absolute pants-shitting fear I'm going to screw it all up.

It's nearly ten minutes past the bell when Sister Helen closes the door to her classroom and heads down the stairs.

"Two hundred seconds," Lucy says, looking a little paler than usual. "No problem."

There's another row of lockers next to the classroom's entrance, which cuts off the line of sight from the door to the rest of the hallway. I'll stand there, watching out for anyone who might be looking for Sister Helen, and of course Sister Helen. My job is to act natural and inconspicuous.

I'm going to throw up.

There's no one else in the hallway as Lucy opens the theology classroom door and takes a first tentative step inside. My eyes are fixed on the hallway ahead when someone taps me on the shoulder.

"Hey," Max says as I recover from my heart trying to jump outside my body. "Avi and Eden sent me to check on you guys."

I'm happy to see him, and not just because he isn't a nun. If Max is here, Lucy's fate isn't solely in my hands.

"Lucy just went inside. I'm going to watch this way—" I point up the hallway, the direction Sister Helen left. "—you can watch the other way."

As Max and I stand by the lockers in silence, my eyes keep darting between the hallway and the theology room door, where Lucy is doing something that could get her expelled. Something that was my idea in the first place. I should be in there, not her, and I don't know what I'll do if she gets caught, because I like her.

I've been trying to pretend like I don't, but I do. I like her. When she touches me—usually by accident, like when she brushes my arm reaching across the lunch table to check Avi's Latin homework, but sometimes on purpose, like when she grabbed my hand to lead me down the stairs to the first HA meeting—it's like every nerve in my body wakes up. Like being on a roller coaster, that jolt you feel the moment you start the biggest plunge.

I've only had one girlfriend: Rebecca Blanchard, in ninth grade. It lasted three months and largely involved watching reality TV shows about weddings (her idea), sloppily making out (my idea), and eating whatever my mom had baked that afternoon (both our ideas). The relationship fell apart because I started to get the feeling Rebecca liked my mom's brownies more than she liked me.

Lucy can't like me either, at least not the way I want her to. I know that. She's waiting for someone, someone as smart as she is, as kind as she is, someone who talks to God and hears something back. I have to tell someone about this. If I don't, I'll explode and do something really stupid. Like kiss Lucy. Or commit arson.

Avi already thinks I'm a bad influence. If I told him I wanted to get Lucy naked, he'd probably have me killed. Eden would tell Lucy everything. Max is my best bet, and who knows when I'll get him alone again?

"Can I ask you something?" I say, peering around the bay of lockers to check for Sister Helen. No one's there.

"Sure."

I take a deep breath and try to ignore the prickling on the back of my neck. "Do you—do you think Lucy's hot?"

Max looks confused. "Compared to who?"

There's a bead of sweat running down my back. It tickles. "I don't know, compared to anyone."

"You can't compare one thing to every other thing. That's not how comparisons work."

"Compared to whoever you want," I say. "Who do you think is hot?"

"Marie Curie."

"What?"

"She won two Nobel Prizes. In two different subjects. She's perfect."

"Max, she's dead."

Max looks offended. "You asked who I thought was hot. She's hot. Was hot."

"Fine," I sigh. "So, do you think Lucy's hot, or not?"

He considers this. "Her hair's kind of messy—"

It's not messy. It's wavy.

"—but her eyes are nice. I like brown eyes."

Me too.

"And she's smart and nice to me. Those things don't make her hot, but they're still important."

Yes. Yes, they are.

"I feel weird talking about this," he admits.

"That's okay," I say. "Forget I asked."

"I can't forget this exact second," Max says. "But probably by tomorrow."

I hear a low, faraway shuffling sound. I poke my head around the lockers.

Sister Helen is walking back our way.

I dash over to the classroom, but just as I'm about to open the door, there's Lucy in the doorway, with a smile and an oddly shaped lump under the arm of her cardigan.

"Come on," I hiss. "She's coming back."

"I'm out, I'm out," she says, closing the door behind her. "Try to look less guilty."

She sidesteps me and breezes down the hallway, past Sister Helen, who doesn't even lift her eyes from the bag of gummy bears. Max shrugs, and we run to catch up with Lucy as she rounds the corner.

"That was really close," I say, my heart still beating too fast.

"I wasn't worried," she says. "You had my back."

There it is again, that roller-coaster jolt in my chest.

Lucy stops outside the door to the dining hall, where Avi and Eden are waiting for us. "And as Saint Joan said: I am not afraid. I was born to do this."

As Max and I follow her inside, he leans over and whispers: "Do you think she knows what *happened* to Joan of Arc?"

I'd assumed Max, who takes computers apart for fun, would edit the video, but when I ask, he laughs. "I don't know how to program. Why would I do it?"

"But didn't the Unitarians give you all their computers?"

"Yeah, so I could disassemble them and recycle the parts," he says. "Did you know we throw away fifty million tons of electronic waste every year? And that only like ten percent ever gets recycled?"

I did not. Luckily, Max has several pamphlets in his backpack. It turns out that Eden's going to take care of the video, and she suggests we do the editing at her house. "I work better on my own computer anyway," she explains. "And my basement's really big."

Eden's whole house is big, I discover after the bus ride we all take together. It's also silent when we walk into the entryway, which makes it seem even bigger. My house has never been this quiet. When Dad was home more, he used to talk with Mom as she made dinner, or quiz Sophia on whatever new language she was trying to learn. And even now, Mom makes a ton of noise cooking, or cleaning, or passive-aggressively arguing with the TV weatherman.

"I have to grab my laptop real quick," Eden says. "I'll be right back."

"Show them your altar!" Max says, taking his shoes off at the door. "It's so cool."

"No one wants to see my altar."

I raise my hand. "I do." Avi and Lucy agree.

Eden glances warily up the stairs. "Fine, but everyone be quiet up there, okay?"

Eden's room is nothing like I'd imagined—the two twin

beds have pink comforters, the walls are sunshine yellow, and there's a big family portrait on one wall. The only thing that looks like hers is the altar, tucked behind a desk. It's only a step stool, really, draped with green cloth and covered in little trinkets.

"Which god is it for?" Avi asks.

"Brighid," Eden says. "Goddess of spring, healing, and poetry. I work with Áine too, and sometimes Lugh, but Brighid the most."

"You make it sound like a business relationship," Lucy says.

"More like a conversation. I talk, they talk. Brighid's a particularly good listener. And she's patient."

I bend down to get a closer look at the altar. It's not like I was expecting sheep entrails or anything, but everything's so simple, normal. It doesn't look much different than the shrine to Saint Clare in the chapel. Eden points out each part. "Candles, because she's associated with fire. She likes roses, so those, too. Tea, for us to share. On Brighid's Day in February, I'll make bread for her."

Lucy scoffs. "And when you wake up, it's half eaten, like cookies for Santa?"

Eden crosses her arms. "I know you think this is all really silly, but you could at least pretend you don't."

"Wait," Lucy says, holding her hands up. "That's not what I—"

"I don't treat your religion like that," Eden says. "That's one of the best things about polytheism—I don't have to treat any religion like it's silly."

"What do you mean?" Max asks.

"If monotheism's true, anyone who doesn't worship that one God is a sinner. If polytheism's true, then any god can be real. You don't have to worship them or think they're good, but they can still exist. I can believe that Brighid's real, and Athena's real, and so is Jesus." She focuses on Lucy again. "He never did a thing for me, but if you want to work with Him, knock yourself out. Just give me the same respect."

Lucy looks embarrassed but says nothing. Time for a rapid change of topic.

"Is this your family?" I ask Eden, pointing at a photo above the desk. There's seven or eight blond and redheaded kids ranging from teenagers to one baby, right in the center.

"Yeah," Eden says, grabbing her laptop off the desk. "Come on, let's go downstairs before—"

There's a voice from somewhere down the hall. "Felicity?"

"Who's Felicity?" I ask.

"Me," Eden sighs, then raises her voice. "In here, Mom."

No one else seems surprised. Avi shrugs. "She's gone by Eden forever."

"Since fourth grade," Eden corrects him. She nods her head over to the family portrait I noticed earlier. "She gave us all saints' names, in alphabetical order. So there's Anthony and Beatrice and then Christopher, Dominic, Elizabeth, and—"

"Felicity," I finish for her, looking at the redheaded baby at the center of the photograph. That must be Eden. Her brothers and sisters are so much older than her. Even in the photo, her oldest brother and sisters look college-aged. That's why her big house feels so empty. She's the only one left.

"I messed up her system," Eden says with a crooked smile.

Eden's mom opens the door. She's small and stout, wearing sweatpants and a robe and looking like she just woke up. She has a lot more wrinkles than my mom, and all-gray hair.

"Oh, it's a whole group of you," she says.

"Hi, Mrs. Mulaney!" Max says from behind Avi, waving his hand furiously.

"Hello, Max," she says, brightening when she sees Lucy. "Lucy! When's the last time we got to talk? It seems like it's been months."

"I think it was on Assumption, in August," Lucy says in a cheery camp-counselor voice I've never heard her use before. "Your son was visiting, and he brought his adorable baby to Mass?"

Mrs. Mulaney barely acknowledges Avi and me as Eden introduces us, still chattering with Lucy about church and babies and what does she think of that new priest, the young one with the long hair?

"Mom," Eden says, glancing back and forth between Lucy and Mrs. Mulaney, her hands dug deep in her cardigan pockets. "We're going down to the basement now."

"To do what, exactly?" Mrs. Mulaney asks with a sharp look at the altar in the corner. Eden clenches her teeth.

"Oh my God, Mom, homework," Eden says. "What did you think, animal sacrifice?"

"We have a group project," Lucy interrupts. "For theology. We're presenting a section of Augustine's *Confessions*."

"That sounds interesting," Mrs. Mulaney says. "Which section?"

"His conversion in the garden—I mean, obviously everyone wanted the story of the pear tree, but our group didn't get to pick first."

The way the story slides off Lucy's tongue, I almost believe we're here for a theology project, too. Mrs. Mulaney nods, and I stand there in awe. Everything tumbles out of my mouth whether I want it to or not, but Lucy is so determined and precise, even when she's lying through her teeth. I've never been a good liar, so I barely ever try. It's my one accidental virtue.

Eden nudges Max. "Let's go," she says, walking past her mom and out of the room. Max bounds after her, with Avi following. I take a couple steps outside the half-closed door but then stop to wait for Lucy.

"I'll see you on Sunday, Mrs. Mulaney," Lucy says.

"I—" Mrs. Mulaney clears her throat, and Lucy stops. "Half the time I don't even know what she's talking about, with— what's it—"

"Celtic Reconstructionist Polytheism?" Lucy says, getting it right.

"Her father says it's a phase," Mrs. Mulaney says, and leaves it there, like she wants Lucy to agree.

"I think it's . . . meaningful to her," Lucy says. "I think she's happy."

"Keep an eye on her, for me. Make sure none of this goes too far."

I can feel Lucy gearing up for her biggest lie yet. "Mrs. Mulaney," she says, "I'd never let that happen."

"They call it Planned Parenthood," the narrator warns, "because it sounds better than 'Infanticide Incorporated.'"

"I bet he spent days thinking up that line," Avi says as the screen goes red.

I remember watching a couple sex ed videos back in middle school. One had two white teenagers rapping about the importance of contraceptives. The other was called *A Child Is Born* and showed the joy of childbirth in all its naked, screaming, bloody glory. It made Amanda Keppler faint. But that was nothing compared to the monstrosity that is *Relationships Without Regret*.

By the time the video moves on to the benefits of "natural family planning" within Catholic marriages, I'm ready to run from the room screaming. How have the rest of my classmates watched this video three years in a row?

The screen shifts to a happy couple, hand in hand, the wife displaying her gigantic belly proudly. "Semen is full of zinc, and a married man engaging in natural intercourse will supply this necessary nutrient to his wife."

"Or she could eat more meat!" Eden yells at her laptop screen, which we've all crowded around.

"I'm pretty sure they're suggesting she eat *his* meat," I say.

Lucy gags. "Michael, ew."

"They're not suggesting that," Eden says. "Blow jobs aren't allowed, they don't make babies."

"Anyway," Lucy interrupts, "obviously that's a silly reason to disallow barrier methods, but also, I looked up the study he cited, and it's from 1947."

"So not only is it a bad reason, but it's a bad reason from before color TV existed?" I ask.

"Exactly."

"So where do you want to put that?" Eden asks, hands above her keyboard.

"We could have it in a speech bubble," Avi suggests. "Like with the husband's dick saying it."

I laugh, and so does Eden. Lucy frowns.

"We're not doing that," Lucy says, like the rest of us don't even get a vote.

If Lucy had her way, we'd be writing a dissertation. With endnotes. "Why not?" I ask.

"It's immature."

I stare at her. "Do you know how old you are? Because I know you like tea and watching *Jeopardy!*, but you're actually not sixty-five."

"Think about your audience," Avi says. "You're not addressing Congress, your audience is Connor."

"Maybe I don't want to play to the lowest common denominator," Lucy says.

"Lucy," I say. "I'm surprised by your indicknation over the penis speech bubble."

She gives me a dark look.

"You're making the rest of us feel like we're being shafted."

"It's not funny," she snaps. "This isn't funny."

"It might be, if you weren't such a prude."

I know it was the wrong thing to say as soon as it leaves my mouth. Lucy stomps up the stairs to the ground floor of the house, shutting the door behind her.

Avi and I look at each other. He raises his eyebrows. I stand up and walk to the stairs.

"You always know just what to say," Avi deadpans as I pass by.

"Shut up."

Lucy's sitting on the hallway floor in the entryway, her back up against the wall, her eyes staring at the ceiling.

We sit for a moment in silence, then Lucy says, "Before you ask, no, I'm not okay."

"I wasn't going to ask."

"That's inconsiderate."

"It was a joke," I say. "The prude thing was a joke."

"It absolutely was not."

She's not even going to let me apologize now? "It was!"

"No, it's true, and I'm fine with that," she says. "I don't think it's some failing on my part if I don't want to wax lyrical about—uh—"

"Penises," I say. "I think the word you're looking for is—"

"*Male genitalia!* God!" She slumps back against the wall.

First storming out of HA, now using the Lord's name in vain. Something's clearly wrong.

"What's up with you?"

She hesitates. "I wanted to do something good, something real and helpful."

"We are."

"Are we?" She looks at me. "Or are we using it as an excuse to mess with people we don't like?"

I consider this. "Why can't it be both?"

"Because! If we're trying to make sure our classmates know enough about sex to make their own decisions, I can justify that. Even if everything goes wrong, even if we get caught, I can live with that."

"We're not going to get caught," I assure her, though I don't know why I think that.

"We could," Lucy says. "This could have real consequences. So we have to make sure what we're doing is worth it."

"We'll make sure it's all important. And that it's worth it, if

81

we get caught. And also that we don't get caught. That's like priority number one."

Lucy laughs, her shoulders relaxing maybe half a centimeter.

We're sitting so close our knees are touching, so close I can smell the laundry detergent on her shirt, so close I can see her lips are chapped, and I wonder if mine are too. I wonder if we kissed right now, both with cracked, chapped lips, if it would feel like sandpaper. I decide I don't really care.

But before I can decide anything else, Eden's mom is standing over us. Lucy jumps away. "Do you two need anything?" she asks.

"Construction paper," I say.

"A copy of Augustine's *Confessions*," Lucy says.

I follow Eden's mom through the kitchen to collect the supplies, still thinking about Lucy's chapped lips.

10

THE LIFE CHOICES assembly is scheduled for fifth period, PE, which is really too bad. Since it's pouring outside, I would have been guaranteed a full hour of hiding behind gym bleachers and playing card games with Max. Instead, I'm following Avi and the rest of our PE class into the auditorium behind the chapel.

"I don't know who decided bright purple was a good look for this place," Avi says as we settle into plush seats in the front row, on the aisle. "But they were wrong."

"I don't know," I say, running my hand over the fuzzy armrest. "Maybe alien vomit purple will be the next big thing."

Theresa, at the head of her class, stops on the stairs to glare at us. "Violet. Our school color is *violet*," she says before swishing her ponytail and continuing up.

"Violet," Avi repeats. "Please. It's Barney." He cranes his neck toward the back. "Do you see where everyone is?"

I twist around, scanning the auditorium. Lucy told everyone to split up, to look less suspicious, so Max agreed to hang back when we lined up. He's sitting in the second row, in the center, chatting up a girl in the row behind him.

"Eden's off to the left," Avi says. "Five rows up."

It takes me a couple seconds until a distinct red ribbon flashes in the second-to-last row. Lucy's wearing her ribbon as a headband today, and she smiles nervously when she sees me looking at her. I don't feel nervous at all. Returning the annotated DVD to the theology room bookshelf went off without a hitch, and there's nothing left for us to do.

Avi nudges me. "It's starting."

Father Peter takes the stage. He clears his throat. "Ladies and gentlemen," he says, as if we're opera patrons, not teenagers about to hear about STDs against our will. "I'm very happy that once again, we're able to host this Life Choices program. We'll be starting with a speech and activity session hosted by Mr. Paul Dwyer—"

"Wait," I whisper to Avi. "Purity Paul's name is *actually* Paul?"

"Why'd you think I called him that?"

"—followed by a short video presentation. Now." Father Peter folds his arms across his chest. "This is sensitive material, and I expect each and every one of you to be mature about this. There are terms used in these presentations you may find . . . uncomfortable."

Father Peter sighs the kind of sigh that only comes from

decades of hearing fifteen-year-olds giggle at the word "vagina."

"I expect the St. Clare's community to be attentive and respectful to those who have given up time in their day to speak to you. On that note, let me introduce our guest speaker, Mr. Dwyer."

Before Father Peter's even finished with the introduction, Purity Paul bursts through the center of the curtains, carrying a mic in his hand and wearing a smile that could only be caused by Jesus or LSD.

"Thank you so, so much, Father Peter." Purity Paul turns to us. "Let's give Father Peter a big hand, everybody," he says, gesturing at Father Peter's hastily retreating back. One person claps like a seal. I'm pretty sure it's Theresa.

"Hello, St. Clare's!" Paul says, too close to his mic. "It's great to be back!"

Paul plops himself down on the edge of the stage in a way I think was supposed to seem casual.

"So, guys. *Sex.*" He looks at us like we should be shocked and awed he's said the word out loud. "I bet you hear a lot about it. On TV, in movies, in books—not to mention the internet. And what do you hear about it? What does our media tell you sex is like?"

He pauses, and I'm not sure if he's expecting anyone to answer, but no one does.

"Everyone says it's the best thing ever, right? Isn't that what you hear? It's a rite of passage. It's amazing. It's fun. And you know what, guys?" He leans in, conspiratorial again. "They're *right*. Sex is an amazing, beautiful thing."

He sits back, looking disgustingly pleased with himself. *You've got them now,* I can almost hear him thinking. *You acknowledged sex is fun! They went in expecting something stuffy and boring, but you're different!*

I have never been more embarrassed for anyone in my life.

"Don't forget," he reminds us, "God invented sex. Like everything else on this earth, it's one of His creations."

Yeah, well, then so is genocide. And mosquitoes. And tangled headphone cords.

"He wants us to be happy, to enjoy sex, but to do it in a way that respects our body, our spouse's body, and His divine plan for life and procreation. He's not"—and Paul smirks a little here—"some kind of cosmic killjoy."

New life plan: form a band called Cosmic Killjoy.

Purity Paul retrieves a black duffel bag from behind the curtain. I wonder what's in it. Enough chastity belts to go around? Miniature statues of the Virgin Mary that weep when you masturbate?

"I know what you're thinking," Paul says, though I'm sure he doesn't. "You're thinking this is all a lot of *blah blah blah*. So how about we mix it up, you guys? See how all this stuff works in the real world?"

"Ugh," Avi says, slumping in his seat. "The object lesson."

"The what?"

Avi opens his mouth, but before he can answer, Paul asks, "I'm going to need a helping hand for this—any volunteers?"

I sense, rather than see, Theresa's hand shoot up. "Maybe someone who didn't help out last year," Paul adds, scanning the room. He points at someone in the back. "How about you?"

I crane my neck, trying to see who he's chosen. Whoever his victim is, they don't seem too eager to get up.

"Yes, you," he repeats. "With the hair ribbon."

Oh no.

Lucy picks herself up, and slowly, stiffly descends the stairs and crosses the stage to stand next to Paul. She looks like a cow walking into a slaughterhouse, except unlike a cow, she knows exactly what's going to happen to her. But I don't.

"What's your name?" Paul asks, tipping his mic down to her.

"Lucy," she mumbles.

"Lucy. A pretty name for a pretty girl. But I bet people tell you that all the time."

She stares at him, unblinking.

"Well. Lucy, you are going to help me with a little experiment."

Handing the mic to Lucy, Paul digs around in his bag of tricks and pulls out a roll of masking tape. He holds it aloft for us like it's Simba in the beginning of *The Lion King*. He tears off a medium-sized section and puts the rest back in his bag.

"What is this, Lucy?" he asks, showing her the sticky side.

"Masking tape."

"And what does it look like?"

"It looks like masking tape."

Paul laughs. "Come on. You can be more descriptive than that. What does this side look like?"

"White. Rectangular. Sticky."

"Does it have anything on it?"

"No," Lucy says. "It's . . ."

"Go on. It's—"

Lucy's looking at him like someone who figured out a joke's punch line too fast and doesn't think it's funny.

"It's clean," she says.

"Exactly right. It's clean." Paul holds the sticky side up for all of us to see. "This is what you are like, when you choose chastity. Pure, unblemished, untouched . . ."

. . . and good at holding packages together? Did this dude compare our virgin souls to masking tape?

"But what happens when we give ourselves to others? What happens to our bodies and our souls? So, Lucy, if you could take this—"

Paul hands the tape over to Lucy, who would clearly rather paste it over his mouth.

"—and pick out someone in the front row." He chuckles. "A *male* someone, please."

I am in the front row. I am male. I am someone.

And while I'm trying to figure out whether I really want

88

to be part of this office supplies experiment, Lucy comes and stands in front of my seat, holding the tape between two fingers. She looks pissed. She looks sad. Mostly, she looks like she'd rather be anywhere but here, and I want that for her, too.

The way she's standing, her body blocks Purity Paul, but I can hear his voice from behind her. "Now stick the tape to his arm."

I hold my arm out for her, palm up, but off Paul's instruction, she flips it over so it's palm-side down. She affixes the scratchy tape above my wrist, smoothing it over with her hand. This is the longest Lucy has ever touched me. My pulse jumps under her fingers. I know we're in an auditorium full of people and taking orders from a man who thinks premarital sex is akin to murder, but I want to keep feeling the pads of her fingers on my arm, all the blood in my body rushing toward her touch.

I wonder what the Catholic Church does to people who get turned on at chastity assemblies. They probably castrate them.

Suddenly, she yanks the tape off and about half my arm hair with it. Paul must have told her to, but she could have done it more gently.

"Ow!" I hiss at her, and for a second, she smiles, a real Lucy smile, before she heads back to the front of the room. Lucy hands the masking tape to Paul, and he holds it up for everyone to see. It's a little wrinkled now, with bits of hair.

"Now, this is what you're like with one partner. One single partner. But that's not what society tells you to do, is it? No, society wants you to *hook up*. Society says it's okay to treat sex like no big deal. So what happens then, when you've given the most precious part of your soul not to one person, but to five, or ten?"

He sends Lucy out to repeat the masking tape trick four more times, using the same bit of tape. After she's done, he holds up the tape again. It's worse for the wear now, crinkled in some places and curling at the ends. With the remnants of five dudes' arm hair stuck to it, it looks gross.

"This," he says, showing the tape off, "is what you are when you choose to live an unchaste life. And for the girls, there's an extra level of danger. Biologically, women develop strong, hard-to-break attachments to those they sleep with. Though we all give away pieces of our God-given soul through unchaste actions, ladies, you give away pieces of your *heart*, too."

My breath catches. Is that what Lucy's afraid of? That someone will love her for a moment and then wreck her forever? What he's saying is awful, and wrong besides that, but does Lucy believe it?

"So, Lucy," Paul says, tearing a clean swatch of tape from the roll and presenting her with both pieces, one pristine, the other wrinkled and dirty. "Which do you choose? Which one do you want to be?"

Lucy's clenching and unclenching her hands like she can't figure out whether to punch or strangle this douchebag. And if she can't choose, I'll do it for her, because I don't know if I've hated someone so much, so instantly, in my entire life. Lucy is not a piece of tape. Lucy is not one or the other, pure or dirty. Lucy is Lucy. She could swim in a sewer, have sex with every single person in the world, and she would still never be *dirty*. I hate him for trying to tell her she could be.

But, like a person who knows she doesn't have a choice, or maybe a person who knows exactly what DVD is already set up on the TV, Lucy sighs and picks the clean, untouched piece of virgin masking tape.

Purity Paul moves on to Purity Platitudes, telling us things like "true love waits" and "chastity is not a burden, it's a crown of triumph" as Lucy stands awkwardly beside him, wiping her masking-tape-sticky fingers on her plaid skirt.

"He's wrapping up," Avi says. "A couple minutes and they'll start the movie."

This is the part of the plan we never quite figured out: the distraction. Lucy said Purity Paul never stays for the video, so he's one less adult to worry about, and Sister Helen can barely hear, but Father Peter usually supervises. And he'll notice if everyone actually starts paying attention to what's on the screen. But as I look at Lucy onstage, I think I have an idea.

I dig out a pencil and scrap of notebook paper from my backpack and start to write.

"What are you doing?" Avi hisses.

"Being brilliant."

"Seriously doubtful."

Just for that, I don't let him read the note I'm writing. Purity Paul's thanking Lucy for her participation, so I have to write fast.

30 sec. into vid, leave like ur upset abt P.P. Take Pete w/you.

As Lucy starts to sweep by me and up the stairs, I catch her hand. She looks surprised.

"Are you okay?" I ask, not because I think she isn't, but in case anyone's listening. At the same time, I slip the folded-up note into her palm.

"Yeah," she says, and tightens her fist around the note before continuing up the stairs.

Purity Paul wishes us the best of luck on our journey with purity and exits the stage to half-hearted applause. Avi looks like he's got a few questions, but the lights dim, and Father Peter walks away from the projector. He's put our DVD in. Well, he's put *a* DVD in. I hope it's ours.

Thirty seconds into the opening credits, right on cue, I hear the soft squeak of patent leather shoes from the back row. I steal a glance backward and see Lucy descending the stairs, head down. A few people turn to look at her, but not many.

As the opening credits continue, a zygote is transformed into a toddler, then into a child at his First Communion. Lucy hurries toward the auditorium doors, nearly crashing into Father Peter, illuminated by the bright hallway light. He throws out a hand to stop her. The cheesy harp music from the video makes it impossible to hear them, but Lucy gestures to the place onstage where Purity Paul had her stand. Her shoulders sag, and there's a chance Lucy's pulled out some Oscar-worthy tears, because Father Peter opens the door and guides her out of the room.

Avi nudges my leg. He looks toward the door, now swinging shut again. I nod, and he sits back, satisfied. Father Peter's out of the way now, and no one can accuse Lucy of plotting to distract him. She has every reason to be upset, and Father Peter has every reason to try to console her.

Finally, the title card appears on the screen:

RELATIONSHIPS WITHOUT REGRET
PRESENTED BY FR. NICHOLAS ANGELO
AND THE ANTIOCH, NE, DIOCESE

Then, scrawled in a much less formal-looking font:

ANNOTATED FOR ACCURACY BY
HERETICS ANONYMOUS

It sounds, for a second, like everyone's taken a collective breath in. But nobody moves, not Theresa and certainly not Sister Helen, who's sitting on a folding chair by the door, deep into her rosary beads.

The movie begins with a low-budget, bad-actor clip of Romeo and Juliet during the balcony scene.

"A rose by any other name would smell as sweet," Juliet says, her terrible costume wig nearly slipping off her head.

"Is all love equal?" the terrifying narrator says. "Two teenagers may, like Romeo and Juliet, desire one another, but is their love *authentic*? Those who follow God's plan for Catholic marriages are rewarded. American Catholic couples who waited until marriage had lower divorce rates than those that did not."

An annotation pops up on the screen:

But guess who had the lowest divorce rates
of all, according to a decade-long study by the Barna
Group? Atheists and agnostics.

A girl across the aisle from me points at the screen, whispering with her friend. There's a low buzz of excited chatter from the whole auditorium. Avi keeps his eyes trained on the screen, poker-faced, but I smile. I was the one who found that study.

The narrator moves on to the section about the nature of "natural" sexual conduct between spouses, and the dangers of birth control.

"You might have heard that the condom—"

Here, they show a limp, banana-yellow condom.

"—is a fail-proof method for protecting against sexually transmitted diseases. But did you know condoms have pores? A virus such as HIV can easily pass through a pore."

Another annotation appears on-screen, in a speech bubble for a friendly cartoon condom.

This is untrue. Standards testing by
groups such as the World Health Organization
show even water molecules (smaller than an HIV virus
molecule) cannot pass through a condom.

A boy in the far right section starts taking a video with his phone. I can't believe Theresa hasn't torn apart the screen with both hands yet, but I'm too scared to look over at her; it might trigger homicidal rage.

Lambskin condoms are a lot more porous,
but seriously, like you're going to buy a lambskin
condom. Who are you, Henry VIII?

There's commotion behind me, and I turn around. Theresa, apparently recovered from shock, is trying to push out of her row. She's dead center, so it's slow going, even as she throws elbows. Someone yells at her for blocking the screen.

As soon as she gets to Sister Helen, still serenely doing a Rosary in the corner, this whole thing will be dead. Theresa finally makes it out of her row, and I can hear the stomp of her shoes as she flies down the aisle, then a crash. Avi and I both twist back. Theresa's splayed on the stairs, her foot caught in the strap of a brown, vegan leather backpack with an Irish flag pin. Eden kneels next to her, apologizing and asking if she's okay.

"I'm *fine*," Theresa snaps, the image of Christian compassion. "Get *off* me."

Her ponytail half undone and one knee sock down, Theresa takes the stairs two at a time, running over to Sister Helen and gesturing wildly at the screen. Sister Helen stares at Theresa for a moment, then slowly rises and crosses to where she can view the screen better, just in time to see a speech bubble from a man's crotch refuting the healing powers of zinc-filled semen.

The joke kills. And to her credit, Sister Helen doesn't faint.

The door bangs as Theresa disappears out of it, returning thirty seconds later with Father Peter, Lucy trailing behind him. He doesn't wait to see the evidence himself, just walks over to the DVD player and shuts it off. There are a couple groans. The lights flick on.

"The rest of this period will be used as a study hall," Father Peter announces. "You will all quickly and quietly proceed to the library. Miss Ambrose, please go warn the librarians."

Theresa scurries off. The rest of us file out quickly, but not quietly. The rain has stopped, and as I pass through the heavy auditorium doors into the sun-drenched hallway, I can hear someone behind me whisper the words "Heretics Anonymous."

11

EVERYONE HAS BEEN whispering about Heretics Anonymous for the past two weeks.

In theology, Leah Davies interrupts Sister Helen's lecture to ask if the *Relationships Without Regret* DVD came with a teacher's guide, because she can't find any info to back up their claims about hormonal birth control. Even super-shy Jenny Okoye wants Sister Helen to know she found the blog of the priest who directed the video, and he thinks girls shouldn't be altar servers, and she's an altar server, so why should she have to listen to him, anyway?

Sister Helen deflects these questions. All the adults at St. Clare's seem determined to ignore the fact that the whole thing happened. I don't know how effective this is, but it does mean HA can relax, at least for now.

Avi's at his weekly lunchtime meeting for the school newspaper, *The St. Clare's Record*, so Lucy and I are sitting together at a four-top table when something hard and plastic bangs into the back of my head.

"Oh, sorry, dude," Connor says when I turn around, pulling back his food tray a little. He and his girlfriend eye the two empty seats at our table.

Lucy opens her mouth, but Connor cuts her off. "There aren't any other tables open, so chill."

Lucy scowls but doesn't object when they sit down, Connor next to me, his girlfriend next to her.

"How'd you like the sex ed assembly this year, Lucifer?" he asks Lucy, shoveling chili into his mouth.

Lucy attempts to disembowel Connor with her eyes before saying, "I didn't see the video. I was talking with Father Peter outside."

"Shit, you missed out. It was hilarious," Connor says, and his girlfriend groans. "Oh, you are such a killjoy, Jess."

"Whatever," Jess says. "I just didn't get the point."

"What do you mean?" Lucy asks.

Jess shrugs. "So they lied to us about sex. No shit. They don't want us to *have* sex, of course they'd make it sound dangerous and awful."

"But you can't think that's okay!" I protest, and Lucy gives me a look that says, *Dial it back.*

"Maybe it's not. But maybe it's also not up to us to decide what gets taught. Half of us can't even drive yet."

"It was fun, though," Connor cuts in. "A lot more

entertaining than that assembly usually is."

Jess looks unmoved. "I'm going to do what I want, no matter what someone tells me in an assembly. Doesn't matter if it's that chastity guy or Heretics Anonymous."

"Like I said. Killjoy."

"I'm just trying to get through this high school bullshit. It's only going to make it harder on everyone else if these people start throwing public tantrums about St. Clare's."

I hear a foot tapping, and we all look up at Theresa, looming over our lunch table with her arms full of pamphlets. She's flanked by two girls I don't know, similarly buttoned up and fresh faced.

"I couldn't help overhearing," she says, focusing her attention on Connor and Jess.

"Sure you couldn't," Connor says.

"And I think you might be interested in these materials I've prepared—" She hands them two of the powder-pink pamphlets. "—to counteract the misstatements made by certain factions during the Life Choices assembly."

"See what I mean?" Jess says. "They've already made it worse."

"A group of us are planning to meet with the school administration this afternoon," Theresa says, gesturing at her friends. "We're asking them to finally make an official statement about the incident. I, for one, think we need swift, decisive action. Would you like to join us?"

"Not interested," Lucy says.

Theresa rounds on her. "Why would I ask you? You're obviously behind the whole thing."

"Excuse me?" Lucy says.

"I know you ruined the DVD, that commentary has you written all over it—"

"Theresa, I wasn't even there," Lucy says, like she's talking to an overtired toddler and not an unhinged future Bride of Christ.

"A *ruse*," Theresa hisses, jabbing a finger at her. "A carefully planned *ruse*."

It's amazing how ridiculous someone can sound when they're saying something true. Except for the "carefully planned" part.

"Really?" I ask Theresa. "You think she planned to be humiliated by some purity douchebag just so she couldn't watch the movie?"

Theresa bends down, putting both hands on the table. "I'll be watching you," she promises Lucy, then turns to Jess and Connor. "Think about it." She leaves with a flip of her braid.

Jess turns the pamphlet over. She doesn't look sold but doesn't look disgusted, either. Connor puts his down immediately.

"Say what you want," he says to Jess, twirling his spoon with an almost philosophical air. "But they had good points. Like about condoms. I know what Sister Helen says, but there's got to be times God's okay with them, right?"

Jess pulls out her phone. "Connor, you hate using condoms."

"Yeah, but that's me and my life. What about people who have like, raging herpes? Or someone who would for sure abort the baby if she got knocked up. What's worse, condoms or abortions?"

"I don't know," Jess says. "I'm on the pill, so, irrelevant."

"It's not irrelevant," Connor says. "Just because it's not about you or me doesn't mean it's irrelevant."

Lucy's looking at Connor with some kind of dazed amazement. I'm shocked, too. I had no idea he knew the word "irrelevant."

"So I'm down with HA," he declares, and, tipping his bowl to his mouth, slurps down the last of his chili.

12

I NEVER THOUGHT of Thanksgiving as a dressy holiday, but apparently, this year is different. Sophia's in her freshly ironed Christmas dress, standing at the kitchen table, trying to build a Thanksgiving horn of plenty out of wire, burlap, and a malfunctioning glue gun. I, of course, am being wrangled into my least favorite article of clothing.

"But I already have to wear a tie every day to school."

"Then you should be better at tying one," Mom says, and reaches over to redo it.

"Mom—"

"I don't want to hear it."

"If we were at Grandma's—"

She tugs too hard on the tie as she loops it around. "We're not at Grandma's. We're here, and this is my Thanksgiving, so Sophia is making a cornucopia and you are wearing a tie."

Sophia struggles valiantly with the hot glue gun. The floor

beneath her feet is sparkling; Mom waxed it this morning. The whole place smells like the inside of a citrus fruit.

"He's not going to notice," I tell Mom. "He's not going to notice any of this."

She suddenly yanks on the tie, dragging me down until I'm eye level with her. "Michael Andrew Ausman, I love you more than life itself, but if you pick a fight with your father tonight, I am going to drive you into the mountains and leave you there."

She hasn't resorted to *that* threat in years.

"Okay?" she says, and her eyes look too bright.

"Okay, Mom. Okay."

She releases her grip on the tie. "Good." She pats my shoulder. "Now help your sister with that chicken wire before she pokes her eye out."

Mom wanted to go to my grandparents' house for Thanksgiving, like we always do. I did, too, if only because that's what we always do. But Dad got the long weekend off, and said that after his twelve-hour flight, a five-hour drive was out of the question. Mom took him off speakerphone after he said that and went into the bathroom to have a hushed, angry conversation. But we ended up staying here for Thanksgiving anyway.

A car door slams outside as I finish laying the festive brown-and-orange tablecloth out, and Sophia picks pieces of dried glue off the ends of her fingers.

"That must be Dad and Alex," Mom says.

Alex is my older cousin, Mom's brother's son. All the family members we speak to are from my mom's side. When we were younger, Alex spent most holidays holed up in Grandma's garage and periodically returned to the house to steal half-baked crescent rolls out of the oven. Now, he's at some grad program in the woods, an hour's train ride from us. Dad picked him up on his way in from the airport.

But when the back door opens, only Alex walks in, wearing at least one article of clothing made from hemp and carrying a Tupperware of brown goo. I hope it's not a communal offering.

"Hey, Alex." I'm not sure if I'm supposed to shake his hand or hug him or what. I settle for sticking my hands in my pockets.

"Michael!" he says, looking me up and down. "Dude, wow, you're like a real person now."

I gesture at the Tupperware. "Should I put that with the rest of the food?"

He looks down at it, as if seeing it for the first time. "Oh. No, it's just for me. Vegan chili. I didn't want to put you guys out or anything."

"Where's my dad?" I ask, looking over Alex's shoulder.

"He got a call in the car. Said he'd be in in a minute."

I catch a glimpse of Dad out the back porch window, talking on his phone. He's got that sour look on his face, the one that says the conversation isn't going well. And when work isn't great, Dad isn't great. When his day is bad, it's bad for everyone. Mom pulls the turkey out of the oven and ignores our conversation.

"We're ready!" she says. "Let's set the table."

"Sophia, please stop picking at the cornucopia."

Sophia looks up at Mom, pulling her hand back from the stray wire she was poking. We didn't do a very good job with the burlap, and now the whole thing's falling apart.

"I'm bored," she whines. "And hungry."

So am I. The bowl of mashed potatoes directly in front of my plate is slowly getting colder and colder. The green beans are getting cold too, and so is the turkey. I guess the cranberry sauce was cold to begin with.

"This is ridiculous," I say. "Can we please start?"

Mom shakes her head. "He said he'd be done in five minutes."

"Ten minutes ago. And he didn't even *say* that, he held up five fingers. That could mean fifty minutes. It could mean five hours."

"He meant five minutes," Mom says, craning her head to see the back porch. Sophia starts picking at the cornucopia again.

My phone buzzes in my pocket. I pull it out and see a text from Lucy.

Did you know they served lobster at the first Thanksgiving?

I've accepted Lucy's never going to text me normal things,

like "hey" or "how are you" or "I don't want to be a girl priest anymore, let's have sex."

Me: what?

Lucy: I'm bored and reading Wikipedia

Lucy: They also served clams

Just then, I hear the back door close, and a voice behind me say, "Put the phone away, Michael."

I glare at Dad as he sits down at the head of the table, next to me. Mom squeezes my leg under the table, so I stick my phone in my pocket and don't say anything.

"All right," Dad says. "We're ready."

"We've been ready," I mumble. Mom takes a sharp breath in through her nose.

"Maybe you should say grace," Dad suggests. "Show us what you've learned at Catholic school."

"They don't teach us that," I say, and make the executive decision to start serving myself mashed potatoes.

Dad goes for the turkey and takes his time selecting a piece. He's weird about food, and way pickier than he'd ever tolerate me or Sophia being. When we used to go on road trips, Mom would pack us all PB&J sandwiches. Except Dad. He got his own sandwich, specially made.

"So," he says to Alex, "what's your major, again?"

"Cinema studies," Alex says, his mouth full of weird vegan paste.

Sophia perks up. "You make movies?"

"No, cinema studies is more about analyzing films."

"I watched a really good movie yesterday," Sophia says.

"What movie, Soph?" Mom asks.

"On TV. It was called *How the West Was Lost*."

"*How the West Was Won*," Dad corrects her. "Henry Fonda. Great movie."

Sophia hesitates. "No," she says. "*How the West Was Lost*. On the History Channel. It was about how white settlers took Native people's land, even when they promised they wouldn't, and they said the West was 'won' when it was obviously really *lost* for the people who'd always been there, which is why the movie's called that. And then they started talking about all these massacres—"

Mom clears her throat. "You know, honey, maybe this isn't the best—"

"And I wanted to know what happened to the Wampanoag— the tribe that was at the first Thanksgiving—and the internet said they got mostly killed or sold into slavery, eventually." She takes a split-second breath. "I like turkey and I like the Thanksgiving parade, but this holiday is *really sad* and I sort of don't get why we celebrate it."

"I'm not sure I like you learning about all this," Dad says.

Sophia blinks. "Why not? It happened."

My phone vibrates again, and I discreetly fish it out of my pocket.

Lucy: What do you think seal tastes like?

Me: im at dinner

Me: shouldn't you be too?

Lucy: Still waiting on the turkey. Cooking isn't my calling.

"I already told you once, put the phone away."

Dad's glaring at me across the table.

"Sorry, I got a text, it buzzed—"

"Who could possibly be texting you at six p.m. on Thanks-giving?"

"Canadians," Sophia suggests.

"My roommate doesn't celebrate Thanksgiving," Alex offers up. "He says it's a testament to, like, American imperialism, so he's in DC protesting oil drilling."

"Imperialism! They talked about that so much in the movie!" Sophia says.

"No more movie talk," Mom says, at the same time as Dad repeats, "Who was texting you?"

"Lucy," I say. "My friend from school, Lucy."

Sophia cuts right to the chase. "Is she your *girl*friend?"

"No, she's—"

"Turn your phone off," Dad says to me. "Your friend can leave a message."

I pretend to but don't. Who turns their phone all the way off, ever? Or leaves messages? Old people.

Mom makes small talk with Alex, asking about his parents (fine), his classes (also fine), and his romantic interests (he doesn't believe in labels and is keeping it casual) until Sophia leans across the table, peering at Alex's Tupperware.

"How come you brought your own food? It looks like primordial ooze."

"Sophia!" Mom says.

"I'm a vegan," Alex says.

"How would you even know what primordial ooze looks like?" I ask.

Sophia shoots me a withering look. "From *textbooks*." She turns back to Alex. "My old best friend, Hannah, didn't eat anything with a face."

"I don't eat anything with a face, either," Alex says. "Or any of the stuff those face-havers make. Like the butter on the green beans. And the potatoes."

"It's actually margarine," Mom admits, then shrugs at Dad. "With your cholesterol."

"Really? Sweet!" Alex shovels several helpings of green beans into his Tupperware, but then stops. "Wait. Is margarine vegan?"

"It doesn't have a face," Sophia reasons.

Another buzz in my pocket. I try to ignore it, then feel another buzz, ten seconds later. Then another. I wish I wasn't sitting right next to Dad. I sneak a glance under the table.

Lucy: This holiday is the worst

Lucy: SERIOUSLY IT IS WORSE THAN ARBOR DAY

Lucy: Talk to me before I start watching the parade highlights out of sheer boredom

I feel a surge in my stomach, and not just from the mashed

potatoes making their way through my intestines. Of all the people in the world, I'm the one Lucy wants to talk to on her least favorite holiday. The moment's brief, though, because Dad smacks the back of my chair harder than he needs to, and I bang my arm on the underside of the table.

"If I see you touch that phone one more time, I'm going to put it in the blender," he says.

And suddenly, I can't take it anymore, and I don't care what I promised Mom. I don't see Sophia anymore, trying to rearrange the disintegrating cornucopia, or Alex, debating whether our green beans are ethical to eat. I'm like a horse with blinders, and all I see is Dad, sitting at the head of the table like he owns it. We leave that seat open at dinner every night. He's never there to sit in it.

"You took a half-hour phone call while we were all waiting to eat, and I can't answer one text?"

Silence. Mom's knife scrapes against her plate. Dad takes a breath in.

"It was a work call. This isn't a holiday in Europe. It's just Thursday."

"So we had to sit here and wait for you because Belgians don't celebrate Thanksgiving?"

"The whole world doesn't revolve around you, Michael."

"No," I grind out. "Just you. It revolves around you."

"Dude," Alex says gently, but I barely even hear him.

"Everything gets set up for *you*," I say, "everything gets

perfectly arranged for *you*, and you still act like a jerk, because you're mad at other people half a world away, and that's not Mom's fault and it's not Sophia's and it's not mine, so *back off*."

Dad halfway stands up then, his mouth open, but Sophia's faster. Her chair squeaks against the freshly waxed floor as she pushes it back and runs from the room. Dad follows after her, but not before he throws a dark look in my direction.

Alex and I sit quietly as Mom removes the dishes one by one from the table.

"You can't abandon me in the mountains," I argue. "He started it."

Mom sets down the bowl of mashed potatoes, as if it's suddenly too heavy to carry. Then she leaves too.

My phone's buzzing in my pants pocket. Alex stares straight ahead. He should have gone with his roommate to protest oil drilling. Even if they got arrested, it would be less awkward than this.

"Alex," I say. "Please tell me you have weed."

"Oh man," he says. "I was about to ask you the same thing."

It turns out Alex does have weed, but I can understand why he wanted to ask me first.

"This is shit," I tell him in between coughing my brains out. "It tastes like burnt tires."

Alex doesn't say anything. He's too busy inspecting the leaves of the giant tree we're standing under. It's not even our tree. It's so big, its heavy branches droop over the neighbor's fence into our backyard. My mom hates it. Alex wants to molest it.

This was a bad idea. It seemed like such a good idea when I was mad, but I'm not as mad anymore. I'm cold. And hungry. And really, really need a glass of water.

"Michael!"

Shit. Dad. I thought we'd have more time. Usually, it takes Dad forever to console Sophia after stuff like this. She's so dramatic.

"Where are you?" I hear him stomping up the stairs, probably checking in my room, which buys me maybe a minute.

Oh crap, and I probably smell like this terrible skunk weed, too. I strip off the hoodie I put on over my shirt and tie and stash it in the bushes. I throw the joint there too, and hope Mom doesn't decide to do any gardening tomorrow. Alex doesn't move.

"Alex," I whisper, gesturing at his jacket. "Take it off."

"Chill," he says, reaching inside his cargo pants and taking out a small purple bottle. I might be hallucinating, but I think it has sparkles on it.

"The fuck is that?"

He uncaps it and starts spritzing himself. "Body spray."

"What, for nine-year-old girls?"

"Whatever, it works."

And it better, because I hear the back door open.

I have butterflies in my stomach. A million butterflies. How did that become a phrase? What caveman was super nervous about trying to kill a saber-toothed tiger and decided it felt like he swallowed butterflies? Why not rocks? Because it does feel like butterflies, but it also somehow feels like rocks. Flying rocks. Maybe the caveman really did swallow a butterfly, so that's how he knew. Maybe he ate it on purpose. Bugs have iron in them, or actually protein, I think it's protein. I wonder what a butterfly would taste like.

I am so screwed.

"There you are," Dad says, clomping down the porch stairs, and I walk toward him, only to keep him as far away from Alex as possible. "Why didn't you answer me?"

"I didn't hear you." I keep my eyes down in case they're red and my hands in my pockets in case they smell and I can't think of anything else to do or I'd do it.

"Oh, like hell," he says.

I don't say anything, because I can feel a tickle in my throat, and if I cough, he'll know, *he'll just know.*

Dad looks over my shoulder. "What's he doing?"

Alex is underneath the tree, letting the droopy branches cover his face. "It's a willow!" he crows.

"It's a willow," I repeat for Dad, as straight-faced as I can.

"I love willows!"

"He loves willows."

Dad shakes his head and focuses back on me. The tickle in my windpipe is getting worse. I clear my throat. It doesn't help.

"What happened tonight was completely unacceptable."

Thanksgiving is all about firsts. The first night Native Americans ate dinner with genocidal dicks who would later steal their land, and also the first time I have to listen to a Dad lecture while high. Not that I'm actually listening. The itch in my throat has evolved into whatever comes after an itch. A worse itch. It feels like poison ivy and mosquito bites and scratchy sweaters all rolled into one, but I can't cough. I won't cough. I think he's figured out something's up with Alex, but Alex isn't his kid.

". . . but this is beyond an adjustment period, this is a full-blown attitude issue . . ."

I'm not going to be able to hold it in. I can feel it. It wants to get out. Like a lion in a cage. Or a butterfly in a caveman's stomach. My chest hitches.

". . . and if you think because I'm not in the house twenty-four/seven, I'm going to let you act this way, then . . ."

It hitches again. *I am not going to cough I am not going to cough.*

". . . because I'm so sick of it, Michael, I'm sick of this disre-spectful, immature . . ."

There are tears streaming down my face. I am crying. I am trying so hard not to cough, my body has found another expressive outlet and that outlet is my tear ducts. If I hadn't already put so much effort into not seeming high, I would be laughing hysterically.

It takes me a second to notice Dad's stopped talking. I glance up at him, and he looks taken aback. I guess by the tears.

"I—" he stutters, and actually looks *sorry* for a second. "I didn't—" He clears his throat, and I take the opportunity to cough. But only twice. Quietly.

"So," he continues. "We're clear, then?"

I nod.

"And you're going to work on this?"

I nod again and swipe at my eyes with my shirtsleeve. Just to rub it in.

Dad claps me on the shoulder. "Good."

He steps away from me, and I think I might actually be in the clear. The butterflies have died down. Or maybe just died. How long could they swim around in a person's stomach acids, anyway?

"I'm getting my keys, and then I'll drive you to the train station," Dad says to Alex. He looks back over at me. "Do you want to come?"

Oh please no. I clear my throat for a full three seconds before saying, "I'll stay." I feel like I need a reason, so I add, "Dishes."

Dad nods in a way that almost looks like approval. "I'm sure your mom could use the help. I'll be out front in five minutes, Alex."

He goes back into the house. I'd breathe a long sigh of relief if I didn't think I'd start coughing again. Alex leans over our neighbor's fence, trying and failing to hug the tree.

"You know what's great?" he says. "This tree."

"You know what's terrible? Your weed."

"I want to take this tree with me. I want to put this tree in my suitcase and take it back with me."

This person is an adult. He can vote. He can buy beer. He can even rent a car.

"Alex," I remind him. "You didn't bring a suitcase."

13

THE DAY WE come back from Thanksgiving break, Eden and Max call an HA meeting. This is new—as long as I've been here, Lucy has set the meetings. When they tell us at lunch, Lucy looks as surprised as I am. And when we arrive that afternoon, they're standing at the front of the room, clearly planning something.

"Personally, I think the video went better than expected," Eden starts off as Lucy, Avi, and I take seats on the couch and chairs. We all agree it did.

"And that just means we have to keep the energy going," Max says.

"Obviously, we can't do a big event every week—"

"—but we don't want the school to forget we exist."

"Did you guys practice this?" Avi asks.

"No," Eden says, at the same time Max says, "Yes."

Eden gives Max an exasperated look. She turns to the rest

of us. "So, I propose we create a symbol—something we can leave around the school for people to find, something to remind them Heretics Anonymous is still here, gearing up for the next thing."

"Sure," Lucy says. "Just the letters HA? Maybe in red?"

"We actually have some thoughts on that," Eden says. "Max?"

Max jogs over to the broken whiteboard pushed up against one wall of the room, its surface gray and dusty. He pulls a whiteboard marker out of his pocket and begins drawing intersecting circles. He steps back, revealing this:

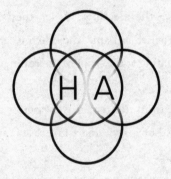

"What is it?" I ask.

"A five-fold," Eden says. "It's Celtic, it's supposed to represent the interconnectedness of things."

"And there's five rings, just like there's five of us!" Max adds.

"It's pretty," Lucy says. "It won't be that pretty when I draw it, though."

"I looked for other symbols from old heretical Christian groups, but I liked the meaning of the five-fold. We're all in this together." Eden shakes her head. "Catholicism never felt like that, for me. It always seemed like I had to squeeze myself in, leave parts of me behind. Now, I feel like my religion wants all of me, because everything and everyone is connected—no matter what we believe."

Lucy's mouth tightens. Is she thinking about the parts she has to leave behind to be a good Catholic? The parts that her own faith doesn't want or value? Lucy with all her brilliant ideas, Lucy with all her steel and softness, Lucy who will never be a priest. I wonder if she'd really shut herself off from everything she could feel, and do, and be, for something that will probably never happen.

I want to think she wouldn't. I know she would.

"It's great," Lucy says. "Thanks, you guys."

"We're not actually done," Eden says. "Max and I have an idea for our next big project."

"Has this ever happened to you?" Max says, sounding uncannily like an infomercial voiceover. "You get dressed in the morning in totally normal clothing that you like, but then—" He pauses dramatically. "They slap you with a dress code violation. Your skirt's too short. Your shirt's not tucked in. Your perfectly normal blazer-alternative's not from the uniform company, which isn't even your fault, because you've written multiple emails about how they should carry cloaks—"

"We'd like to do something about the dress code," Eden interrupts smoothly.

I'm down. But when I look over at Avi and Lucy, they don't look the least bit enthused. Eden presses on.

"Little things," she says. "Figuring out small ways to subvert the dress code and sharing them with the school. There are tons of loopholes, and it would show just how silly our uniform policies are."

"Works for me," I say, but Avi and Lucy stay quiet.

"I don't mind the uniform," Avi admits.

"This is Catholic school," Lucy adds. "They have uniforms, it's kind of their deal."

Eden's mouth drops. "It's their *deal* that you can wear a saint medal, but I can't wear earrings with my religious symbols on them? It's their *deal* that girls have to constantly check how much skin they're showing, and get shamed if they don't?"

"Eden, come on," Lucy says.

"It's not fair. We shouldn't have to look—"

"Or act," Max adds.

"—like everybody else just to be taken seriously. That's something we deserve no matter what. Everybody deserves that."

"I know," Lucy says. "But is this really the best we can do? It's just the dress code."

"Oh, whatever," Eden snaps. "You only feel that way because this is how you'd dress regardless."

Lucy scoffs. "You think I'd wear the same outfit every day? Like a cartoon character?"

"The dress code just seems like . . . the smallest thing," Avi says.

Eden throws up her hands. "The smallest— You guys are being ridiculous! This is important, it's—"

"No," Max says quietly, and Eden stops. "They're right."

Everyone turns to look at him.

"It *is* the smallest thing," he repeats. "We can't even have the smallest thing."

Then there's silence. Avi looks at his shoes. Lucy folds her hands.

"I think we should do it," I blurt out.

"Yes, we all know you hate your tie," Avi says.

And then I realize it. "We should do it because it's important to Eden and Max. It doesn't matter why. If it's important to one of us, it's important to all of us. Isn't that what our symbol means?"

Lucy and Avi share a glance. Lucy nods. "You're right," she says. "We should do it."

Without even having to look at each other, Eden and Max share a high five.

"Any other business?" Lucy says, looking around the room. I raise my hand.

"I think we should add Eden's symbol to the club manifesto," I suggest, and everyone agrees.

Each armed with a marker from a box of abandoned school supplies, one by one, we draw a circle at the top of the sheet. Eden's first, with a green circle in the center. Then Avi, with gray, then Max with purple, like his cape. The circles overlap, the ink bleeding through and melding into an odd-looking brown. Lucy and I go last, her with blue, me with red, like her ribbon.

We all stand back to look at it, five mismatched, misshapen circles that somehow transform into something that matters.

We've got a symbol, and we've got a plan.

Over the next week, five-fold circles begin popping up around St. Clare's. There's one in purple on a cafeteria table. One in my math classroom, drawn perfectly with a compass. On Tuesday, after lunch, every library computer has an HA symbol as its desktop background. Just as theology class starts on Friday, I notice one on the empty desk behind mine.

"When did you draw that?" I ask Lucy and Avi. It had to have been them—Eden and Max have a different theology teacher. Lucy looks at Avi. He shakes his head.

"We didn't," she says.

14

EDEN'S THE ONE who sees it.

I'm standing with her and Max by the locker bays before first period on December 7. Max is explaining the plot of his new favorite fantasy series when Eden looks up over his shoulder and tilts her head to the side.

"What?" I say, searching the stucco ceiling for whatever it is she's staring at.

"Look," she says, and points. "There."

It's a little glass dome tucked in the corner of the hallway ceiling, with a bright red light on the side.

"What is it?" Max asks.

"It's a camera," Eden says. "A security camera."

"I don't remember that being there before," I say.

Eden frowns. "I don't think it was."

"Did there used to be cameras at all?" Max asks.

"A few by the gate, I think." Eden shrugs. "They're more

123

worried about people outside St. Clare's than people in it. Or were, I guess."

I bet I know what changed their minds. "Will this be a problem for . . . study group?" We have a meeting set for after school.

Eden considers. "I don't know. I'll look around. Maybe tell Avi and Lucy not to go down until I check it out."

We have new lab groups in chemistry, and two minutes into class, I'm already sick of mine. Connor and his girlfriend, Jess, keep trying to play footsie under the table but end up kicking me. Theresa doesn't have to do anything to annoy me besides exist.

The morning announcements are the same as always—track-and-field tryouts are on Friday, talk to Sister Joseph Marie about attending the local March for Life, we still don't have a football team—but at the end, instead of signing off, the student anchor hands the mic over, and Father Peter's voice comes through the loudspeaker.

"Good morning, all. I wanted to take a moment to address some changes to the St. Clare's campus. You may have noticed the addition of several security cameras in the school building. These were implemented due to safety concerns and with full approval from the board of directors and the Student Communication Committee. The security of our students is my greatest concern, and these cameras are there to ensure a safe environment for the entire community.

"St. Clare's is known for its rigor and for the quality and discipline of its students. Certain standards have recently become relaxed. As the semester continues, staff has been instructed to enforce all dress code requirements, rules concerning academic integrity, and attendance policies. If you feel unfamiliar with any of these procedures, please consult the student handbook. I look forward to a wonderful Advent season with you all."

The mic clicks off, and everyone in the room whispers at once.

"Seriously?" Jess says to Theresa, the only person in the room looking pleased. "You let them put cameras up?"

"I didn't let anyone do anything," Theresa says. "The cameras were going up regardless, and the Student Communication Committee supports that decision, because there are factions within this school actively trying to destroy it."

"Oh my God," Jess says.

I stay quiet. It would be suspicious if I talked. Or is it more suspicious if I don't talk? I don't know.

"Do you think they aren't trying to destroy it?" Theresa asks.

Jess considers this. "I think they're trying to change the school, but that's different."

"It's not different!" Theresa says. "I like St. Clare's the way it is. I'm at St. Clare's *because* it has a good reputation, *because* it's traditional. A lot of people chose this school for that reason, or at least their parents did. What would you say to them?"

"I guess I'd say, 'Get a grip, it was just a video'?"

Theresa sniffs. "First it was the video. Then the vandalism. What will it be next time? Arson?"

She stands up and stalks to the front of the room to get our lab materials.

"Maybe that's what makes her skin so blotchy," Jess says. "The paranoia."

"Bitches are crazy," Connor says, elbowing me in the ribs in a way I think was supposed to be friendly. "You know what I'm talking about."

"Um," I say.

"Excuse me," Jess says. "I know you did not lump me and all women *ever* in with her."

"It's just something people say, Jess."

"Yeah, well, a crazy bitch probably wouldn't call the attendance office for you and pretend to be your mom, so maybe say something else."

Connor shuts up. Theresa returns with the lab materials and proceeds to do the entire lab herself. All three of us are perfectly happy to let her.

Lucy's waiting for me outside history, like she usually does. We go into the classroom together, like we usually do, but don't get far before Sister Joseph Marie swoops down in front of us, blocking the way to our seats.

"Hold on, Miss Peña," she says, and Lucy stops. "Did you

hear the announcement this morning, about how the staff is required to enforce all aspects of the dress code?"

"Yes, Sister." Lucy glances down at herself like she needs to confirm she is, in fact, wearing a uniform.

"And do you know what the requirements are for St. Clare's skirts?"

"They have to be plaid, Sister?" Lucy says, right on the edge of snapping.

"They have to be no less than three inches above the knee when kneeling." Sister Joseph Marie gestures in the general direction of Lucy's knee. "And that looks a little short."

"It's not." This time Lucy does snap.

"I have to make sure." She motions at the classroom floor. "Go ahead."

Lucy makes a small, disbelieving sound. It's not until Sister Joseph Marie pulls a tape measure from her pocket that I understand what's about to happen.

"You want her to kneel?" I say to Sister Joseph Marie, louder than I mean to, and the room quiets. "You can't do that."

"Sit down," she says without even looking at me.

"You can't, that's messed up. It's humiliating and—"

"Michael," Lucy says, glancing past me at our quiet, watching classmates. "Please sit down."

And only because she asked, I stomp over to my seat on the aisle.

Everyone watches as Lucy slowly, silently kneels down on the dusty classroom floor. She stares straight ahead, her mouth set and her face blank, like she's waiting through one of the kneeling parts at Mass instead of indulging some power-tripping nun. I don't want to watch her. It feels like someone's pulling out my intestines bit by bit, every millisecond she kneels there, as Sister Joseph Marie crouches down to measure the gap between the floor and the hem of Lucy's skirt.

A girl sitting in the row to my left nudges her friend and snickers, and I glare at them both until they notice and turn away. Both of their skirts are shorter than Lucy's.

When I turn back, Sister Joseph Marie is putting away the tape and Lucy is awkwardly getting to her feet. Her skirt was long enough. Of course it was. Sister Joseph Marie didn't stop Lucy because of any announcement or new rules. She did it because she doesn't like Lucy. Someone is pulling at my insides again.

Lucy sits down in front of me. Sister Joseph Marie is already going on about the new semester and how much ground we have to cover before Christmas. Lucy's back is straight and rigid. I touch her shoulder as gently as I can, wanting to ask if she's okay and how she'd like Sister Joseph Marie to meet her untimely demise.

Lucy turns around. She looks at me the way she did the first day I met her, after history class. Like she's trying to decide something. "Hey," she says. "Do you want to come over tonight?"

✦ ✦ ✦

"Don't judge me on the state of the house," Lucy says to me as we climb the steps of her porch, her two younger brothers behind us. "It's been a busy week."

"I won't judge you," says her smaller brother, straining for the top of the mailbox.

"You're the reason it's so messy." Lucy grabs mail out of the box with one hand and unlocks her front door with the other, ushering us inside.

"Mateo, put your shoes on the rack," Lucy says, dropping her keys back in her cardigan pocket. "No, J.J., your backpack doesn't go on the floor. Show me where it goes."

She helps the littler one, who looks about seven, hang his backpack up on a hook by the shoe rack. "Is there anything for me?" he asks as she rifles through the mail.

"I have an electric bill, a furniture catalog, and a mortgage payment notice. Any of that interest you?" He shakes his head. "Me neither."

I survey the house. Based on Lucy's locker I expected bookshelves organized by color, but it's more like controlled chaos. It's clean, but the floors are a little dusty, and the recycling bin by the door's close to overflowing. The entryway table is covered with coupons, library books, and—oddly—medical tape and a bunch of single-use alcohol wipe packets. There's a basket of folded laundry by the stairs to the second floor, like someone meant to take it up but got distracted.

129

"Go start on your homework," Lucy tells her brothers. "I'll call you when everything's ready."

Mateo, who's older, maybe ten, narrows his eyes at me. He gave me that same look when Lucy and I picked him and J.J. up from their after-school program earlier this afternoon. I don't think he approves of my presence. He tilts his head up at Lucy and mumbles something in Spanish.

Lucy raises an eyebrow. "Your dad doesn't care who I have over. And maybe *I'll* tell him you were the one who finished all the ice cream in the freezer last month."

Mateo huffs and heads off. Lucy tucks the electric bill into her book bag. "Remind me that I have to deal with this tonight," she says. She writes JAKE in capital letters on a sticky note, affixes it to the mortgage notice, and sets it on the entryway table.

"What's with the alcohol wipes? And the tape?" I ask.

"Their dad's a nurse. He's always bringing stuff home in his pockets."

Lucy leads me to the living room, where we sit on the comfy, pea-green couch. From underneath the couch, she pulls out a plastic box full of craft supplies—glue, scissors, and slightly yellowing white paper.

"Where are they?" she mutters, rummaging through the box. "Hey, can you look through that"—she points to a dresser set against the wall—"and see if there are any candles? Try the second top drawer."

"What's this all for, again?" I ask as I open the dresser drawers.

"Día de las Velitas. Day of the Little Candles. It's how Colombians celebrate the Immaculate Conception."

"So today's the day God and Mary got it on and made Jesus."

She shoots me a look. "No. Today's not about Jesus at all; it's the day *Mary* was conceived in her mother's womb, immaculately sinless. So we make paper lanterns and light candles to celebrate her."

I find the candles in the third drawer, half burnt down and all different sizes. I hold them up for Lucy.

"Oh, good," she says. "As far as my brothers are concerned, it's not really the Christmas season until they can light something on fire. Boys."

I close the drawer, but when I straighten up, I notice what's on top of the dresser. A woman's watch, a couple rings, and a set of house keys with a bunch of grocery and pharmacy loyalty cards attached. It's all covered in a layer of dust, like it hasn't been touched in a long time.

"Is this your watch?" I ask Lucy, and her face falls for a moment, then washes into a kind of cheerful blankness.

"That's my mom's."

Why wouldn't her mom take her keys on her trip? "Lucy," I say, sitting next to her on the couch, "how long has your mom been traveling?"

Lucy looks away, and the cheerful blankness fades. "A year." She swallows. "Nearly a year."

She's not on a trip at all.

"I'm so sorry," I say, but then have no idea what to say next. "That's . . . that's so shitty, how could she—"

"She's not a bad mom," Lucy interrupts me. "I don't want you to think she's a bad mom."

I nod, but I don't believe her. My mom would never up and leave me the way Lucy's has. My mom probably wouldn't make it past the county line without worrying about what Sophia would eat for lunch the next day, or whether I'd turn all the sheets pink trying to do laundry, and would speed back home in a panic before we even noticed she was gone.

Lucy gets up and quietly shuts the living room door. "They don't need to hear . . ." She sits back down next to me. "She's always been a good mom, a really good mom. She was young when she got pregnant with me, and everyone treated her like she'd never do anything else with her life. Her boyfriend bailed. No one expected her to finish college, but she did. She worked the whole time, so it took longer, but she did it." Lucy smiles. "Sometimes she had to take me to class with her, and I'd draw in someone's spare blue book.

"My mom worked so hard, for so long, and it was all for me. She said that a lot, she was doing all of it for me. After she graduated, she got a really good job at the hospital. That's where she met Jake, and they got married fast, and had the boys fast. They bought this house. It all worked out, fairy-tale ending."

"So what happened?" I ask. Fairy tales start with child

abandonment. They don't end that way.

"I don't know!" Lucy shakes her head. "She had a husband, kids, a house she owned. She got everything she wanted and . . ." Lucy falters. "I guess it wasn't enough. I guess she looked around and saw everything she'd missed out on, instead. She had a—breakdown, sort of, at work, and her boss said Mom should take all her vacation days, take some time away. And Jake and I, we were like, go for it, because she needed it. She deserved it. It was only supposed to be a month."

"And then she just didn't come back," I say.

"Every time I talk to her on the phone, she says she's not ready, yet. She needs more time."

"More than a year?"

"All her stuff is here," Lucy says, nodding at the dresser. "It's not like she won't—she told the boys Christmas. She wouldn't lie about that."

And like he knows we're talking about him, J.J. pokes his head around the door. "Luuuucyyyy," he says, drawing the word out like it has eight syllables.

Lucy plasters on a smile. "What's up, Jay?"

"I'm bored."

"What about your homework?"

"I did it at after-school, and now I'm bored."

"Pobrecito," Lucy says, and I wonder if her brother's old enough to understand sarcasm. "Don't worry, I'll find something for you to do. Stay there while I get the vacuum."

133

J.J. disappears behind the kitchen door. Lucy laughs. "Works every time," she tells me, and spreads the craft supplies out on the floor by the couch. She's clearly done talking about her mom, and I won't push it.

"Is this something you guys do every year?" I ask. "Like a tradition?"

"A pretty recent tradition," Lucy says. "I think church holidays are fun, and now that the boys are older, it's important they get to celebrate more than Christmas and Easter. So we'll light the candles, eat chocolate from the Advent calendars, and listen to the Magnificat. It'll be nice."

"What's the Magnificat?" I ask, and Lucy looks excited.

"It's a song," she says. "It's Mary's song."

"There're songs in the Bible?"

"A bunch, but this is my favorite. Mary sings it right after she's told she'll give birth to the son of God. She goes to her cousin, Elizabeth—who's pregnant with John the Baptist—and she sings about the greatness and glory of God."

I'm disappointed. People singing about how much they love God? Big deal.

"And it's also a revolutionary anthem," she adds. "That's why it's my favorite."

The most revolutionary thing I know about the Virgin Mary is that sometimes people see her face on toast.

"She's Jesus's mom," I say. "What would she revolt against? She was basically the most important woman in the world."

"Mary was a peasant. A poor, female, Jewish peasant. She

gave birth to a son who preached all people were equal in God's eyes, and she saw that son tortured and executed by the Roman Empire. She had a lot to revolt against."

"She didn't revolt, though."

"But other people did. In Argentina in the 1970s, the mothers of people killed by the military used the Magnificat as their anthem, so it was banned. Francisco Franco banned it in Spain in the 1930s. It's dangerous, a song about the poor and lowly being raised up and the rich and powerful falling."

I think of all the statues of Mary at school, all docile and pretty, her eyes downcast, holding flowers or a smiling baby Jesus in her arms. "*Mary* says that?"

Lucy nods.

"Tell it to me," I say, suddenly eager to hear Jesus's mom talk about overthrowing the state.

"Really?"

"Yeah. I want to hear it."

"Okay." Lucy adjusts herself on the couch so she's facing me head on. She takes a breath. *"My soul magnifies the Lord,"* Lucy recites, half whispering. *"And my spirit rejoices in God my Savior."*

There's a stillness to her body as she goes on with the song, talking about the glory and mercy of something I know doesn't exist. Lucy's always moving around; even when she's sitting in class, she's taking notes quicker than teachers can spit out information. But she's still now, calm and unmoving, like water in a pond.

✦ ✦ ✦

135

> *He has cast down the mighty from their thrones,*
> *and has lifted up the lowly.*

She wasn't kidding about the revolution parts. I think about all the famous Christians, all the kings and presidents and televangelists in thousand-dollar suits. Do they know this? Do they know this is in their holy book, that the mother of God proclaimed their downfall?

> *He has filled the hungry with good things,*
> *and the rich he has sent away empty.*

I know why this is Lucy's favorite song. Lucy believes in a world that's fair. As she recites, clear and crisp, I realize I believe in that world, too. I just don't believe in a god who will create it for us. I think we'll have to do it on our own.

Lucy takes a breath, prepping for another verse, and I grab her hand. She looks up at me with wide eyes but doesn't pull away.

"Michael," she whispers. "I—"

There's a scraping sound in the kitchen, then a bang.

"Lucy, I'm gonna get a snack," J.J. calls from behind the door. "I can do it myself. I didn't knock over the cereal. Don't come in."

Lucy sighs and jumps up. "Let's make those lanterns."

As the sun sets, I stand with Lucy and her brothers outside, helping Mateo put his softly glowing lanterns around the porch ledge. J.J. holds his hand over one of the lanterns, feeling the heat of the candle inside, and I think about the Magnificat, playing from inside the house. For J.J., God is something warm and innocent, Christmas presents and stories from his big sister. Lucy's God is one of revolution and justice, someone who can set a damaged, difficult world right. But they're the same God, from the same book—the same unbending, authoritarian God that Theresa believes in. Can one God be all those things to all those people?

J.J. hands me a lantern and points at the highest spot on the porch ledge. "Put it there," he commands. "So that Mary can see it."

Lucy smiles at me. The glow from the candles makes a halo around her, and she almost looks like Mary, herself. I set the lantern on the ledge.

15

EVERY MONDAY MORNING, all St. Clare's students get an email delivered to their school email address with the subject line: "Did You Know?"

It never says anything important, mostly a rehash of the previous week's morning announcements. And at the end, without fail, are several "Fun Facts," though how fun they are is debatable. They usually have to do with saints' lives and squeaky-clean tidbits from Catholicism's long, boring history.

On the second Monday in December, all St. Clare's students get an email at 7:22 a.m.

SUBJECT: Did You Know
FROM: Heretics Anonymous

Happy Monday, St. Clare's! We hope you enjoyed your weekend of wearing whatever you pleased. But we've been thinking—why should that stop the second you walk through the school doors? Here are some fun facts to get *you* thinking:

* *The school handbook tells us that uniform policies "create an equal playing field for students regardless of economic resources."*

DID YOU KNOW? Students from economically disadvantaged backgrounds are far more likely to be required to wear a uniform, and also more likely to be removed from class or suspended for dress code violations. So who exactly does that benefit?

* *Our uniform policy has different guidelines addressed to "young men" vs. "young women." As Deuteronomy 22:5 says, "A woman shall not wear a man's garment, nor shall a man put on a woman's clothing; for anyone who does such things is an abomination to the LORD."*

DID YOU KNOW? More things that are abominations, according to Deuteronomy:

—Not abandoning your wife after she's been raped

—Sacrificing a defective sheep to the LORD

—Rock badgers

* *"The St. Clare's uniform is designed to uphold and promote modesty for both young men and women. Saint Padre Pio tells us that 'By the virtue of modesty the devout person governs all his exterior acts.'"*

DID YOU KNOW? Saint Padre Pio also allegedly burned himself with carbolic acid to mimic Christ's crucifixion wounds and thought that dancing was "an invitation to sin," so it's possible he's wrong about this one.

In the name of comfort, style, and personal freedom, Heretics Anonymous declares the next five days Dress Code Week.

Stay tuned, St. Clare's.

Eden promises that we're totally safe from detection. "I set the email account up so it looks like the sender's in a different country," she tells me and Lucy at lunch, as our classmates whisper about the email, reading it on their phones under the dining hall tables.

"Where does it look like it's coming from?" Lucy asks.

"Vatican City."

"Very cute, Eden."

The next day, all St. Clare's students get another email, but this time there aren't any words. Instead, embedded in the email is a short animation. Rosary Rita, a cartoon girl in a St. Clare's uniform who bears a passing resemblance to Theresa, is chased through the school by monsters from her worst nightmares: dress code infractions. First she's pursued by a miniskirt with fangs. Then, an untucked shirt with evil eyes and a hole in the sleeve. She's finally felled by a baseball cap (*worn indoors*) that I still say looks more like a platypus.

"Screw you," Avi says when I tell him that. "Sorry I can't draw hats. I don't even wear hats."

"Who says you couldn't wear a platypus as a hat?" Max adds.

In my second-period math class, a girl at another table defends getting her uniform skirt custom-tailored by declaring,

"It's not like I'm Rosary Rita, or whatever."

During last period, while I'm in Spanish class, Father Peter comes on the loudspeaker to announce that school email accounts will now automatically filter out messages from non-approved addresses.

On Wednesday, Heretics Anonymous takes to the streets. Or really, the bathrooms.

Through the staggered use of bathroom passes, the inside of both the girls' and boys' bathrooms are soon plastered with brightly colored posters, designed by Eden and Avi and secretly printed by Max using his dad's home office. They read:

"That girl's visible collarbone
is distracting me from calculus."
—No Person Ever

Jesus Wore Open-Toed Shoes, So Why Can't We?

You Are a Person, Not a Distraction

OUR EDUCATION IS MORE IMPORTANT
THAN OUR CLOTHING

"Dressing in enforced business casual
makes translating Virgil easier."
—Seriously, No Person Ever

"I saw Theresa and her friends taking the ones in the girls' room down," Lucy says as we eat lunch.

"Too late," Avi says, scrolling through his phone. "They're up online. She can't get rid of that as easily."

If you were reviewing security camera footage of St. Clare's on Thursday morning, the main hallway would look normal. The statues of Mary and Saint Francis with his animal menagerie cast their watchful eyes over the central locker bays, the ones juniors and seniors get priority access to. The underclassmen's assigned lockers are less conveniently located, tucked into side corridors out of view of the cameras.

On each freshman's and sophomore's locker is a note that reads:

RULE #17: Shoes must be closed-toed and entirely black.
. . . But they didn't say anything about the laces.

Tied to each regulation combo lock is a pair of neon-colored shoelaces.

"Nice of the guy at the dollar store to give you that discount on the two-hundred-pair set," Lucy whispers just before first period, as we watch one freshman trade his lime green shoelaces for a friend's radioactive red pair. Not everyone's shoes have laces, so plenty of juniors and seniors are wearing the laces too, even before they start finding them in other places, tied to the inside doorknobs of bathroom stalls and the railings of out-of-the-way staircases. Everyone looks ridiculous in the best way possible, pops of neon on shiny black dress shoes.

Max is the only HA member wearing the laces at lunchtime, when staff members comb the lunch tables, confiscating the contraband. We figured it would be more suspicious if he wasn't participating. And as expected, no one gets detention. There are just too many people to deal with.

Friday morning passes without incident, and a kid in my math class complains that HA promised a whole week devoted to the dress code, not just four days. I hope that he has PE fourth period, because when that class walks into the gym locker rooms, they're greeted by more presents, courtesy of HA. On the boys' side, this note is attached to each locker:

RULE #22: Young men's ties must be plaid and purchased through St. Clare's official uniform supply company.
. . . But they didn't specify which type of plaid.

As it turns out, the uniform supplier has a veritable bounty of available plaids to choose from. Eden, putting on her best mom voice, arranged for us to purchase an assortment of their worst-selling ties at a steep discount. It's clear why those ties didn't sell, I think as Avi and I scatter the ties throughout the boys' locker room. Who would put dark purple and buttercup yellow together, anyway?

On the girls' side, a different note is attached to the lockers:

RULE #26: Young men must be clean-shaven, without sideburns, mustaches, or goatees.
. . . But they didn't say anything about girls.

Underneath each note is a gift from the owner of the seasonal Halloween store across town, who was happy to get rid of his excess stock of fake handlebar mustaches and furry sideburns.

There are extras of everything, and by fifth period, it seems like just about every girl has one article of fake facial hair on and most boys have traded in their St. Clare's plaid for a garish, horribly clashing tie. Me included—that pea green and fire engine red number just called to me.

The confiscated neon shoelaces showed up in the locker rooms, too, since we had some left over, and between that, the plaid, and the Halloween costume mustaches, St. Clare's looks vaguely like a clown college. Teachers are doing their best to restore order to the dress code, but there are too many kids to corral—especially when people start arguing that their accessories are technically allowed.

"But it *is* from the uniform company, look at the tag," one freshman boy says to Father Peter in the hallway. "And this is unrelated, but Padre Pio was a jerk."

"I don't think this is an abomination," a girl in my theology class tells Sister Helen when told to remove a fake mustache. "And neither are rock badgers. They're adorable."

"Connor," Theresa says in chemistry Monday morning, as the rest of us struggle to figure out the spectrophotometer, "you're Irish, right?"

"On my mom's side," he says. "I think my dad's, like, Czech? Somewhere with pierogis."

"Have you ever seen *this* before?" Theresa whips out a very poorly drawn version of Eden's five-fold.

"Um, yeah, it's all over school," Jess says, turning back to the experiment. "The HA people drew it, it's their symbol."

"And I think you're missing a circle," Connor adds. Jess stares at him. He busies himself with the lab equipment.

"It's not their symbol," Theresa says. "They coopted it; it's from Ireland, before it was a Catholic country. So I'll ask again—" She pushes the paper closer to Connor's face. "—have you seen this symbol before?"

"Wow, ethnic profiling, that's always gone well," I mutter, and Theresa fixes her eyes on me. "Before you ask, my family's not Irish." Although, come to think of it, I have no idea where Dad's ancestors are from. Just Mom's.

Theresa turns to Jess, who rolls her eyes. "Are you serious? I'm Filipina."

Theresa sniffs. "Wouldn't want to *profile*." She gets up and takes the bathroom pass from our teacher's desk.

"Didn't I say this would happen?" Jess says to Connor. "The HA cult gets weirder, Theresa and her cult scream louder, and the rest of us suffer."

"Relax," Connor says. "Last week was fun. You should have put on the mustache, I think it would be a good look for you." He nudges her under the desk.

Jess doesn't look amused. "I actually spend a lot of money to not have a mustache, thanks."

"I was kidding."

"We couldn't even go over our quiz in French because Ms. Dieng had to run around confiscating Halloween costumes, basically. They're turning the school into a circus. And it's only going to get worse."

Connor looks at me and raises an eyebrow. I shrug. "I think you're being a little dramatic, Jess," he says, and turns off the spectrophotometer.

But as the week goes on, I'm starting to think Jess might have been right, after all. On Wednesday, Sister Helen tries to engage the class in a discussion about the role of saints in our daily lives, but this quickly devolves into a full-on showdown over whether everyone's favorite saints were sexist (all the male ones), anti-Semitic (all the medieval ones), or just plain weird (all of them, in my opinion), and whether they should have a role in our lives at all.

"They wouldn't be saints if what they said was that terrible," argues one of Theresa's overly earnest followers, a pale girl with lots of freckles. "Do you think you know more than, like, the pope?"

"Saint Tertullian said women are 'temples built over sewers,'" says Maura Kearney, a girl I've never heard speak before. "I read it when I was looking up Padre Pio. He called women literal sewers, and he's a saint. That's messed up. How can you defend that?"

"That was so long ago," Theresa's friend argues. "It was different then. You're not being fair!"

"But that's—" Jenny Okoye says, then hesitates when she notices all our eyes are on her. She takes a breath. "Okay, so they canonized him a long time ago. But they *just* made Junipero Serra a saint, and we know that he and his followers were horrible to Native people in California."

"They thought they were doing the right thing," Theresa's friend says.

"Then they were wrong," Jenny says. "My grandparents were born in colonial Nigeria. I don't care about Britain's *good intentions*. Good intentions don't excuse destroying somebody's culture. Good intentions don't excuse anything. We can't judge dead men by our standards, fine, but we choose who we canonize, and we can do better. Shouldn't we want to do better?"

Half the room shouts her down. Half the room agrees.

Avi, Lucy, and I sit in the back and say absolutely nothing.

In the cafeteria the next day, Avi shows us the article he's been working on for *The St. Clare's Record*, the school paper, about Dress Code Week.

"I'm not happy you're writing this," Lucy says. "Couldn't you give it to another reporter?"

"It was assigned," he says. "It's not like I was thrilled to have to get quotes from Our Lady of Perpetual Outrage."

I'm guessing that's Theresa. "What'd she say?"

He flips through his notebook. "She said—on behalf of all her fellow students—that Heretics Anonymous was a radical hate group whose clear mission was to turn the St. Clare's student body against their school and their church." He closes the notebook. "It went downhill from there. She wanted to write her own op-ed, but Jenny said no, thank God."

"Jenny Okoye?" I ask.

"Yeah, she's the editor in chief of the paper."

"That mouse?" I say, but then I remember how she spoke up in theology.

"She's a good writer, and she's organized."

"But she could probably use some backup," Lucy says, looking over my shoulder. I turn around to see Jenny, backed into a corner by Theresa, who has several pieces of paper in her hands. Probably that op-ed. Lucy starts to stand, but Jenny, apparently having heard enough, shoulders past Theresa without a word.

"This is anarchy," Avi says, shaking his head.

"If this is The Anarchy, do you think Heretics Anonymous is more like Queen Matilda or Stephen of Blois?" Lucy asks. We look at her blankly. "Guys. The Anarchy? The twelfth-century English civil war that ended in the rise of the Angevin dynasty?"

"Super-accessible joke, Lucy," Avi says. "And I'm serious. People are going at each other's throats."

"At least they're talking about things now," Lucy says. "At least this stuff is out in the open. Isn't that what we wanted?"

Avi nods but looks doubtful.

✦ ✦ ✦

On Friday, Avi goes to pass out the paper to all the classrooms and Lucy has a Model UN meeting, so I eat lunch with Eden and Max. If anything, the dining hall's more chaotic than it was on Wednesday.

"It's like we flipped a switch," Eden says, watching two boys at another table argue over an article in the school paper. They must have gotten an advance copy. "I know you only just got here, Michael, but this never would have happened before."

"Is that a good thing, or a bad thing?" I ask.

"I think it's good," Max says. "So people are yelling. People disagree with each other, that's okay. Just because you put everyone in the same clothes and make them do the same things doesn't mean they think the same, and they shouldn't have to. That was the point of Dress Code Week, right?"

He looks to Eden for support, but her eyes are by the salad bar, where Theresa is plastering a giant butter-yellow poster.

TAKE BACK YOUR SCHOOL
JOIN THE ST. CLARE'S CRUSADERS

"Yikes," I say.

"That's a bad name for a club," Max says as Theresa flits around the dining hall, wallpapering every flat surface with another poster. "That seems like a really bad name."

"Why does she care so much?" I wonder aloud.

Eden sighs. "Her parents are . . . hardcore. Like, extremely traditional Catholics."

"So are yours," Max says, "and you're not a Crusader."

"You don't understand," Eden says. "Her family used to go to our parish, but now they drive an hour south so they can go to a Mass in Latin. The girls wear veils to church, and that hasn't been a thing since the sixties. They don't have *cell phones*. Hard. Core."

"You think her parents put her up to this?" I ask.

Eden shakes her head. "No way she's told her parents what's going on."

"Why not?"

"Theresa's the oldest, I think," Eden says. "Definitely the oldest girl. All her siblings are homeschooled; she practically had to beg to come to St. Clare's in ninth grade. Her parents were worried about what she might be exposed to, I guess. If she told them about the school being in chaos—oh my God, if she told them about the sex ed assembly? They'd yank her out in a second."

"She needs everything to stay the same," I say as Theresa plasters up another poster. She doesn't have any say in who her parents are or what they do, but she has a say in this. There's a twinge in my chest that feels almost like pity but isn't. Oh shit. Do I *identify* with Theresa?

"She's scared," Eden says. "I'd be scared, too. St. Clare's isn't perfect, but it's better than her house. I've been there."

"Here comes her backup," Max says as Father Peter stalks past us, carrying a yellow poster under his arm. But to my surprise, Father Peter walks right up to Theresa and stops her from putting another poster up. It looks like he's trying to explain something, gently but firmly. Theresa looks heartbroken. She waves her arms wildly at everyone in the dining hall, pointing out a couple people—including Jenny—in particular. Father Peter rubs the bridge of his nose and gestures at the poster, motioning for her to take it down.

"Oh man," I say, watching Theresa hesitate. "She's not going to do it."

But she does, with a huff and an expression of utter betrayal. Father Peter helps her remove the rest.

"I don't get it," Max says. "She's standing up for him; why doesn't he want that?"

I think back to the knockdown, drag-out theology debate. Theresa trying to ferret out HA members. Even Connor and Jess, who probably really love each other, sniping in chemistry.

"He doesn't want people to make trouble," I say. "It doesn't matter which side they're on."

Max nods, but Eden's not paying attention. She's still looking at Theresa, who has returned to her lunch table and is complaining to her surrounding lackeys.

"God," Eden says. "She must be so lonely."

I don't feel bad enough for Theresa to agree with *that*. "What are you talking about? She's practically got an army."

Eden nods at Theresa's table. "Look over there, and tell me what you see."

"I see a bunch of girls wearing ancient Roman torture devices around their necks."

"*Really* look."

Well, there's Theresa, smoothing her now-crumpled posters and complaining to the dark-haired girl next to her. Except— Theresa's not even bothering to look at her friend while she rants. She's too focused on her posters to notice that her friend is sharing a meaningful glance with another girl, the freckled one from my theology class. The dark-haired girl raises her eyebrows and tilts her head at Theresa. The other girl rolls her eyes. And when I look at the rest of the girls at the table, their expressions range from bemused disinterest to silent judgment.

I turn back to Eden. "They don't like her. Even they don't like her?"

"I've known those girls since kindergarten," Eden says. "Rose, Marisol, Grace. They're nice. They were raised to be polite. They might agree with Theresa, but no way they like her."

As we pass by their table to bus our trays, I wonder how many things and people I've looked at but haven't seen at all.

By the time the following Friday rolls around, and with it, the last day before Christmas break, I'm convinced that the teachers are happier about it than the students. Maybe they think a solid two-week vacation will cleanse the school of an impending emotional apocalypse, but I'm not so sure.

Either way, I'm excited to be away from school for four-teen days, but that presents me, Lucy, and the rest with another problem—with the school locked for two weeks, where should we meet for Heretics Anonymous?

"My house won't work," Eden says as we all walk through the park across from St. Clare's after early dismissal. "All my siblings and their packs of kids will be in and out. My parents are giving my bed to three of my nephews. I'm sleeping on the basement couch."

I'd offer up my house, except Dad has been home nearly every night for the past week and won't be traveling again until after New Year's. Apparently, the Belgians take Christmas seri-ously. Luckily, Avi jumps in.

"My parents are going out of town for a few days," he says. "So I've got the whole place to myself."

"They're letting you stay home alone for that long?" Lucy asks.

"They're under the impression I'm very trustworthy. Ms. Katz next door is supposed to check in on me, but she's old and goes to bed at eight." He arches an eyebrow. "Meetings are great and all, but I think it's time we had a Heretics Anonymous *party*."

My parents are, as suspected, not entirely cool with this plan, even with some creative storytelling on my part.

"A sleepover?" Dad says. "Aren't you kind of old for that?"

"The day after Christmas?" Mom says. "Are you sure you wouldn't be imposing on Avi's parents?"

"They're Jewish. And I don't think we'll bother Mr. and Mrs. Einhorn at all." Both these statements are technically true.

"Who's going to be there?" Dad asks.

"Avi and Max. They're in my PE class." *And Eden, who casts spells, and Lucy, who will hopefully be wearing the flimsiest of pajamas.*

"And Avi's parents will supervise?" Mom asks.

"Their bedroom is right above the living room," I assure her while not actually answering her question.

Mom glances over at Dad. "Michael, I don't know," she says. "Dad's not here very long, and I was hoping we could spend that night as a family."

"But we're going to be spending Christmas Eve and Christmas and the whole *week* as a family," I protest. "It's one night."

"Maybe after the holidays," Dad says, and goes back to his newspaper.

I didn't want to have to do this. It's manipulative and weird, but they've left me no choice.

"St. Clare's is really small. Everyone made their friends years ago," I say, trying to sound cut up about it. "It's not like I've gotten tons of offers to hang out."

"You don't have a great track record with sleepovers," says Dad, who never misses an opportunity to remind me of the time I accidentally blew up David Englander's mailbox in sixth grade.

"Avi's the first friend I made. Like, the only one who talked to me for weeks."

"What about that girl?" Mom asks. "Lucy?"

And I don't even have to fake it, because as soon as I hear her name, the back of my neck gets hot. "That's different."

The mention of a possible unrequited crush has dropped Mom's resistance down by half, I can feel it. If I can knock her down a little bit more, she'll override Dad.

"If I tell Avi no, he might think I don't like hanging out with him and Max."

Mom reaches out to me. "They won't think that—"

"They might! And, I don't know, for the first time it almost feels like I—"

I break off here and wait for Mom to ask me to finish the sentence. Which of course she does.

"You what, honey?"

"Belong somewhere."

Mom's heart breaks. I can also *see* Dad roll his eyes, but broken hearts trump all.

"Oh my God, *fine*," he says. "Try not to blow up anyone's mailbox this time."

16

I REALLY LIKE the day before Christmas Eve. It's close enough to Christmas that the tree's already been bought and decorated, but not so close to Christmas that you have family things to go to or new sweaters to pretend you like. I was planning to spend today holed up in my room with hot chocolate, peanut brittle, and video games, but Dad has other plans.

"You're not going to leave all your homework until the night before you go back to school, like last year," he says, turning off my console before I've even had a chance to kill anything. "I want you to accomplish something today."

Fine. I'll start with my chemistry project, purely because I can complain about it the most.

"This can all be done at home," Mr. Pierini assured us last week, passing out a set of complicated-looking instructions. "And please get pictorial evidence of your experiment before it's consumed."

And then he laughed. Like the vacation-ruining monster he is.

"My teacher didn't even say what it's supposed to be," I tell Dad as I follow him to the kitchen, clutching the assignment sheet. If he wants me to get this project done, he's going to suffer through it right alongside me. "How can I do an experiment if I don't know what I'm proving?"

"You get the materials and follow the instructions," Dad says, already sounding weary. Good. I think if parents had to do all the time-wasting busywork their kids have to get through, they'd riot. At least they get paid to do their stupid, time-wasting busywork.

"The materials are weird, though, look—sodium hydrocarbonate? Does he think people have that lying around the house?"

"Well," Dad says. "Most people do." He reaches into the cabinet behind him and pulls out a box.

"What's that?"

"Sodium hydrocarbonate. Baking powder."

Baking powder?

"Can I see the materials list?" Dad asks, and I hand him the paper. He reads it over and starts to laugh.

"What's so funny?" I ask as he opens up another kitchen cabinet.

"This won't take long," he promises. "Maybe an hour. I'll help you."

And I almost tell him no, that not only am I not supposed to be getting help on this, I don't *want* his help in the first place. But he starts whistling as he rummages around the kitchen cabinets, and I haven't heard him do that in forever. Besides, the faster I'm done, the faster I can go upstairs and kill CGI Nazi cyborgs.

He pulls out each item on my list of materials, naming them as he goes.

"Sucrose—sugar. *Mentha peperita*—peppermint extract. $C_6H_{10}O_5$—cornstarch."

I stare at the pile of ingredients. "What, do I have to make a cake?"

Dad looks down at the instructions. "I don't think a cake, exactly."

The first step is to heat the starch with water and baking powder until it boils. After the mixture boils and I've checked and written down its temperature, we leave it to sit.

"How do you know all of this?" I ask, because I can't remember Dad once using the kitchen for anything other than making himself a sandwich.

"The chemical names? I loved science. I minored in chemistry. Didn't you know that?"

No. I didn't. The earliest picture I've seen of my dad is from his and Mom's engagement. We have tons of photos of Mom as a kid, going to the beach, opening presents on Christmas, graduating from high school. But none of Dad. And for the first time, I wonder why.

"The cooking stuff, too," I say as he takes the mixture off the stove and adds in the peppermint. "I didn't know you knew how to cook."

"I used to cook all the time, when your mom was at the teachers college and I was working nights. I'd make dinner for both of us, then she'd go to bed and I'd go to work."

I knew, I guess, they'd done that, before Dad landed a job that could support all of us. As I watch Dad pour one half of the mixture onto the cookie sheet, I try to imagine them young and exhausted, sitting at a table without me or Sophia, loving each other enough to work graveyard shifts or to go to sleep alone every night.

"Grab some food coloring from the cabinet," Dad tells me. "That's the last thing on your list."

I open the cabinet where Mom keeps all the decorating stuff—food coloring and cookie cutters and birthday sprinkles. "What color?"

"Personally, I'd go with red, for the traditional look."

I'm about to ask him what that means when I turn around and see him twisting the now-thickened mixture into long, thin cords.

"Candy canes?"

"The final instruction is 'form into a J-shape,' so that would be my guess."

Mr. Pierini thinks he's so funny. *Be sure to get pictorial evidence before the experiment is consumed.* Ha.

As the candy canes bake, I realize that this is the first time

Dad and I have been together, just us, in a really long time. Even before this last move, he wasn't home much, and when he was, he spent most of his time in his office upstairs. Being alone with him feels good but awkward, like getting on a bike for the first time. It shouldn't feel like that; it should feel normal. It used to be normal.

"Hey," I say, "do you remember that time you said we were going to the dentist, then took me to the water park?"

A grin spreads across his face. "Sure."

"What about—" I pause, pulling a memory from somewhere dark and dusty. "I was eleven. We were in the Agnes Street house. And there was that monster snowstorm."

"Oh yeah," he says. "Everything shut down. Even my office."

"The schools, too. So you drove me and Sophia to find a place to sled, but we couldn't spot a decent hill, so you stopped the car in an empty field. And you took this long rope out of the trunk and tied our sled to the car bumper."

He laughs. "I forgot about that. Probably wasn't very safe—I couldn't have been going more than ten miles an hour, but still."

"It felt like we were flying," I say.

The oven timer dings. He reaches in to take the tray of candy canes out. "If I remember correctly, I made you promise to never, ever tell your mother."

"I never did."

"Obviously not, she would have murdered me—Sophia was what, four? Five?"

Something like that. She asked to go again and again until it was almost dark out.

"She was too young." I pause. "It's not fair."

"What's not fair?"

"She doesn't remember the way you used to be." He freezes, the tray still in his hand. We stare each other down, both of us hurt, neither of us knowing what to say next. Dad takes a breath in, but then there's a click as the front door unlocks, and we both look away. He sets the tray down on the breakfast bar. Sophia bounds into the kitchen, her eyes going wide when she sees the candy canes.

"Ooh," she says, dropping the shopping bag she's carrying in her rush to get to the candy.

"Sophia! There are *ornaments in there*," Mom says. She scoops up the bag, and Dad scoops up Sophia before she can get to the candy canes.

"Hey, let them cool first, you'll burn yourself."

"They look kind of weird," she says as Dad sets her down.

"That's because they're homemade," I snap. "And who said you could have any?"

Sophia whirls around to look at Dad, who raises an eyebrow at me. "You can have some."

"Fine, but I have to takes pictures first," I say.

"Why?" Sophia asks, clearly picking out which candy cane to eat first.

"Because otherwise I'll fail chemistry."

161

"That doesn't make any sense."

I snap a couple of pictures on my phone before Dad places all the candy canes in a basket. Sophia immediately grabs the fattest one. "Can I eat it in the living room? By the tree?"

Mom, putting away groceries, hesitates. Food outside the kitchen is her third-greatest fear, after bees and members of her family being harmed. But she looks over at the three of us standing together and closes the fridge door. "Yes," she says. "Let's all do that."

So we sit in the living room all together, something we've never done in this house. Dad pulls out the box of half-broken ornaments Mom set aside when she was decorating the tree and we all listen to Sophia sing a song she's learned to list all the elements in the atomic table. In order.

"There's hydrogen and helium and lithium, beryllium. Boron, nitrogen, and—"

"Slow down, Soph," Dad says. "You forgot oxygen."

The doorbell rings, and Mom leans over to me. "Can you get that? It's Sophia's gift from . . ." And then she mouths the word "Santa."

Sophia is ten. Sophia can describe exactly how tectonic plates work. But Sophia still pretends she believes in Santa, and my mom still pretends to believe her.

I roll my eyes and walk to the door. I'm in pajama pants and have the last bit of a candy cane sticking out of my mouth, but I figure a FedEx delivery guy doesn't care what I look like.

Except when I open the door, it's Lucy.

"Hi," she says. I realize this is the first time I've seen her out of uniform—she's in jeans, winter boots, and a green coat that's a little too long in the sleeves.

"Hi," I say back, wishing the first time she'd seen *me* out of uniform didn't involve pajama pants and a hoodie I've had since middle school. From the living room, I can hear Sophia trying her song again, and my mom and dad laughing. Lucy hears it, too.

"Are you guys—is this a bad time?" she asks.

"It's fine, we were just hanging out by the tree."

"I should have texted," she continues, like she hasn't heard me at all. "I realized I wasn't going to see you until after Christmas, so—" And then I notice a package, wrapped with snowman paper and tied with red yarn, under her arm.

"Michael?" My mom pushes open the door from the living room. "Do I need to sign for—" She stops when she sees Lucy. "Hello."

"Mom, this is Lucy." Lucy waves awkwardly with the hand not clutching the package. "From school."

"Oh," Mom says, suddenly *very* interested. "Of course, Lucy! It's nice to meet you, we've heard so much about you."

"It's very nice to meet you, too," Lucy says, shooting me a curious look.

Mom turns to me. "Michael, aren't you going to invite her inside?"

She says it like it's a question, but it's definitely not. "I was about to."

"That's okay," Lucy says. "I was dropping something off."

Mom is undeterred. "Just for a minute," she says, steering Lucy out of the doorway and toward the living room. "Until you warm up."

Lucy looks back over her shoulder at me, panicked, but this is now out of my control, so I follow behind them into the living room. Sophia is standing on one of the kitchen stools, trying to find a place for a newly repaired ornament. Dad's on the couch with the basket of misfit ornaments, trying to fix the wing on a particularly accident-prone angel.

As soon as we step into the living room, Lucy gets the strangest look on her face. At first I think it's embarrassment, because *I'm* embarrassed by my pushy mom and my gross clothes, so it must be way worse for her. But as she glances around the room, at the tree that's almost too tall for the ceiling, and its lights, and the small mountain of presents piled up underneath, I realize she's not embarrassed. She looks sad.

She puts on a smile fast, though, as Mom introduces her to Sophia and Dad, and she shakes his hand. "It's a beautiful tree," she tells Mom.

"It's a noble fir," Sophia says. "*Abies procera.* It used to be called *Abies nobilis*, but it turned out another tree already had that name, so they had to change it."

"I did not know that," Lucy says.

"So," Sophia says, latching her ornament on to a branch way up top, "are you Michael's girlfriend? He said you're not, but I think you are."

Lucy's mouth drops open and I brainstorm the best ways to kill my sister in her sleep. Mom rushes toward the tree before Sophia can say anything worse, though I can't imagine what would be worse. "Don't hang it there, sweetheart," she says, throwing a *sorry* look back at me. "It's way too heavy for the branch."

"We're about to eat lunch," Dad says to Lucy. "Would you like to stay?"

"Thank you, that's so nice, but I should probably be heading back home to get lunch ready myself," Lucy says, and it sounds like something my mom would say, not something a sixteen-year-old would. "It was really nice to meet you all. Merry Christmas."

"Merry Christmas!" Mom calls out after us as I lead Lucy back toward the front door.

"I'm so sorry," I whisper to her as we walk. "I am so, so sorry—"

"Don't be," she says. "You have a really nice family."

At the front door, I peek outside the window. It's overcast and so windy the trees are bending a little under the weight. "Are you going home?" I ask Lucy. "I could probably drive you."

"Yeah, but it's not far, and my coat's warm."

Her house is at least a mile away. "Let me take you home."

Inside the house, Sophia is trying her elements song again.

"No, you should stay with your family," Lucy says. "But before I go—" She hands me the present. "Here, open it."

It's been wrapped and tied so carefully and cleanly that it feels wrong to rip it open, so I take my time as Lucy buttons her coat all the way to the top. I can tell it's a book, but it's not until the wrapping paper is in a pile at my feet that I flip it cover-side up to read the title.

It's a Bible. I am holding a Bible.

"Lucy," I say as calmly as I can. "What the fuck."

"Oh, chill out." She digs a pair of mittens out of her coat pockets. "I'm not trying to convert you."

Either all the sugar from the candy canes has gone directly to my brain, or Lucy's given me the worst present ever. I don't believe in God. I don't want to believe in God. I spend five days a week surrounded by God. "Why?" I ask. *"Why?"*

"Look," she says. "You believe what you believe, and that's great. I don't think you should stop believing what you do. But you go to a Catholic school and exist in a world shaped by this book. You should know what it says."

"I do know what it says. It says gay people are sinners and women are chattel and people like me should be burned at the stake."

"That's not all it says! For better and worse, it says a lot more than that." She gestures at it. "It's a pretty thick book."

I'm still not convinced, and I think Lucy can tell, because she sighs. "Think of it this way. The better you know the Bible, the better you'll be able to argue against the parts of it you don't like. 'Know thine enemy,' right?"

"Let me guess. That's from the Bible."

"That's from *The Art of War*." Stepping very close to me, she opens the Bible to a random page. "And I forgot to say—it's not a regular Bible. I marked it up for you."

I flip through, and sure enough, on nearly every page are annotations in red pen, carefully written out in Lucy's perfect, loopy handwriting. And I understand, then. I'm not holding a Bible. Not really. I'm holding a little part of Lucy, something she wants me to see.

"It's a great present," I tell her, and she smiles. "I wish I had something to give you."

"I'll give you a grace period," she says. "Until the party."

She flips her coat hood up, covering her red-ribboned pony-tail, and turns the doorknob. "Happy holidays."

"Merry Christmas," I say, and watch her walk out into the wind.

17

IT TAKES SOME wheedling, but I convince my parents to let me take one of the cars to the HA party tonight. Dad's rummaging around in a file cabinet upstairs for proof I'm on the insurance for Mom's car, and Mom is helping Sophia explore the research database she got for Christmas when my phone vibrates. Avi's sent a group text to everyone.

> Avi: so we didn't talk about this before but people are going to have to provide alcohol if they want it tonight bc i checked my cabinets and there's not a lot
>
> Eden: totally OK, I can bring some
>
> Lucy: Should we say a bottle from each of us? That seems fair, right?

My heart stops for second. I hadn't even considered Lucy might be drinking. It seemed like one of those things she wouldn't do, though I know Catholic Jesus can't have much problem with alcohol, since his blood's made out of it. But I also know drinking can be dangerous, and not just because you could drive drunk or throw up or eat an entire Carvel ice-cream cake and *then* throw up. Alcohol makes you impulsive and honest, and I'm scared of what impulsive and honest Lucy is like, but excited, too.

She might say she secretly hates me.

She might kiss me.

I need a drink.

My parents are both upstairs, so now is my best chance for getting the alcohol. Creeping over to the cabinet next to the dishwasher, I forage through the dozen or so bottles of liquor as quietly as possible.

My phone buzzes in my pocket, but I ignore it. I also ignore the wine at the front of the cabinet, because my mom will notice it's gone, and I also hate the way it tastes. Ditto with Dad's scotch. I settle on the dusty bottle of vodka way in the back. Neither of my parents like vodka, so it must have been some gift my mom felt too guilty to throw away.

I stow the bottle behind the potted plant on the back porch, where I can pick it up before I leave tonight. My phone buzzes again. There are a couple texts from Eden and Max agreeing to both bring alcohol, then a few from Avi.

Avi: cool sounds good

Avi: any alcohol is fine but NO WEED bc my mom has a super-natural sense of smell

Avi: MICHAEL

Tell someone *once* that reading Latin might be more fun if you were high, and they act like you're running your own personal growhouse.

Everybody knows you're not supposed to show up to a house party right on time. This is a universally accepted fact. The problem with befriending members of a secret society, though, is they don't know anything about parties. Which is why, when I show up at eight thirty, only a half hour after Avi said, Lucy opens the door to Avi's house and says, "We were wondering where you were."

"Is everyone else already here?"

I think about the last party I went to, before we moved. It was at Becca Conover's house on the Fourth of July. Someone burned a hole in the fence with off-brand Mexican sparklers, and two people later developed staph infections from Becca's improperly cleaned hot tub.

This is not that kind of party.

"Max is here and Eden's on her way—she got held up at home." Lucy takes my coat for me and hangs it over the banister in Avi's clean, beige entryway. The sweater she's wearing— cornflower blue, soft-looking, and a lot tighter than her school cardigan—rides up in the back as she does. I don't know why that tiny sliver of tan skin is so mesmerizing, but it is. Probably because I've memorized and cataloged every little part of Lucy, and this is a new part.

I sound like a serial killer. I hate myself. I love that sweater.

I've seen enough stuff on the internet to know a lot of people really like the Catholic schoolgirl thing, with the knee socks and the plaid. I don't get it. I like seeing Lucy like this, in jeans and a sweater I hope she owns ten of, dressed like every girl I've liked before, girls I somehow managed to kiss and go on awkward dates with. Catholic schoolgirl is okay, but regular girl is a lot better.

She turns around and catches me staring. "What?"

"Uh—" My brain stumbles around like it's already drunk. Then I remember what's in the shopping bag next to me, nestled against a bottle of vodka. "I have something for you."

It's not a great gift. I know it's not. But I had to get Lucy something after she gave me the marked-up Bible. So, when Mom decided the tree needed more colored lights the day before Christmas, I offered to go pick some up. And I did, but I also stopped by the section of the mall where they sell makeup and perfume. I was so embarrassed to be there, I blew off the saleslady's offer to help me "pick out something nice," grabbed pretty much the first thing I saw, and left, trailing colored Christmas lights and shame.

I hand Lucy a red box and think about telling her I picked that box because it was the same color red as her ribbon but don't.

She opens it. "It's . . . is it perfume?"

I considered finding Bible quotes about perfume and sticking them in the box, too. But after flipping through Lucy's carefully annotated Bible and using Google, the only ones I could find referred to prostitutes, and that wasn't the message I wanted to send.

Instead, I nod, affirming that yes, it is perfume, and that yes, I know why she's asking. Perfume is not a gift you give your friend whose boobs you don't sometimes stare at.

"Thank you," Lucy says. "It's— Thank you."

I want to think she's at a loss for words because she's overcome by the specialness and not terribleness of my gift.

"I appreciate you keeping your Christmas promise," she says, putting the perfume bottle into her overnight bag. She grimaces. "Not everyone does."

Oh no. "Your mom—she didn't—?"

"She called. Just a *little* more time. She just needs a little more time. Yeah, well, my brothers need their mom. Jake needs his wife."

"What about you?" I ask. "What do you need?"

We lock eyes for a moment. Then she stands and adjusts her sweater. "I need to check on Avi."

"What? Why?" I ask as I follow her into the kitchen.

"He's a bit ahead of us." Avi and Max sit at a polished, dark-wood table, a half-empty bottle next to Avi.

"Michael!" Avi says as we enter, happier to see me than he has ever been in his sober life. "You made it!" He holds up the bottle. "Would you like to try the drink of my people? My

Jewish people, not my gay people."

"What is it?" I ask, eyeing the bottle.

"Manischewitz," Avi says. "The only thing my parents drink ever." He begins to pour himself another glass.

"Hey, okay, maybe pace yourself," Lucy says, pulling the bottle out of his reach.

"It's *four* glasses, Lucy. You have to drink four glasses, that's the rule."

"Yeah, on Passover. It's Boxing Day."

"Why is it called Boxing Day?" Max asks. His cape is new; it's a darker color and less frayed at the edges. "Maybe because one year, some person in, like, medieval France tried to return their Christmas present—a cloak, probably—and the store wouldn't take it back, so he got into a fistfight with the store owner and now it's called Boxing Day."

"I think it's actually because servants would get Christmas boxes from their masters that day," Lucy says, putting the Manischewitz on a high shelf, despite Avi's protests.

"My story's better," Max says.

As Max and Lucy argue over the etymology of Boxing Day, I search for the bathroom. Everything in Avi's house is nice, a carefully planned kind of nice. Curated. Like a museum people live in. I nearly burn my hands on the heated towel rack in the bathroom.

The thing that makes Avi's house not like a museum, though, is all the family pictures. They're almost all of Avi, usually looking vaguely uncomfortable, often flanked by two beaming older people. Baby photos, childhood photos, an actual kindergarten diploma framed and mounted on the wall—I take it back. Avi's house is less like a museum and more like a shrine. To him.

Max appears in the doorway. "Did you get lost?" he asks. "It's not a big enough house to actually get lost, but when I was six I got lost in a clothing rack at JC Penney, so I guess you can get lost anywhere."

"I was just looking around. There are . . . a lot of photos of Avi."

Max nods. "Yeah. His parents really like him. I mean, all parents love their kids, I guess, but his parents *really* do. Avi thinks it's weird, but he told me once his parents tried forever to have kids and his mom had a bunch of miscarriages and so he thinks they're just happy he actually made it." He pauses. "Should I have told you that?"

"Probably not, Max."

The front door opens behind me, and Eden comes in, wearing a weather-inappropriate long, gauzy dress under her winter coat and carrying five beers out of a six-pack under one arm. She hugs us hello, and we all head to the kitchen, where Lucy is struggling to open my bottle of vodka.

"Here," she says, holding it out to me. "Can you try?"

I will open this bottle even if I have to smash it open over the sink. Luckily, it doesn't come to that. I open it, then go to the fridge.

"What kind of mixer do you want?" I call over my shoulder to Lucy. "There's orange juice and, um, Mountain Dew—"

I turn back around to see Lucy has already poured herself a shot. She downs it and then looks at me with supreme satisfaction. "What?" she says. "I've been drinking wine every Sunday since I was seven, you think I can't do a shot?"

"Uh, so have I," Eden says, "but I'd like some of the orange juice, please, Michael."

I reattach my dropped jaw to the rest of my face, reexamine every assumption I have ever made about Lucy, and fix Eden a drink.

"We should play a game," Lucy suggests, once we're all settled in Avi's living room, drinks in hand.

Avi nods so hard he spills his drink. "Scrabble, let's play Scrabble, I am kickass at Scrabble."

"I meant like a drinking game," Lucy says. "Though you should switch to soda."

"Which one do you want to play?" Eden asks. There's silence, and then they all slowly turn to me.

Sometimes I wonder how Heretics Anonymous had any fun before I showed up.

"How about Never Have I Ever?" I suggest.

Neither Lucy or Max have ever played it before, so as we all get in a circle on the rug, I explain the rules.

"We go around the circle, each saying something we haven't done. Like, 'Never have I ever been to London.' So, if you have been to London, you take a drink."

Avi demonstrates by taking a drink.

"We're not playing yet," Eden says.

"And they shouldn't be boring like that," I add. "You're supposed to get people to admit stuff they've done, not where they went on vacation."

But four rounds later, the only one who ends up admitting anything is me, because in the second surprise of the century, it turns out Max, Eden, Lucy, and Avi collectively haven't done *anything*. They have never smoked weed *or* a cigarette. They have never snuck out of their house at night. They have never been drunk enough to throw up, though Avi might get there soon. On Max's turn, he asks if anyone has ever accidentally lit themselves on fire, and thankfully, I don't have to take a drink on that one.

Eden's next. She swishes her drink around in her cup. "Never have I ever made my parents proud of me."

Max puts his head in his hands. "Wow, Eden," Lucy says. "Way to be a downer."

"That's mine and I'm sticking to it," she says. "Who's drinking?"

We all do, even me—my parents were very proud of my preschool macaroni art.

"Oh, you jerks with your happy home lives," Eden says. Lucy stiffens, and I know she's thinking about her mom. Lucy must not have told Eden. Lucy's got so much to complain about, so much to be angry about, but she keeps it somewhere out of sight, like a box in the basement. I can't do that. I spread all my problems out on the lawn, like a yard sale.

"My parents are weird, too," Avi says.

Lucy scoffs. "Please. They adore you."

"They're obsessed with me. Not in a stalker way, but— actually, almost in a stalker way."

"You don't want your parents to be proud of you?" Eden asks.

"Maybe if I deserved it."

"You do," Max insists. "You're smart and a good artist and other things I can't think of right now."

"It's not about me, it's about them." Avi looks at the ceiling. "Everything I do, even who I am—it's like a checkmark for them, something they can drop into conversations at parties." He sighs. "They spent all their time . . . I don't know, *cultivating* me—"

"Cultivating?" Max says. "Like a garden?"

"Yeah," Avi says. "Watering and weeding and making everything look perfect. But I'm not perfect." He sighs. "They're proud of me. But I'm not sure they actually know me."

"My mom and dad are great," Max announces. "Zero complaints."

"Good," Eden says. "Someone should have a functional family."

"I didn't say my whole family," Max says. "My grandparents think we're total weirdos, and I kind of get that, but also, we're really awesome, and I wish they thought so, too."

Eden laughs. "Your mom wears sweater sets. Your dad collects baseball cards. They're the most normal people I've ever met."

Max shrugs. "My grandma and grandpa—my mom's parents—are hard to please, sometimes. And I think I embarrass them."

"Why?" Avi says. "Just because of the cape?"

"Everything," Max says. "I talk too much, I talk too loud, I talk about the wrong things. It makes them go quiet. They look at each other and whisper. Like there's something wrong with me."

"There's nothing wrong with you," I tell him.

"I know that. My parents know that. But—" He hesitates. "I think my grandparents had a really specific idea of who I was going to be, and I'm not that person."

"That's so shitty," I say.

"It's not," Max says. "They only want what's best for me; we just don't agree on what that *is*. I don't know. I wish they didn't make me feel so bad. I wish I didn't make *them* feel bad."

We sit there, no one saying anything, until Lucy clears her throat. "Let's play a new game," she says. "It doesn't have to be a drinking game, it could be a regular sleepover game. Maybe Truth or Dare?"

I hate Truth or Dare. It's always physically painful or

emotionally scarring. The last time I played, in eighth grade, I had to jump from the roof of Justin Bennes's dad's home office, and the time before that, I had to kiss Rachel Markowitz, who had very sharp braces. I do not want to do this.

Lucy can tell, too, because she turns on actual, full-blown puppy-dog eyes.

"Come on," she pleads. "It'll be fun."

I didn't even know Lucy was capable of puppy-dog eyes. I thought she'd find them demeaning. But hers are amazing, and maybe there's a reason she wants to play. Maybe that reason involves me.

"I'm game," I say.

"Okay, Lucy," Eden says, clearly with something already in mind. "Truth or dare?"

"Dare."

"I dare you to follow Connor Zetsner on the social media platform of your choice. And leave him a nice comment."

"What?" Lucy yelps. "Why?"

"Because it's funny and you don't want to," Eden explains, and it is, but I'm disappointed the dare didn't involve me. I'm relieved, too. "Go on, get out your phone."

Lucy digs her phone out of her pocket. "He'll block me, just watch."

"Quit stalling," Avi says.

"I'm not, I can't find him on— Oh." She grimaces. "Is his shirt off in all his photos?"

Avi grabs the phone from her. "Holy shit," he says, and keeps scrolling.

Lucy snatches the phone back, types for a moment, then holds the screen up for Eden to see.

"'You are an adequate human being,'" Eden reads aloud. She looks at Lucy. "That's your idea of a nice comment?"

"He doesn't believe the pay gap exists," Lucy says. "Adequate is as far as I'll go."

Eden is the first to choose truth. I jump in, because there's something I genuinely want to know. "What's the weirdest spell you've ever cast?"

Eden raises an eyebrow. "I don't do spells, that's not part of my practice."

"You used to," Lucy insists. "You *totally* used to, you carried around that giant spellbook for all of seventh grade."

"Ugh, that book was horrible. The author named herself Sapphire Lonewolf. I didn't know any better yet."

"Okay, so," I press on. "What was the spell you did then, even if you don't do them now?"

Eden blushes down to the roots of her hair. "A love spell."

"On *who*?" Avi asks.

"His name was Daniel."

Lucy bursts out laughing. "Danny the Dragon."

Eden gets redder. "He liked dragons, so what?"

"No, Eden, he didn't like dragons, he seriously believed deep down in his soul he *was* a dragon."

"I liked dragons, too," Eden says, ignoring Lucy. "But he barely noticed me and I was too shy to talk to him, so I went through that book and decided to try a spell. It was called Aphrodite's Elixir, and I had to gather all this stuff—rose petals, cloves, lavender, and kosher salt for some reason—and ask Isis and Hecate to help me 'ensnare my future lover,' which even I thought was over the top, and I was twelve."

I don't get why Eden thinks that's weird, but worshipping ancient Irish gods is a perfectly normal thing to do. Lucy thinks it's weird Eden follows ancient gods, but has no problem living by the whims of an itinerant street preacher. I don't understand either of them.

"So the spell didn't work?" I ask.

"Of course not. Danny started going out with Kristin O'Donnell, who was convinced she could talk to horses. I started reading more about Celtic Reconstructionist ideas and decided spellcasting wasn't for me."

"Because it's not real," I say.

"Because it wasn't real for me. I had to read, and talk to other people, and change my mind a lot before I figured out exactly what I did believe in."

"How can you change your mind about what's real?" I say. "Either something exists or it doesn't."

"But that's so limiting," Eden says. "You can decide you were wrong about something, and it doesn't mean you were stupid. You just know more now. If I still thought the same as I did in seventh grade, I'd be worried."

I mean, sure, in seventh grade I thought girls were gross and one day I'd be tall enough to dunk a basketball, but that's kid stuff. The bigger things, though, those stay the same.

Don't they?

"It's your turn," Lucy says to me. "Truth or dare?"

My mouth is dry. My stomach is doing somersaults. I have to pee.

"Come on, truth or dare?" Avi asks, sitting up. I don't like the way he's looking at me.

"Um." I swallow. "I need some water."

I stand on shaky legs and escape to the kitchen. I'm pouring myself a slightly less-stiff drink when Avi materializes at my side like a horror movie jump gag. I almost spill the drink.

"Hey," he whispers, as if we're plotting something.

"I don't think you need another," I tell him, sliding the vodka away.

"You should talk to Lucy," he says.

I look back into the living room. Lucy hasn't moved from her spot on the carpet. "Why?"

"Dude," he says, too close to my ear, too loud. "Dude. You know why." I shake my head. "You *like* her. So tell her already."

A wave of nausea overtakes me. "I don't—"

"I'm not blind," he says. "If I have my glasses on, I'm not blind. At first, I didn't think it was a great idea, but you're a good guy, mostly. And I like you, mostly. And Lucy should be happy, she deserves to be happy. So, tell her."

"Of course she should be happy," I say. "But—"

"I'll get her," Avi decides. He turns to the living room. "Lucy!"

My nausea is instantly joined by panic. "Wait, no—" I grab for Avi's arm, spilling my drink onto the floor in the process.

"I can be a wingman!" Avi insists, trying to pull his sleeve out of my grip. "Let me be your wingman!"

When Lucy walks through the door, what she sees is me and Avi yelling at each other, locked in a battle for his flannel shirt, and standing in a puddle of vodka.

"Uh," she says. "Everything okay?"

"We're fine," I say.

"Michael has something to tell you," Avi says, louder.

Lucy turns and looks at me expectantly, adjusting the collar of her amazing sweater. Once, when I was nine, I fell out of the tree in our backyard and broke my arm. Before I felt any pain, I lay there, the wind knocked out of me, knowing there was air all around me but unable to get any of it into my lungs.

This feels worse.

"I—" It's all there, everything I feel, and Lucy's right here, bright-eyed and smiling, but all I can say is "I have to throw up."

And then I run out the kitchen door, like the absolute coward I am.

The light in Avi's bathroom is way brighter than it was an hour ago, and it hurts my eyes. I stay in the bathroom longer than I need to, trying to figure out whether I feel sick because I drank on an empty stomach or because I couldn't, wouldn't tell Lucy how I felt. I could have said I loved her, I think about taking off her clothes layer by layer, I wish she'd trade loving God for loving me. I didn't say anything.

There's a knock at the door.

"Avi," I say, "do not talk to me right now. Consider not talking to me ever."

"It's Lucy."

I turn the doorknob without getting up from the rug. I avoid looking at Lucy as she shuts the door behind her and sits down next to me.

"So," she says. "That was . . . weird."

"What did Avi tell you?"

"He just kept saying, 'I can be a wingman, why won't anyone let me be a wingman.'"

"He's drunk. You should get back to him."

"I've got a minute. I told everyone I needed to take a call outside." Her hand brushes my arm, just for a second. "Michael. What's going on?"

"Avi wanted me to tell you something."

She shrugs. "So why didn't you?"

"It's not important," I say, but that's a lie. "I felt sick." That's only half a lie.

"If you hadn't felt sick," Lucy says slowly, like she's cracking a riddle, "what would you have said?"

I take a breath. Then another. "I would have said . . ." I start off, and no room has ever been quieter than this one. "I would have said that on my first day in history class, I walked right past you. I sat behind you without even looking at you or anybody else because I was pissed I had to be there in the first place. I thought no one at a school like that could possibly be like me, be friends with me. I walked right past you."

Lucy smiles at me, and I smile too, thinking of the way she glared at me when she caught me following her through the hallways. But I have to keep going. There's more I have to say.

"I would have said—when you started to talk about saints, that's when I knew I was wrong. I wasn't alone. I could have friends, real friends. And you chose to be my friend. Even though I was a jerk about your religion, you still wanted to be my friend, and you let me join the group even though I'm not a heretic at all, and you fixed my theology homework and stole from a nun and gave me your Bible and I can't believe I walked right past you. I should have known, before I even knew your name, that you were going to be important."

Lucy has stopped smiling. She's staring at me with her mouth half open. She doesn't look embarrassed, like I thought she might. Or overcome with joy, like I hoped she might. She looks overwhelmed. She looks like she's seeing me for the first time.

"I'm so glad you said something, that day in history. Because I could have kept walking past you, and I might not have known you until later, or maybe not at all. And I can't—I can't imagine not knowing you."

I exhale, drop my eyes to the carpet, feel the knot in my shoulders loosen. I'm done. Silence is filling up the room again, and soon there's going to be no air to breathe.

"Quick question," Lucy says. "Did you actually have to throw up?"

I shake my head.

She nods. "Okay. Good."

She yanks me forward by my shirt collar and I'm kissing Lucy, or really, she's kissing me, and the fluorescent bathroom lights dim and so does the party noise outside the door, because there is nothing, nothing else but her. Her hands balled in my shirt, her hair brushing against my neck, her mouth on mine. Life can't possibly exist outside of this moment. What would be the point?

Someone bangs on the door, and we break apart. "Michael," Max says. "We're going to watch a movie. Come out when you feel better, okay?"

Lucy and I look at each other. No one knows she's in here. No one knows what happened—except us. Do we want them to know? Does she?

"Be out in a second," I call to Max, and listen as he pads away from the door. Lucy looks like she's holding her breath. "What do we do now?"

She considers this. "I think we should watch a movie." She

gets up and offers me her hand. I let her pull me up, and before she opens the door, she kisses me. It's quick. But the way she kisses me, it feels like she might do it again.

Lucy leaves the bathroom first, and I follow her after a minute. The sleeper sofa in the living room has been folded out and Avi's sprawled on top of it, already half asleep. Eden and Lucy are setting up floor cushions and sleeping bags, and Max is rummaging through Avi's DVD collection.

"Why are all your movies from the 1940s?" he complains to Avi. "That's just bizarre."

"Nghhh," Avi says, rolling onto his side.

"No film noir," Eden decides. "Pick something we'll all like."

Max frowns, rummages some more, then holds up a DVD of *The Breakfast Club*.

"Seems appropriate," Lucy says, settling herself on the far side of one of the cushions.

I hang back as Eden and Max set up the movie. I figure I'll sleep on a pad with Max, if there's room, or on the floor. I don't mind sleeping on the ground. Dad and I used to go camping when I was younger. Mom wouldn't come—she hates dirt and bugs and a lack of showers—but I always liked sleeping close to the ground, hearing crickets and frogs and smelling the grass under the tent, like the whole earth had swallowed you up.

But as the movie starts, there's a space on the sleeping pads, big enough to be on purpose, and it's not next to Max. It's next to Lucy. I'm not sure if I should. We might switch around to go to sleep, but still, I don't want to make this weird for her. She looks up at me.

"You're missing it," she says, and doesn't tell me to sit next to her, but doesn't object when I do.

18

"MICHAEL."

My mouth feels like cotton and someone is shaking me out of a great dream, one where Lucy and I are stranded on a desert island with lots of privacy and little clothing. I try to slide back into sleep, but the shaking gets more insistent.

"Michael, wake up."

I open my eyes to see the real Lucy, the one wearing pajamas instead of a palm-frond bikini, kneeling over me.

"Sorry," she whispers. "But it's almost nine. Can you drive me home?"

"Uh" is all I can say, because not only did I wake up five seconds ago, but Lucy's right hand is about five inches away from my leftover dream boner. This would probably freak her out, if she knew, because it's really freaking *me* out, and I'm attached to it.

"No one else is up yet," Lucy says.

"I AM UP," Leftover Dream Boner says.

I sit up in my sleeping bag and draw my knees to my chest, because maybe that will help. Lucy's shirt slips a little off her shoulder. That does not help.

"So can you drive me?" Lucy asks.

"CARS ARE PLACES PEOPLE HAVE SEX," Leftover Dream Boner reminds me.

I clear my throat. "Sure," I say to Lucy. "Totally. I just have to get ready. And stuff."

"Okay," she says, but stays right there, like she's expecting I'm going to climb out of my sleeping bag and start getting ready, which I can't do because she's still right there. So I stare at her helplessly and wonder when death will come.

"Okay," she says again, sounding suspicious and confused. She picks herself up off the floor and starts for the kitchen. "I'm going to get a glass of water. In there."

As soon as the kitchen door closes, I bolt out of my sleeping bag and down the hall to the bathroom.

"DID YOU NOTICE SHE WAS ONE HUNDRED PERCENT NOT WEARING A BRA?" Leftover Dream Boner asks.

"Shut the fuck up," I tell Leftover Dream Boner.

Five minutes later, with my face washed, teeth brushed, and Leftover Dream Boner mercifully gone, I join Lucy in the living room and pack up my bag. Lucy is already packed, and she's put on a sweatshirt and sneakers. As I put on my shoes, she leans over Avi, still sprawled across the sleeper sofa, and nudges him awake.

"Avi."

He makes a sound like a dying sheep and pushes her hand away. She nudges him again, harder.

"It's nine, I'm going home now. I put out some Gatorade for you on the kitchen table."

"Why are you yelling?" he mumbles, even though she isn't.

"Michael's driving me."

"Okay."

"So we'll see you later."

"Okay."

"Do you want us to take the bottles out?"

"Please," Avi says, and buries his face in his pillow.

I retrieve the bag full of empty bottles from under the kitchen table. As I pass by the couch, a hand snakes out and grabs my ankle. I drop the bag on the floor, right by Avi's head.

Lucy's head turns as the bottles clatter against one another. Eden stirs in her sleeping bag. Avi claps his hands over his ears and buries his head farther into the pillow. And Max, eyes still closed and hand still on my ankle, mumbles, "Don't throw the bag in the recycling."

"What?"

"Only recycle the bottles. They can't—" He yawns. "—process plastic bags."

He snuggles back in his sleeping bag.

Outside, Lucy and I dutifully separate the bottles from the trash bag before getting into my car.

"Is this weird?" Lucy asks as I start the ignition.

I hesitate. Maybe she's thinking about last night. "Is what weird?"

"Leaving a sleepover this early. What's the etiquette, are you supposed to wait until everyone's awake, or—?"

"Have you never had a sleepover before?"

"My mom wasn't into the idea. Whenever I'd ask, she'd act all confused and say, 'But you have a bed here, *mija*.'"

I'm relieved it wasn't our kiss she thought was weird, but I wonder if we're going to talk about it. I don't know if I want to. I mean, I *do* want to, at least part of me does. The part of my brain that wants things—like pizza or Lucy with her shirt off— is screaming at me to talk about it. But another part of my brain, the part that keeps me from touching hot stoves, is holding that first part back. It must have a name.

"What's the part of your brain that makes you want things?" I ask Lucy as we drive down Avi's block.

"The limbic system," she says, because of course she knows. "Why?"

"No reason."

We drive in silence for a minute. When I shift gears, she shakes her head.

"I can't believe you can drive stick," she says. "Who even has a stick shift anymore?"

"Lots of people," I say. "Like my dad. He says the car responds to you better, and you have to focus more, so you drive safer."

"More safely."

"You probably shouldn't correct your chauffeur's grammar." She laughs.

"So you'll only drive an automatic?" I ask.

She picks at her nails. "I actually don't drive anything."

"You don't *drive*?"

I know Lucy's family only has one car, the one her stepdad takes to work every day, so I assumed that's why Lucy never talked about driving.

"Didn't your mom teach you?" I ask, remembering too late that Lucy's mom hasn't been around for over a year. She missed Lucy turning sixteen. The back of my neck gets hot. Why did I say that?

"Or your stepdad," I add, trying to recover. "What about your stepdad?"

If the mention of her mom bothered Lucy, it isn't showing on her face. "Oh, he tried. A couple times. But I don't want to drive."

Sometimes I don't understand this girl at all. "Why not?"

She looks at me, then back at the road. "I do a lot, you know? For my brothers, and Jake." She lists it off on her fingers. "Most of the cooking, all of the cleaning, the laundry, picking them up from after-school. But there's some stuff I can't do, like get the groceries and take them to doctor's appointments, because I don't drive."

I don't even know how to do laundry. Everything Lucy does for herself and her brothers, my mom does for me. Lucy's mom left and Lucy took her place. The weight of that sinks into my hands, and when Lucy reminds me to make a left, the steering wheel feels heavy.

"I don't mind doing what I do," Lucy says, like she's trying to convince both herself and me. "I love them. But if I learned how to drive—I'd have to do even more. And I guess I don't really want to." She sighs. "Is that selfish?"

Lucy has never been selfish in her life.

"No," I say. "It's human."

And she nods and looks less worried.

"I don't drive that much anymore, either," I say, trying to make her feel better. "My mom always needs hers, and my dad's is a company car, so I can't drive that." I shrug. "Just one more way he ruined my life."

Lucy laughs, but not like she thinks it's funny. "You have a really low bar for life-ruining."

"What?"

She looks at me like I'm a kid who can't quite figure out basic addition. "Your dad didn't ruin your life."

She's barely even spoken to my dad; how would she know? "He moved us here—"

"—so he could take a better job, right?" she says. "So you

194

could live in a nice house, and your nice mom could stay home and cook you breakfast every morning, so you could go to a really good high school, so you could go to college and not even worry about how to pay for it." She looks out the window. "I think he did this *for* you."

If we hadn't moved again, if Dad hadn't done this to me—or for me—I wouldn't be sitting in this car with Lucy at all. I'm glad I'm here, but I'm still mad at my dad for the way it happened. And maybe that's not fair.

We drive in silence for a minute.

"Hey, so," I say, not sure if I want to hear the answer to my next question. "Do you want to talk about it?"

Lucy glances over her shoulder. "Talk about how you just missed the turn?"

Shit. I brake, put the car in reverse. "Talk about last night."

"I—" She wraps her arms around herself. "We don't have to. It's okay."

"I want to."

Lucy nods, looking all at once hopeful and terrified.

"I shouldn't have done that," she says, and my heart plummets. "Without asking, and we were both a little drunk, but you were drunker, I think, and—"

Wait. Does she think she took advantage of me? "Hold up," I say. "I wanted you to do that. I'm glad you did that."

"Yeah?"

"Yeah. Obviously."

"It's just—" She hesitates. "No one's ever wanted me to do that before. And—I've never wanted to do that before."

She's never had a crush? Or has she never *let* herself feel that way? Lucy wants to be a priest. Though she knows it's on the far side of unlikely, it's still what she wants. Priests don't have crushes, they don't kiss people, they don't date or have sex or get married. With any other girl, a drunken bathroom makeout would be a solid foundation for a relationship, but with Lucy, I'm not so sure.

"What do you . . . want this to be?" I ask, feeling my pulse in my fingers as I flick on the turn signal.

She gulps audibly. "Be?"

"I mean, was this a one-time thing? Or do you want to, I don't know—go steady?"

She bursts out laughing. "Only if we can get milk shakes and go to the sock hop afterward. *Go steady?*"

"You know what I mean." I can feel my hand slipping on the steering wheel. "Do you . . . want to be my girlfriend?"

Then, silence. I keep my eyes on the road, waiting, just waiting, for her to say no.

She clears her throat. "Do *you* want me to be your girl-friend?"

"I asked first!"

I steal a glance away from the road. Lucy's smiling the way she did before our first theology class, like she knows something I don't. Did she know that day? Not just that she'd bring me into

Heretics Anonymous, but that she'd bring me into her life?

"I want to," I tell her. "If you want to, I want to."

She nods. "Okay. Me too."

I pull the car over.

"Michael, this isn't my block."

"I know."

I kiss her, and I don't care that my seat belt's practically strangling me, because it's even better than last night. She wants this, even without alcohol and the world's worst wingman egging her on, she wants to do this. It feels almost like being underwater, quiet and dark, the rest of the world just above the surface, but so far away. It's a long time before we come up for air.

"About last night," she says. "I wanted to say, it was—it was a really nice Christmas gift."

"The perfume?" I ask.

She shakes her head. "Not the perfume."

We go back under.

19

WHEN WE RETURN to St. Clare's in the second week of January, I half expect the place to be on lockdown, with barbed wire and nuns with metal detectors, weeding out any hint of dissent. But everything looks the same—if there's another crackdown coming, no one's letting on.

When I get to history, though, Lucy looks uncomfortable. For a second, I wonder if it's my fault. We spent a lot of winter break together, at her house and mine, but maybe it's strange for her to see me at school, in my tie and blazer. But what she says is "Something really weird happened in Latin."

Before I can ask her what, Sister Joseph Marie calls the class to order, and Lucy turns back around.

At lunch, I meet Avi at our usual table. He's staring into his soup. Not eating it, just poking at it with his spoon. Lucy throws him a worried glance as she sits down, and I remember what she said at the beginning of history.

"What happened in Latin?" I ask.

Lucy grimaces. Maybe she didn't want me to ask right then. "We have a new teacher," she says, looking at Avi out of the corner of her eye.

"Halfway through the year?" I've seen the Latin teacher, and she's too old for maternity leave.

"Ms. Simon resigned," Lucy says.

Avi looks up from his bowl of soup. "She did *not* resign."

"She left voluntarily," Lucy says. "They said she agreed to—"

"That's bullshit. They found out she got married and they made her leave."

I know the Catholic Church has a strong celibacy message, but I thought they were generally cool with weddings. "They fired her for getting married?"

Avi stirs his soup. Lucy sighs. "For getting married to another woman."

Oh.

"That's obviously not what they told us," Lucy continues. "But Jason Everett knew because his mom did their flowers, and so now everyone knows."

"That sucks," I say.

"No shit," Avi mutters.

"It does," Lucy says. "It really does. And everyone's upset about it, especially since apparently Ms. Simon was with her wife for ages, and it wasn't a secret, but they only made her leave when she got married. Some contract the teachers sign. A morality clause."

"Nothing more moral than firing someone for having a wedding," Avi says. Jenny from history class approaches our table, nervous and clutching a clipboard in her right hand.

"Hi," she says, eyes darting from Avi to Lucy. "We're sending around a petition about Ms. Simon and how unfair it was, and once we have all the signatures we're going to show it to Father Peter. Do you want to sign?" She thrusts the clipboard out at them.

Avi stares her down. "What do you think is going to happen?"

"Huh?"

"When you give that to Father Peter, what do you think is going to happen?"

Jenny blinks. "We're going to try to get Ms. Simon her job back."

Avi laughs, and it sounds awful and bitter. "A bunch of children signing a piece of binder paper is not going to get her job back. Every single person in this school could sign that and Ms. Simon would still be out of a job, because she is gay, and the church you *choose* to belong to thinks gay people are 'intrinsically disordered' and should *suffer* through that disorder, chaste and alone, for their entire lives. Ms. Simon didn't. So she's not coming back." He pushes the clipboard back at Jenny. "Petitions are a joke. You are a joke."

Jenny's mouth drops.

"Avi, unnecessary." Lucy grabs the clipboard and signs. "I'm signing your name, too," she tells him. "Sorry, Jenny."

"You can sign even if you weren't in her class." Jenny's staring down at her shoes, but I think she's talking to me. "Anyone can sign."

"Yeah," I say. "Of course." I sign the petition and hand the clipboard back to Jenny. She hugs it to her chest but doesn't leave. She draws her head up and looks straight at Avi.

"You don't know me," she tells him, quiet and clipped. "You shouldn't act like you do."

Avi opens his mouth, but before he can respond, Jenny's moved on to another table.

Avi is quiet during theology and goes to the school nurse with a "headache" during PE. By the end of the day, I hope he's gotten all the anger out of his system, because Angry Avi is like regular Avi on sarcasm amphetamines. When I meet up with him after sixth period, he's calmed down. But only a little.

"What bothers me the most is the hypocrisy," he says as we walk past the chapel on our way to HA. "So okay, Ms. Simon works at a Catholic school. And the Catholic Church thinks gay people should lead lonely, lonely lives. But if you're going to go there, the Catholic Church thinks no one should get divorced, and I know Mr. Cartwright is on his second wife. I'm also pretty sure he only coaches lacrosse because he likes creeping on teenage girls in flippy skirts, but that's beside the point."

"Yeah, I think the Bible might be okay with that," I say.

"So why fire Ms. Simon but not Mr. Cartwright?" Avi continues. "If Catholics believe sin is sin, like Sister Helen always says, why is what Ms. Simon did so much worse? She's not even Catholic. What did they expect her to do? Be alone forever because she wanted to keep her *job*?"

"I'm sure she'll find another one."

He shakes his head. "That's not the point. You don't get it."

I open my mouth to argue, because of course I get it. I'm an atheist surrounded by priests and portraits of popes. Of course I know what it's like to feel alone, to feel closed in by people who want me to change to fit their worldview. I almost say that, but then I stop. Because Avi's right. What happened to Ms. Simon will never happen to me. No one will fire me for not believing in God. No one will kick me out of school, or it would have happened already. No one will stop me from living my life exactly as I want to, without religion. People might want to convert me, or think I'm going to hell, but they can't hurt me, not really. Not like people hurt Ms. Simon. Not like they could hurt Avi.

"You're right," I say to Avi as he pushes open the door to the janitor's closet and the stairs down to the HA room. "I don't. I'm sorry."

Avi looks back at me, shocked, then promptly falls headfirst into the closet.

I step in and close the door quickly, scared someone could

hear the crash and find us.

"Ow. Shit," Avi says. I can't find the light. I turn my phone's brightness up as far as it'll go. Avi's still sprawled on the floor.

"Are you okay?"

"Yeah." He takes his phone out too, and shines it right next to him. "Watch out, somebody put all these boxes right in front of the stairs."

I shine my light at the cardboard boxes. They're all labeled HUMAN RESOURCES. I open one of the boxes and pull out some of the folders. The dates are old, some from almost ten years ago, and each folder is labeled with a name.

"What are they?" Avi asks.

"Records, I think." I rifle through the papers inside. "It looks like for teachers. Staff."

Avi takes a stack, too. "God, it's everything, tax forms and notes from meetings . . ."

"Why would they leave this stuff in here?"

"It's a storage closet. I guess they're storing it." Avi puts down his stack. "Come on, let's move it out of the way so the others don't trip over it."

I don't move. People talk about gears turning in their heads, but that makes everything sound so orderly. When I have ideas, the pieces rub against each other, but never line up right at first. That's what's happening right now. I know I have an idea, but I'm not sure what it looks like.

"Avi."

"Yeah?" He stops moving a box.

"You were talking before about hypocrisy, about how there's probably lots of things teachers here have done that *didn't* get them fired from St. Clare's."

"So?"

I put the folder back and pick up the whole heavy box. "So let's find out what those things were."

"No."

"Lucy—"

"No. Absolutely not."

"Absolutely not to what?" I ask as Lucy returns a stack of files to its box. "We haven't planned anything; I'm only saying we should look through them."

"But we shouldn't," Lucy says. "These are private documents, with people's pictures and social security numbers, and you shouldn't have even touched those boxes."

"Yeah, didn't have much choice there, Rosary Rita," Avi says. "I tripped over them."

"I don't see what the big deal is," Eden says to Lucy, sitting cross-legged on the couch and thumbing through a file. "It's not like Michael's suggesting we steal their identities."

"I'm not sure what Michael *is* suggesting we do."

I didn't expect Lucy to be such a wet blanket about this, but as soon as she, Eden, and Max got down to the HA room and Avi and I filled them in, she immediately shot everything down.

"What happened to Ms. Simon wasn't right," I say. "And it wasn't right especially because other teachers get away with stuff the Catholic Church isn't okay with, like divorce, and they don't get fired. And that's not fair." Lucy just blinks. "So I'm suggesting we let all the students know about how unfair it is, and let the administration know that we know."

"And how are you going to do that without throwing those teachers under the bus?"

Avi shrugs. "Casualties of war."

"Avi, no," Lucy says, with a hard shake of her head. "You can't."

"Well, you can," Eden says, looking up from her stack of files, "but you don't want to."

"Yeah, well, maybe I do," Avi says.

"You don't," Eden repeats. "Because that's exactly what St. Clare's did to Ms. Simon, you know? They took something private that was her business and they used it to hurt her and set an example for us." She picks up another file. "So I really don't think that's what you want to do."

"Thank you," Lucy says, her hand outstretched at Eden. "I know this is a tough situation, but us playing investigative reporter isn't going to help. Let's be rational about this."

"Just because you don't like the plan doesn't mean it's irrational," I protest.

"That's so fucking easy for you to say." Avi interrupts me, zeroing in on Lucy. "This is *your* church. What they did is something *you* choose to believe in."

Lucy looks taken aback. "What? I don't think she should have gotten fired."

"Because she isn't Catholic."

"Right. Why should she have to follow the rules of another person's religion?"

"What if she were Catholic?" Avi asks. "Do you think she should be able to get married then?"

"I believe in marriage equality, you know that."

"Do you believe in it in *your* church, though? Do you believe in two men or two women standing at *your* altar, not just at city hall?"

Lucy hesitates. "That's—"

"What about two years ago, when the school found out that senior girl got an abortion? They kicked her out; do you believe in that?"

"No!" Lucy throws her hands up. "Of course she shouldn't have been kicked out."

"But do you believe she did something wrong?"

"It's not what I would have done."

"That's not what I asked."

Lucy stares at him. "I don't know why you're acting like this. What happened to Ms. Simon isn't my fault."

"If you put money in their collection plate, you're supporting them. You're literally financially supporting what they do."

"You're being a jerk, stop it," I tell Avi.

"Why?" Avi snaps back. "Because it hurts her feelings? Her

feelings aren't the only ones that matter."

Lucy spins back on Avi. "What do you want me to do, Avi? I'm not the pope. I'm not Father Peter. I'm not *allowed* to speak for my church; what exactly do you think I can do?"

"You could leave," Eden says softly. Lucy stops short. "The church isn't going to change. The only thing you can do is find something better."

"I'm not going to leave," Lucy says. The way she says it, it's like Eden asked her to sacrifice her firstborn.

"Why?" Eden asks. "It hurts people you care about. It hurts you. Why can't you leave?"

"Because it's my home!" Lucy bursts out. "And it's a mess. I know it's a mess. But it's my home, and I'm going to stay, I have to stay, and make it better." Her voice wavers. "I won't run away from my home."

Everyone's quiet.

"I don't think we're really mad," Max says. "At least, not at each other. There's just no one else we're allowed to yell at." Avi and Lucy glance at each other, then away.

"But while we're still mad," Max continues, "we probably shouldn't make any big plans. Like, angry dancing is fun, but angry baking isn't, because you burn yourself on the stove and forget the baking soda and then your cookies are all flat. And I think planning's a lot like baking."

"Yeah, me too," Eden agrees. She starts to pack up the box of files. "Let's all sleep on it."

✦ ✦ ✦

Lucy and I walk together after the meeting's over, me on my way home, her to pick up her brothers. Lucy is weirdly quiet.

"What's wrong with you?" I ask after ten solid minutes of silence.

She sighs, long and hard. "It feels like everything's falling apart."

"Avi will come around. Max is right, he's not really mad at you."

"It's okay for Avi to be mad," she says. "But people do stupid things when they're upset. And now the whole school is upset, and you want to add in all the teachers' personal lives—"

"A very select few. And fine, we won't do it, I'll tell everyone tomorrow. So what's the problem?"

"We have to do something, I know that. But when people get upset," she repeats, "they go to extremes. Can you promise that's not going to happen? Like, swear to God?"

"Can't swear to something I don't believe in."

"What do you want to swear to?" she asks. "Science? Deductive reasoning? *The ghost of Friedrich Nietzsche?*"

"You," I say, and her face softens. "I swear to *you*. I won't let this go too far."

"Cross your heart?"

I'll do the next best thing. "I promise."

20

BY THE LAST week in January, we still haven't had another HA meeting. Eden proposes it once, but Avi and Lucy make it clear they aren't interested. They've warmed up to each other, and Lucy told me that they had a conversation and worked things out, but maybe they're afraid another meeting about Ms. Simon will bring it all out again.

On my own, I go down to the Heretics Anonymous room and start sifting through box after box. If I can show everyone—but especially Lucy—what our anti-hypocrisy project would look like, I know they'd get on board. If it's laid out in front of them, the research already done, they'd see that this is the perfect response to Ms. Simon getting fired.

"Do you want to come over today?" Lucy asks, for the second time this week. "I got the boys a build-your-own-castle set at a yard sale. It's only missing a couple pieces."

And for the second time this week, I say no. "I have Spanish tutoring," I tell her, and wish I didn't have to lie. But if I told

Lucy I was doing this, she'd make me stop. She'd remind me that I promised her I'd leave it alone. Though, really, what I promised was not to take it too far, and I haven't. All I've done is make some posters.

They aren't great—I'm not an artist—but I found some posterboard and made them anyway. They've got each teacher's name, their sin, and the hard copy of the evidence taped up, along with their picture.

MR. MARTEL (AP Government)
SIN: Adultery
—First married to Marion Martel.
—Ten years ago, had his health insurance benefits switched to a girl named Chelsea Cantlin *three months* after her graduation from St. Clare's.
—Yes. You are reading that correctly. He married his eighteen-year-old former student.

MS. POPLAWSKI (Math, Grades 9–12)
SIN: Greed (and paranoia)
—Repeatedly stole colleagues' lunches from the communal fridge.
—Maintained that she only wanted to test them for radiation poisoning.
—Caused 9th grader to have a panic attack after asserting the Chilean government was messing with the school's water supply.
—Forced 12th grade class to build a model of the Twin Towers out of Legos . . . to prove it was an inside job.

MR. CARTWRIGHT (English, Field Hockey Coach)

SIN: Lust

—Seven separate incident reports over twelve years
from female students.

—In every case, complimented the students' shampoo
and invaded personal space.

—In one case, confided in student about his failing
marriage and asked for advice.

—In another, straight up texted a student and asked if
she wanted to get gelato. At 10 p.m.

—All students were switched into alternate classes and
the incidents closed.

I bet if I did more digging, I'd find teachers who used birth control or teachers who used IVF centers to have their babies, but I don't think I should make posters for them. I know Lucy said the Catholic Church considers those things sins, but I don't get why. Someone who wants a kid shouldn't have one, and someone who doesn't want a kid should, just because God's sitting on his hands?

"Is that what you believe?" I asked Lucy when I brought up the topic last week.

"I believe everyone should be able to make choices, and I believe that that choice is none of my business," she said, then put her book down. "Why do you ask?"

"No reason."

When the posters are done, when the time's right—then I'll tell her.

✦ ✦ ✦

To my surprise, Avi calls a Heretics Anonymous meeting, something he's never done before. He proposes Thursday, after he's done with his after-school newspaper meeting. They print every other Friday, so it's their most important day. Lucy and I head to the newspaper adviser's classroom to meet Avi and go down together, but when we approach, I can hear Father Peter talking to someone inside.

"I feel like I've been patient. I've heard you out," he's saying. Lucy grabs my arm to stop me from going farther, but I poke my head into the classroom. It's empty, except for Father Peter, whose back is to the half-open door, and Jenny, who has her hands balled at her sides. She looks terrified, but she also looks furious.

"I know, Father, you did. But . . ."

"Yes?"

"I heard *you* out, too," she says with the barest hint of an edge, "and I still think we should publish it in *The Record*."

He shakes his head. "Jenny—"

I've never heard him call a student by their first name. It sounds oddly intimate.

"This happened," Jenny says. "It happened, we can't say it didn't, everybody knows."

"If everyone already knows, I don't see why you need to write an article about it."

"She was a part of St. Clare's! Her students deserve to know the whole story, not just rumors." Jenny sets her jaw. "She was a part of our family. Wasn't she?"

I duck out of the doorway and turn back to Lucy. I mouth, "Ms. Simon?" and she nods.

"This is a very sensitive issue," we hear Father Peter say. "It's been a hard couple of months around here. This would only exacerbate things. I know you and Ms. Simon were close, but I need you to trust me on this. We can't have an article on her departure."

There's the squeak of patent leather shoes on linoleum. "I'd quote you; you could explain why it happened. But not writing about it at all, it's like you're asking me to lie."

"I'm not asking anything. I am telling you, there will be no article in tomorrow's paper or any other. Are we clear on that?"

Silence. He prods again. "Jenny?"

"Yes!" she says about eight decibels louder than I've ever heard her speak. "Father," she adds. Her footsteps get close to the door, so Lucy and I escape down the hall.

"Man, I didn't think she had that in her," I say to Lucy as we descend the stairs to HA.

"She's quiet," Lucy says, pushing open the door, "but Jenny has *principles*."

Everyone's already there, so Lucy and I waste no time in telling them what we heard Jenny and Father Peter saying. Avi nods, like he already knew.

"Father Peter kicked us all out of the newspaper office early. Everyone except Jenny."

"What does she want to do?" Eden asks. "Write an editorial

213

saying it was wrong to fire Ms. Simon?"

"Not even, that's what's so messed up," Avi says. "She wanted to write a *news* article about Ms. Simon leaving. Just confirm that she did, and why she had to. Father Peter said no."

"Because it would be 'divisive,'" I add. "He doesn't want anyone to talk about it." Avi nods.

"What about your article, back in December?" Lucy asks. "About Dress Code Week. That wasn't divisive, but this is?"

"Did you actually read that article, when it came out?" Lucy looks suddenly guilty. "It started out about Dress Code Week. By the time our staff adviser and Father Peter were done with it, the article was about the new security cameras and how much safer everyone feels."

"You can't write what you want?" I ask. My old high school didn't have a real paper, just a student-run blog, but no one was censoring those articles. Or spell-checking them.

"Everything goes through Father Peter at least once," Avi says. "So our articles get rewritten and sanitized and end up boring as hell. That's why I called this meeting."

We all look at each other, confused. Avi elaborates.

"A school newspaper is more than something to put on your college application. It's one of the only places we have to talk about our school, to voice our opinions without getting in trouble. That's what it should be, anyway, and I think HA should make it that way."

"You want to protest the paper?" Max asks.

"No," Avi says. "I want to make one of our own."

21

LUCY AND I haven't told anyone we're dating, not yet. She worries that it'll upset the group dynamics, and I'm worried Avi will think he possesses any skill at being a wingman. But this secrecy doesn't even last two months. One day, Eden and Max join me, Lucy, and Avi for lunch. Eden and Max seat themselves on one side of the table with Avi, like some of kind of jury, and tell us they know.

"We totally support you guys, but we're kind of hurt you didn't tell us," Eden says.

"There shouldn't be secrets in a secret society," Max says.

Lucy looks unconcerned. "We were just waiting for the right time."

"How did you even know?" I ask.

"Please. It's not like you two were subtle," Avi says.

"Give us a little credit," Eden says.

"I saw you making out by the teacher parking lot yesterday and I told them," Max says.

Eden and Avi glare at Max.

I decide to use this newfound group honesty to my advantage and call an HA meeting for February 14. But when Lucy arrives to the room that afternoon, we're the only ones there. I've set up the camping lanterns on the bookshelves and the broken desks in the corner but turned the other lights off, so the whole room is bathed in a low glow that I hope looks romantic, not creepy.

"What is this?" Lucy whispers as she shuts the door behind her. "Where's everyone else?"

"They were nice enough to give us the room," I say. "Happy Valentine's Day."

She drops her bag and goes to inspect the V-Day spread I've arranged on the least damaged desk I could find. It's all Lucy's favorite things: off-brand Dr Pepper, cheddar popcorn, and of course, some Valentine's Day treats.

"*Chocoramo!*" she says, scooping up the Colombian chocolate cake I had to buy on the internet. "I haven't had this in forever, how did you know?"

"Eden said you used to bring one in your lunch every day."

"It's a national treasure. Like Vegemite in Australia," she says, sitting down on the couch to unwrap it. "I can't believe you did all this."

"It's our first Valentine's Day," I say, sitting next to her and helping myself to a handful of candy hearts.

"I feel awful, I don't have anything for you."

This is the first time we've been alone—really alone, without my mom downstairs or Lucy's brothers in the next room—since the night of the party. "I feel like we can figure something out."

"I thought you wouldn't be into Valentine's Day," she says. "It's about a saint, after all."

"I like free candy. I don't care if I get it because of some saint who was into hooking people up."

"The day's not supposed to be about chocolate, you know," Lucy says as she shoves half the chocolate-covered sponge cake in her mouth.

I already heard the whole Saint Valentine's story in theology, and it didn't exactly get my heart pounding.

"Yeah, yeah," I say, "Saint Valentine married a bunch of Christians in secret and the Romans chopped his head off. Boring."

"Oh yes, decapitation. Super boring."

"It's the same story with all the saints. They're Christian, they won't stop being Christian, they get executed, the end."

"When I was in elementary school, that was always the boys' favorite part, learning all the gross ways saints died."

"Decapitation's not so bad," I say. "When Mount Vesuvius erupted, Pompeii got covered in ashes, everybody knows that, but in Herculaneum, which was closer, the air got so hot so fast everyone's heads exploded. Literally exploded. *That's* gross."

Lucy stares at me, horrified and impressed. For once, I know something she doesn't. Finally, all those books about natural disasters I read as a kid have paid off. I can't wait to tell Mom. She thought they'd turn me into an arsonist.

"That's . . . awful," Lucy says.

"I know. Nature's awesome. None of your saint stories can top that."

"Saint Lawrence was roasted alive on a spit," she says. "And guess what they made him the patron saint of?"

"What?"

"Cooks."

Touché. That's extremely messed up, but I'm not conceding defeat. "In the eighteen hundreds, a volcano called Krakatoa erupted with four times the strength of a Russian hydrogen bomb. I don't know if people's heads exploded there, though."

"Pope John XII died of a massive heart attack while having sex with his mistress. Or her husband killed him. Nobody's sure."

"One time in Boston, a tank carrying molasses blew up and a fifteen-foot tidal wave of molasses covered the whole city, wiping out buildings, taking out trains, and legit murdering like twenty people."

Lucy thinks for a moment. She puts her cake aside. She folds her hands in her lap. "In 897, Pope Stephen VI dug up a previous pope's dead body, brought it to a courthouse, conducted a trial against the corpse, found it guilty of illegally ascending to the papacy, and threw the decaying skeleton into the Tiber River."

Holy shit.

This girl gets me.

"See, this is what Sister Helen should be teaching us," I say. "That's awesome. I want to know about that, not the Chief Spiritual Works of Mercy."

"It's theology. Were you expecting sex, drugs, and rock and roll?"

"One out of the three would be nice."

Lucy looks like she's considering something, then says: "There's Saint Daniel the Stylite."

"Isn't that a kind of rock?"

"No, that's—a stylos is a really tall pillar. And stylites were these holy men who would go live on top of the pillars."

"They'd *live* on top of the pillars? Like eat and sleep and live on top of a pole?"

"Yes. So Daniel—"

"How did they go to the bathroom?"

"Do you want to hear the story, or not?"

I nod.

"One day," she continues, "Daniel was sitting on his stylos, minding his own business, when someone leaned a ladder up against the pole and climbed to the top. People did that sometimes, to talk to Daniel and seek his wisdom. But that day, some of Daniel's enemies sent a prostitute to climb the ladder and seduce him."

"They wanted to get him laid?" I ask.

"Daniel was celibate," she explains. "If he was seduced by a woman, it would wreck his holy reputation."

"What kind of prostitute?"

"What do you mean what *kind*—"

"Are we talking a high-priced call girl, or . . . ?"

"Yeah, I don't know how much this ancient Byzantine woman charged for her services, Michael."

"I'm just trying to create a visual."

"So the girl climbs onto the pillar, next to him," she continues, and scoots closer to me. "He sits there and stares at her." She shoots me a sharp glance. "Weirdly. Very weirdly."

I avert my eyes, focusing on the sound of her voice, soft and rolling, like ripples in a lake.

"Daniel tries to look away from her, but he can't. And Daniel knows if she stays there for one more second, he's going to end up kissing her." Her knees are touching mine, the chocolate cake abandoned on the desk. "He wants to. Even though everything he's ever been told tells him he shouldn't, it's all he wants."

I snake my hand around her waist, pulling her closer. This is almost better than kissing, the way her body presses against my hand when she breathes in. I can feel the edge of her tights under my fingers. I think about what it would be like to unwrap her layers, sweater vest, crisp white shirt, and all, like the world's greatest Christmas present.

"Would it really be so bad?" I ask. "If Daniel did kiss her?"

"Well," she says, "I don't think he would have become a saint." She loops her hand around my tie and pulls us both down onto the couch. "But he might have been happy anyway."

22

LIKE ANY GOOD editor in chief, Avi assigns each member of Heretics Anonymous a piece for our secret newspaper. With only five of us, it's bound to be small, but Avi's fine with that.

"It's the content that matters, not how many pages we can fill," he says. "I mean, *The Record* prints the weekly lunch menu, for God's sake. Doesn't mean we have to."

As Avi works on the actual, school-sponsored newspaper, he secures the things we'll need—a bootleg copy of the computer program used to lay out the paper, and *The Record*'s official template, complete with the right fonts. Then, one sunny Thursday afternoon in late February, we all gather at Max's house, our assigned articles on flash drives.

Both Max's parents work from home, and their industrial printer's just what we need to produce our newspaper—we're calling it *Off the Record*. Max's mom and dad both have afternoon appointments, so we've got full access to our own private print shop. We crowd into Max's bedroom, look over the articles, and lay everything out.

Eden and I have cowritten an article titled "Interfaith Is Integral," exploring how St. Clare's could better include non-Catholic students and their religious traditions. "I get that this is a religious school," Eden says. "But if you're cool with accepting kids who aren't Catholic and taking their tuition money, you could at least not insult their beliefs." I suggest that the theology textbook could stop describing atheism as "one of the most serious problems of our time" and not suggest that agnostics suffer from "a sluggish moral conscience." Eden suggests acknowledging other faiths' holidays during the school year.

"If people who aren't Catholic can sit through mandatory Masses, St. Clare's could at least *acknowledge* Ramadan or Yom Kippur."

"Rosh Hashanah would be good," Avi says. "Everyone can get behind eating apples and honey."

"Which holiday's the one where you get to build a hut?" Max asks.

"Sukkot. My family tried to do it once, but our sukkah kept collapsing, so we built a pillow fort, ate some dumplings, and called it a week."

Lucy's contribution is a forceful, thoroughly researched, excessively long opinion piece on why women should have institutional power in the Catholic Church. She hovers over

Avi's shoulders as he edits it.

"You can't cut that!" she protests as he slices and dices with his red pen.

"Lucy. This paragraph alone has eight separate quotes from feminist theologians."

"So?" she says. "Everyone should read Sister Elizabeth Johnson. She's a genius."

He crosses something else out. "No one will read it if it feels like homework."

She pouts but lets him edit.

Max gets very concerned that this paper is going to turn out too serious. "*The Record* has an entertainment section," he points out. "We should, too."

Everyone agrees. Max puts together a quiz called "Which St. Clare's Nun Are You?" and we all have fun taking it—well, except Lucy, who is horrified by her result.

"Sister Joseph Marie?" she yelps. "This can't be right. I must have scored it wrong."

"I can see it," I say, and she glares at me.

"Better than who I got," Max says. "Sister Joan. She's the most boring one. Even her name is boring."

Together, we come up with a word search puzzle that asks readers to locate all the words we've heard people using to describe Heretics Anonymous. These words include "atrocity," "hilarious," and "blasphemous." We tried to fit in "basically the eleventh plague of Egypt," but that was too long.

The centerpiece of the issue, though, is Avi's article. It's not exactly the paragon of journalistic integrity he wanted it to be.

"How can you get quotes from people if the reporter's anonymous?" he points out. "And besides—I'm too biased for it to be a real article, anyway."

So what he creates isn't quite an investigative exposé and isn't quite an opinion piece. It's an impassioned defense not just of Ms. Simon, but of the human rights we all have—the right to walk our own path, the right to strive for our own happiness. The right to be ourselves without fear.

"Saint Clare of Assisi herself said, 'We become what we love. Who we love shapes what we become,'" Avi writes in the closing paragraph. "And I would add something else: The way we treat others proves who we've become. Who are we, St. Clare's? What do we want to become?"

The next day, Avi and I sneak out of the dining hall at lunch with overstuffed backpacks, leaving out the school's side entrance and skirting around the track, where the cross-country team is doing a lunchtime practice. We exit via the metal gate by the basketball courts. I still can't believe this is against the rules. At my old high school, we could go wherever we wanted for lunch. Though, granted, the suburban neighborhood surrounding St. Clare's doesn't offer many dining options.

We take the long way around, eventually looping back to the park across the street from the school's main doors. "There,"

Avi says, pointing out the biggest tree in the far corner of the park, near the county courthouse. "That's the one."

Obviously, we couldn't distribute the paper on campus, and not just because we'd get caught. Avi wanted it delivered exactly 150 feet away from the school.

"Father Peter kept saying that, when he told Jenny she couldn't publish her article," Avi explained yesterday as copies of *Off the Record* churned out of Max's printer. "Anything distributed within 150 feet of school property has to have his approval."

After some discussion, we settled on the park's largest, oldest oak tree—it's a solid landmark and far enough away. As a bonus, it provides excellent cover from anyone who might be looking for us.

"Avi, come on," I hiss as we stand behind the tree. We've been here five minutes, weighing down stacks of newspapers from the wind with rocks. "They're fine; can we go already?"

"You have no appreciation for presentation, you know that?" He stands up. "Okay. Let's find Eden."

Waiting through seventh period is agony. Not that I cared much about mastering the subjunctive before, but today, I can't even hear my Spanish teacher, much less understand her. I'm too busy watching the clock. 2:52. 2:53. 2:54.

The minute hand hits 2:55, five minutes before the final dismissal bell. It should be coming any second now. Sure enough, to my left, I hear the muffled sound of someone's phone vibrating deep in her backpack. Just once.

At this moment, Eden is walking back from the girls' bathroom, the cheap burner phone we all chipped in for carefully concealed.

To my right, a girl fishes her phone out of her cardigan pocket and looks at it under her desk. She frowns. She just got a text, and I know what it says:

FROM: UNKNOWN

Have you heard the Good News, St. Clare's? It's waiting for you in Evergreen Park, under the tallest tree—our letter, written on our hearts, to be known and read by all.

—HA

The girl nudges her friend and shows her the text. The friend cocks her head. Even with Eden, Max, Avi, and Lucy pooling their contacts, there's no way we could have texted everyone. But I think we got enough, because as soon as the final bell rings, half my Spanish class bounds out of their seats, meeting up with their friends in the halls before making a beeline for the main entrance. Usually, people hang out by the lockers for a while, especially on a Friday. Not today.

It seems like all of St. Clare's has streamed out the doors and across the street to the park. By the time I find Lucy and we go over together, the newspapers have been found and are being eagerly passed around.

Avi sidles up to us. "There aren't enough copies," he says, almost gleeful, as we watch our classmates huddle around our tiny newspaper. Out of the crowd emerges Theresa, white-knuckling her own copy, the pages crinkling under the pressure.

"*Christ* on the *cross*," she whisper-screams as she passes by us.

"Wow," Lucy says. "That almost counts as swearing."

Avi nods. "Mission accomplished."

When we come back to school on Monday, everyone's still buzzing about the newspaper. A few stray copies of *Off the Record* are stuffed into backpacks and strewn under the benches by the front door, though the teachers are quick to confiscate any they see.

"Did you take the quiz?" Connor asks Theresa as we prep our chemistry experiment. "Because you're such a Sister Agatha."

"I burned the one I found," Theresa says.

"Jesus, couldn't you just throw it away like a normal person?" Jess asks.

"Fire is cleansing," Theresa says, lighting the Bunsen burner. The rest of us push our lab stools back a little.

St. Clare's feels different than it did when I first got here. Exciting, maybe. But also tense and dangerous, like walking across a fraying tightrope. The security cameras. The staff members patrolling the halls on the lookout for newspapers and dress code violations. The new posters for the St. Clare's Crusaders that Lucy says have popped up in the girls' locker room. The HA symbol on the third-floor staircase, the ink still wet.

Halfway through Sister Helen's customarily boring theology lecture, Jenny Okoye stumbles into the classroom clutching a hall pass, her eyes red and her mouth quivering. She takes her seat, puts her head on her desk, and doesn't look up for the rest of class. Sister Helen lets her. When the bell rings and the rest of us leave, she stays behind.

Lucy's called an HA meeting for after school to discuss and assess last week's project, so we head there together after sixth period. Eden and Max have already settled in, but Avi's missing. He finally shows up fifteen minutes late, his tie askew, looking ashen.

"Sorry I'm late," he mumbles.

"What's wrong?" Lucy asks as Avi slowly lowers himself onto the couch.

"I ran into Jenny Okoye."

"She looked so upset in theology," Lucy says. "Do you know what happened?"

Avi looks up at the ceiling. "She spent lunch in Father Peter's office."

Eden laughs. "Her? For what?"

Avi doesn't laugh. "For creating and distributing a secret newspaper called *Off the Record*."

There's a heavy, horrible silence.

"Oh no," Lucy says. "They don't really think—"

"They do," Avi says. "Or they did. She got Sister Helen to confirm her alibi during lunch, so."

"That's horrible," Eden says. "Just because she's the editor in chief of the real newspaper?"

"They found it very suspicious that *Off the Record* used the same template and the same font as the real newspaper," Avi says.

We all look at one another. Shit. No one thought of that.

"Anyone on the newspaper could have gotten that, though," Max says. "Right?"

"Jenny started the petition. Jenny pushed for the article," Avi points out. "Father Peter interrogated her for an hour about Heretics Anonymous, which, you know, she knows nothing about . . ."

"Okay, okay," Lucy says, diving straight into damage-control mode. "This isn't great. But if Sister Helen can vouch for her—"

"Jenny's flipping her shit," Avi says, "and it's all our fault."

"This one was *your* idea," I remind him.

He glares at me. "Thanks, I'd forgotten."

"Not helpful," Lucy says to us both. "Let's talk about what we can do to fix this."

"Oh, I'm not done," Avi says. "There's more, so buckle up." He pauses. "I sent Ms. Simon the newspaper."

"What?" Lucy says. "We didn't talk about that, you didn't ask—"

"This one was my idea," Avi cuts in, looking at me out of

the corner of his eye. "Like he said. So I sent it to her, using that old email address Eden set up for Dress Code Week."

"Did she write you back?" Eden asks.

Avi picks at his shirt collar. "Yes."

Why is he acting so weird? "And?"

"She wants us to stop," Avi says. "She said—she didn't want this. She appreciated what we were trying to do, that we cared about her, but it wasn't helping her. She told me we should stop."

Eden sighs. Max wraps his cloak tighter around himself. Lucy sits down next to Avi.

"Hey," she says, "think about it, though. The school probably made her sign something saying she wouldn't sue or complain. She's just protecting herself; it doesn't mean you did something *wrong.*"

"She didn't want Jenny's article or petition either, she just wants to move on." He throws up his hands. "I don't know, I don't—Jenny's freaking out, she thinks she's about to be expelled, and Ms. Simon never wanted this in the first place, so what was the point? Who are we helping?"

"But it's not about Ms. Simon," I say, and Avi and Lucy turn to look at me. "It's not only about her, I mean. It's about the hypocrisy of what they did when they fired her, that's what we first talked about, it's about the larger issues—"

"This is somebody's life," Avi says. "Someone's life isn't a *larger issue.*"

"I'm just saying, maybe the paper wasn't enough. Maybe it wasn't clear. If we looked through the files—"

Everyone groans. Avi covers his eyes with his hands. "Enough with the files, Michael!"

"Let's all calm down," Lucy says, holding up her palms between us. "Okay, so this wasn't perfect."

"We're hurting people," Avi insists. "The whole point of going public with Heretics Anonymous was to make it easier to be at St. Clare's, and I'm starting to think we made it harder."

He shoots me a look, and I cross my arms in front of myself. Okay, so it was my idea to have us go public. But I didn't do it alone, did I?

"No one made you do this, Avi," I snap. "No one put a gun to your head."

"I said from the very beginning that going public was a bad idea. This isn't on me."

"It's not on anybody!" Max says, so loud that Eden shushes him. "Why does it have to be someone's fault? Heretics Anonymous is all of us, it doesn't have a leader."

"Um," Lucy says. "I do think it has a leader."

"But why does it need one?" Max presses her. "I know, I know, this is America and if you aren't in charge, you might as well leave everyone else and do your own weird thing. The Pilgrims did it and also PETA."

Max looks between me and Avi. "What's happening right now sucks, and it's scary, and it belongs to all five of us. Whatever happens—good or bad—we all have to own it."

"If something bad even happens," Eden cuts in. "It might not. Yeah, it's pretty heated right now—"

"Heated," Avi repeats. "Theresa Ambrose launched a literal crusade."

"You don't mean literal," Max says. Avi stares at him. "A literal crusade would have horses."

"Theresa launched a *figurative* crusade, we just about threw Jenny Okoye under the *figurative* bus, and the school is maybe two days away from a full-on revolt—yes, *literally*, Max."

"You're being ridiculous," I tell Avi. "Sorry you regret doing this, but that's not our fault."

"We never should have done this. And someone's going to get seriously hurt." He turns to Lucy. "Would you back me up here?"

"She doesn't agree with you," I say. Lucy's an idealist, she believes in revolution and change. She believes in the Magnificat. "Right, Lucy?"

Her eyes dart back and forth between us. "I . . ."

Avi and I both wait, tense, watching her struggle. I can't believe this. She's not going to take my side? I know her, I know how she feels. Why won't she just say it?

"You guys," Eden says, looking first at me, then at Avi. "What's wrong with you? Don't make her do this."

Avi and I share a glance, then drop our eyes.

"Sorry," I mumble. Avi does the same.

Lucy sighs and gets up from the couch. "I think we could use a break."

"From the meeting?" Max asks.

"From HA. In general. And I think maybe the school could use a break, too."

We put it to a vote, and miraculously, it's unanimous. Heretics Anonymous is officially on hiatus.

23

ON THE THIRD Tuesday after Valentine's Day, Lucy
and I are in my room, again. We're stuffed from the lemon bars
Mom made and Lucy is telling me that despite the scare with the
newspaper, Jenny hasn't given up on her petition to rehire Ms.
Simon. She's gotten signatures from almost the whole school,
but Father Peter still won't look at it. I only half hear what she's
saying, because I still can't believe she's here. That we're *us*. I
keep expecting her to change her mind and walk out. Maybe I
wouldn't feel that way if she'd let me take her shirt off.

I rest my hand on her knee, drawing circles with my fingernails. Lucy laughs, gives up on her story about Jenny, and
kisses me. I let my hand run up her thigh, away from her knee
socks, closer and closer to the edge of her hiked-up plaid skirt,
to where there is no skirt.

Lucy sits up suddenly, drawing her legs away from me.
"Wait."

I knew that was too much, going under the skirt. "Sorry, do you—?"

"It's fine, I— Maybe we should have some rules, though."

Great. Rules. My favorite.

"Sure," I say, because here is Lucy, in my house, on my bed, and I'll agree to whatever she wants as long as she doesn't ever move. "Like what?"

"Well, for now, I think it's better if we don't—if *you* didn't . . ." She hesitates. "Okay, so pretend my body is the United States of America—"

"What?"

"Like if my head were Alaska, and my neck were, uh, Utah—"

I like the Fourth of July as much as any person into fried food and explosions, but this is taking patriotism a bit far. "Head, Alaska; neck, Utah. Got it. So?"

"So for now—for now—maybe stay out of . . . Florida."

I bring up a map of the United States in my head. "Wouldn't Florida be your feet?"

Lucy screws her eyes shut. "Kentucky? You know what I mean!"

It's just like Lucy to come up with a weird metaphor to get out of talking about sex, but I do know what she means. She doesn't want to be the piece of unsticky masking tape. There are parts of her I can't have.

But wait—she said "for now." She said it three times. And

maybe that's to keep me off her back and my hands away from her skirt hem, but maybe it's not. Maybe, somewhere beneath a lifetime of Purity Pauls telling her how to feel and who to let in, Lucy is changing her mind.

"I will stay out of Kentucky," I promise. "And the bordering states. What's your position on the Dakotas?"

She wrinkles her nose. I know I'm pushing it here, but I can't help it. "The Dakotas?"

"Yeah, you know, North and South. The two . . . Dakotas."

She takes a breath in, then lets it out slowly. "I would be amenable to that."

And while I'm cycling through my SAT vocab flashcards in my head, trying to remember whether "amenable" has a plus sign for positive connotation, Lucy grabs my hands, nods, and pulls me back down onto the bed.

The Dakotas are beautiful this time of year.

A very satisfying half hour later, Lucy and I lay across my bed, her head resting on my chest. We haven't spoken in at least five minutes, and nothing has ever felt more peaceful. I look down at Lucy, her eyes closed. Her shirt is wrinkled and buttoned up wrong. I reach over and fix it, and my fingers brush up against Lucy's necklace, a medal on a simple chain that she wears every day, but always under her shirt. I've never gotten a close look. Etched into the silver is what looks like the Virgin Mary, a crown on her head, baby Jesus in her arms, and surrounded by the words NUESTRA SEÑORA DE CHIQUINQUIRÁ.

"It was my great-grandmother's," Lucy says, pushing herself up on her elbows. "Then my mom's. She left it for me."

"What's it mean? Our lady of—"

"Chiquinquirá. It's a place. That's where my family's from in Colombia. Close by, anyway."

"What's it like?" I know Colombia has beaches and jungles, but that's about all I know.

Lucy shrugs. "I've never been. It's in the west, north of Bogotá. My mom says it's foggy in the morning, like San Francisco. And green, really green. The city's most famous for el imagen, though."

"The . . . image?"

"Of Mary," she clarifies. "Short version: A painting of the Virgin Mary was abandoned in this chapel and pretty much ruined by rain leaking in, sunlight, whatever. Years later, someone moved it to Chiquinquirá, and the day after Christmas, it was miraculously, perfectly restored. It's a big deal—the Virgin of Chiquinquirá is Colombia's patron saint. Supposedly, some of my ancestors are buried in the cemetery there, but who knows if that's true."

I let go of the medal and she eases back down, closing her eyes again. That's Lucy in a nutshell—everything is more than it appears. A necklace isn't just a necklace, it's a miraculous painting and a green, foggy town. And religion isn't just religion. It's a link to places she's never been, people she's never met. People who are gone. It's something passed down to her, no different than the medal around her neck. It's where she comes from. It's who she is.

But there has to be more than that. God has to be more than a family heirloom.

"Why are you religious?" I ask.

She opens an eye. "Seriously?"

"You're smart enough not to be, if you wanted to." She opens both eyes now, just so she can roll them at me. "I mean, you're smart and you *know* enough to see the inconsistencies and the uncertainties and you *know* it might not be true. But you believe anyway. Why?"

"This is really bad pillow talk."

I don't know if you can call it pillow talk if you didn't have sex. "It's a big part of who you are. I want to know."

Lucy sits up. She thinks for a moment, then starts.

"When I was eight, I went to Easter Mass. Not at St. Clare's; Mom and I went to a different parish then," she says, slow and halting, not like her usual stories. I don't think she's told this one before.

"It was a family Mass, so Father Al called all the kids up to the altar. And he told the Easter story, with the women coming to Christ's tomb and seeing the stone pushed aside. The disciples were all in hiding, too frightened to leave, but the women came. Jesus came to Mary Magdalene and comforted her, and *she* was the first to see Him as the Risen Lord, *she* was the first person to preach the Resurrection. When Father Al asked us, 'Where is Jesus now?' I raised my hand, and he called on me, and I said 'Heaven!' Because that's what the pictures show."

I can picture Lucy, smart and cute and in a fluffy dress, wanting to show the priest how much she knew. That's pretty much who she still is, minus the fluffy dress.

"But then," she continues, "a voice from the back of the church called out, 'Here I am.' And then another in the balcony. And another from the choir. 'Here I am.' 'Here I am.' And I understood—even though I knew one of the voices was Mr. Mascareñaz, our neighbor, I understood. God goes where I go. He is always with me.

"The Gospel of John says, 'Whoever does not love does not know God; for God is love.'" She picks at the threads in my bedspread. "And I love. So I know God. And even before I did know God, He knew me and loved me. He knit me in my mother's womb and gave me life, and no matter how hard or chaotic that life becomes, He will never, ever leave me."

Lucy looks up at me. She must wonder if I understand her at all. I do. I don't understand God, but I do understand not wanting to be alone. She grabs onto my hand.

"I believe in God because I believe in what I feel. And when I'm in church, or praying, I *feel* loved. I feel safe. I feel like someone knows me."

I squeeze her hand, trying to say, *I know you too, Lucy. Maybe not like God, but I do.*

"So, yes. I know it might not be true," Lucy says. "But I don't think I'd care if it wasn't."

That part still doesn't click for me. And I still don't think any of it's true. But if Lucy, the smartest, most logical person I know, can *feel* something real and powerful when she talks to God, then the whole thing is a lot more complicated than I thought.

And that's how we're sitting, holding hands and thinking about God, when Dad walks in my room without knocking.

Lucy jumps up. "Hi, Mr. Ausman," she says, her hand flying up to check the buttons on her shirt.

"Hello, Lucy." Dad looks at me the way he used to when I'd sneak Halloween candy before dinner. "What have you two been up to?"

"Watching TV," I say at the same time Lucy says, "Homework."

"Uh-huh," Dad says. "Michael, your mom's almost got food on the table, so if you need to drive Lucy home—"

"Oh no, I'm walking," Lucy says, and I help her gather up her things.

"Normally, we'd love for you to stay," Dad says to her. "But we wanted to have a family dinner tonight."

This is Dad's first dinner at home in a while. A couple months ago, Mom suggested video conferencing him in for meals. He laughed, and then she did too, but I could tell by the way her lips tightened that it hadn't been a joke.

"I actually should have left fifteen minutes ago," Lucy says, pulling on her green coat. "Chamber orchestra concert. I mean, we're awful, but I'm first chair for viola, so."

I wanted to go, but between the special family dinner and Lucy's insistence that I didn't have to watch the orchestra struggle through Bach's Fugue in G minor, I'm staying home.

"Break a leg," Dad says as Lucy and I pass by him and down the stairs.

I walk Lucy to the door, kiss her good-bye, and watch as she walks away, her book bag slung over one shoulder and her viola case over the other.

I close the door and turn around to find Dad standing there, his arms folded, smiling a little. He looks at me but doesn't say anything.

"What?" I say. Am I in trouble for having Lucy upstairs with the door closed? No one ever said I couldn't.

"Do I need to be worried about anything?" Dad asks.

"Like what?"

"Like grandchildren before I'm fifty."

It takes me a second to figure it out. And when I do, I want to unzip my skin and climb out of it.

"*No*," I say. He raises an eyebrow. "She's Catholic." He opens his mouth, but I cut him off. "Very Catholic."

"Either way. I'm guessing your school doesn't pass out birth control like candy."

Oh, now he cares about the quality of my sex education.

Don't worry, Dad, Purity Paul covered all of this.

"So," he continues as I stare past him, through him, to the kitchen where there is food and no one is talking about sex. "If you ever need anything, to be safe—for both of you to be safe—I want you to come to me, okay?"

I was wrong. Lucy was right. There is a God, and he hates me. There is a Hell, and I am currently in it.

"Okay?" Dad repeats.

"Okay," I say, and then for no reason at all, add, "Thank you."

I can tell Dad wants to do something fatherly like ruffle my hair, but in an act of true mercy, he lets me walk past him into the kitchen.

"Did Lucy leave?" Sophia asks me, clearing her books off the already-set kitchen table. "I wanted to talk to her about the Merovingian dynasty."

My sister has decided she likes Lucy, mostly because Sophia's been on a huge medieval Europe kick lately and Lucy knows a lot about any time period when everyone had to be Catholic.

"She had to go to a concert," I tell Sophia.

"Merovingian, that's Charlemagne, right?" Dad asks, uncorking a bottle of wine.

Sophia gives him a pitying look. "No, Daddy. That's the *Carolingian* dynasty."

Mom brings out the food. It's two main dishes instead of one—eggplant parmesan *and* beef stroganoff—which seems like a weird combo, but I love eggplant parmesan, so I'm not complaining.

I'm almost done with my second helping when Dad, noticing a lull in the conversation, says, "What do you kids know about Belgium?"

Sophia and I look at each other. I shrug.

"You fly there all the time," I say.

"The capital is Brussels, the national bird is a kestrel, and it's illegal not to vote," Sophia adds.

"Don't forget the waffles!" Mom says, twisting her napkin in her hands. "And the French fries. But I guess they don't call them *French* fries in . . ."

Dad clears his throat. "Well. How would you both like to go there?" He glances from me to Sophia.

And that's when I know.

This isn't how they usually do it. They usually tell us we're having a family meeting in the living room of whatever house we're about to leave. They usually give us some kind of warning. But I should have guessed from the meal—eggplant parmesan for me, beef stroganoff for Sophia. Our favorite foods.

"We're going to Belgium? Like for vacation?" Sophia asks.

Don't say it, I plead, and this is the closest I've ever come to praying. *Don't say it.*

Mom and Dad share a glance, steel themselves for the avalanche of shit about to come their way, and Dad says, "Actually, Sophia, we're going to live there."

All the blood is gone from my body. I didn't feel it drain out and puddle at my feet, but that's where it must be, because all I can do is sit lifelessly in a chair that traveled in four different moving vans and will now fly across an ocean along with me, Sophia, and all my parents' other possessions.

Sophia is frozen for a moment, too. An egg noodle falls off the fork, which never made it to her mouth. She puts the fork down. Looks at her plate. And then bursts into tears.

Mom rushes to comfort her. "Honey, we're not going for months. Not until summer's over."

Mom looks over at Dad, panicked, because Sophia hasn't cried before. She's always excited—this is all she knows. "Young kids are so resilient," Mom told my uncle once. As if that excuses anything. Mom's eyes move to me, and maybe she's expecting me to be a good big brother and help her, but I don't have any blood, so I can't.

"Soph, you'll like it there," Dad says. "I've seen the neighborhood we're going to live in, it's beautiful, and we'll be so close to Paris and all the places you know so much about. You can be our tour guide."

"And we'll be together," Mom adds. "In one place. We'll all be together."

Sophia takes a couple hiccupping breaths. "But I'll have to learn *Dutch*," she sobs. "And it has a *very complicated* system of compound nouns and *I don't want to!*"

She jerks her arm away from Mom and runs up the stairs to

her room. Mom doesn't follow her. She just sits. Maybe all her blood is gone, too.

"You don't have to learn Dutch," Dad assures me after a moment of silence. "Some people speak English. And most people in Brussels speak French. For God's sake, Sophia already speaks French."

"Fuck. You," I say.

Mom's jaw drops. "Michael!"

"I understand you're upset," Dad says.

"Upset? I'm—" Angry, surprised, and scared, all rolled into one. The Belgians might have a word for that, but I don't.

"And I understand why," he continues, rolling right over me. "But we are going to talk about this calmly and rationally like adults, okay?"

He couldn't drag an adult over an ocean. He doesn't want me to act like an adult. He wants me to act like a doormat.

I take a breath. Then two.

"How," I say, and my voice sounds raw and ragged. "How could you do this to us?"

Dad sighs. Mom lays her hand on mine. "This was not only Dad's decision; it was mine, too."

"But not mine or Sophia's," I point out.

"It's been hard for you, for all of us, to be apart so much," Mom says, her eyes wet. "I know it has. This is better, trust me."

I can't believe it, she's as much of a traitor as Dad is. Mom didn't want to move here in the first place. She's far from her family. She misses her friends and hasn't made any new ones. Then again, maybe that's why she doesn't mind going. She isn't losing anything she hasn't already lost. But Sophia's made friends, and I have Eden and Avi and Max and—

Lucy.

Dad is talking again, something about his job and the fantastic international school, which is secular, by the way, but his voice sounds underwater. Something cold and heavy is sitting on my chest and I can barely breathe. No blood, no breath. I'm practically not even here.

There is no Lucy in Belgium. How was she not the first thing I thought of? She was here, in my house, on my bed, a half hour ago, and she already seems a million miles away. No. She's not gone yet. I'm not gone yet. I just have to make my parents see reason.

"What about the house?" I blurt out.

"We've got some great leads," Mom says. "I've seen pictures. One has this amazing kitchen—"

"This house," I clarify. "What about this house? We only moved in five months ago; how are you going to sell it in time?"

Mom and Dad look at each other again. I hate that. I hate that they know so much more than me.

"It's a rental." Mom looks down at the tablecloth. "We won't renew the lease."

A rental?

I pull my hand out from under Mom's.

"You *knew*." When they look at each other again, I know I'm right. "You knew this wasn't forever, you knew we were going to leave!"

"We knew it was a possibility," Mom insists. "We didn't know for sure."

"Then you should have *told me that*!"

Dad jabs a finger in my direction. "Don't yell at her. If we'd told you, you would have blown off your new school, you wouldn't even have tried.

"You're constantly complaining about St. Clare's," Dad says. "I didn't think you'd be so upset about leaving."

Mom tries to grab my hand again, but I pull away. "Your senior year in Europe," she says with fake sunshine. "It'll be so much fun for you. An adventure."

"You're already legal to drink there," Dad adds, and Mom swivels her head around to stare at him.

Fine. I tried, and they would not listen to reason.

"I'm not going," I tell them.

There's a half beat of silence, then Mom starts talking about this one house again, with its amazing kitchen, like I'd care about a kitchen. Dad overlaps her, describing the city of Brussels and how walkable it is, and the architecture, as if I'd care about architecture. Did they hear me at all? Does anything I say matter, or is it white noise they can wash over with stainless-steel appliances and Romanesque cathedrals?

"I'm not going," I repeat, louder this time.

"Of course you're going," Dad says.

I shake my head. "I'm staying here."

Mom and Dad are watching me, tense and ready, like I'm a dangerous virus under a microscope. They're waiting for something. They're waiting for me to crumble like a rockslide, wash away in a flood of tears like Sophia, erupt like a volcano. They're waiting for a disaster.

"When you get thrown in the deep end, you can drown or you can swim," Dad says, and I have never, ever wanted to actually drown someone as much as I do him right now.

"You threw me in the deep end!" I yell. "You've thrown me in the deep end *four times* and told me to swim and I *did* and I'm not leaving just because now you want to throw me in the Pacific Ocean!"

Mom wipes her cheek with the back of her hand. Dad turns his face away.

"I have a life here," I say. "I made one. I have friends. I have a—"

And I stop there, because I'm too close to crying, like Mom is, and I won't.

Dad turns to look at me again, the hard lines around his mouth and eyes saying that this is not how he wanted this to go. He wants to make me feel better, but he can't back down.

"Michael," he says. "There will be other girls."

The disaster wheel spins and lands on "volcano." I stand up

248

and shove myself back from the table, knocking over my chair and the glass next to Dad, spreading dark red wine all over the white, ironed tablecloth. I'm out of the kitchen and to the front door before anyone can stop me. I slam the door so hard I think the house might collapse, and then, staring at the still, dark street in front of me, I wish someone *would* stop me. I don't know what to do now.

Lucy will know what to do. I'll find Lucy and everything will be okay.

At first, I'm looking behind me every few steps, waiting to see Mom's slightly dented green Volvo pull up beside me, but it doesn't. Neither does Dad's shiny company car, but I didn't expect it to. They're probably happy I'm gone, thinking I'll calm down, cool off. They're happy to wait for the volcano to stop spewing molten lava and retreat into the ground, dormant.

But I'm not calming down. I'm not feeling the magma reduce to a simmer inside my stomach. Instead, it's getting bigger and hotter and ready to explode again. They didn't even listen to me. Nothing Sophia or I could have said or done would have changed anything, and that's really what's making my hands twitch and eyes prick and blur as I round the corner to St. Clare's. I don't have any say in my own life. Not even where I live.

I've never been at St. Clare's after dark before. It makes the whole thing creepier, the way the pointed bell tower juts into the night sky, the saint statues lurking in dark hallways, and the silence. It's so quiet, except for the whine of string instruments somewhere in the distance. There's a sign by the admin offices:

SPRING CHAMBER ORCHESTRA CONCERT
7 PM, CHAPEL

It's seven thirty now. I don't know how long these things last. Sophia's recitals would go forever, at least an hour. I might be here for a while, which isn't good, because I still feel like smashing things, and there are so many things to smash here. That statue of Saint Francis surrounded by birds and animals on the second floor, for instance. He looks so smug for a man who's probably covered in bird shit.

I'll wait for Lucy by the chapel. There's a bench outside and no statues to smash. I make my way over there, passing by the admin building and the dining hall and the back hallway leading to the HA room.

I stop.

Someone is going to hear me tonight. Maybe it won't be Dad, but someone is going to listen to me, for once, because I'll make them.

I'm running down the hallway and I don't have a plan, but I have molten lava and someone is going to hear me even if I have to melt the whole place to the ground like Herculaneum. My hood starts to slip off my head and I fix it. I need it; I don't know what I'm doing, but I know I need it.

I throw open the supply closet door and nearly trip over the boxes of records like Avi did— What are Avi and everyone going to say if— I don't care, I don't care—and I switch on the HA room's flickering light—it flickers like it did on Valentine's Day, when Lucy— Not now, I can't think about that now.

Scotch tape in my right pocket. Red spray paint in my left pocket. The posters, the ones I hid behind the bookshelf, in my arms. Heart pounding, head pounding, too.

I fly up the stairs again, forget to turn the light off but what could it possibly matter and I'm twisting and skidding down past my chemistry classroom and does this hallway have a security camera? I can't remember, but my hood's up and my head's down.

I slide to a stop across from the main chapel entrance, where the big bulletin board is, protected by glass, the border decked out in blue and green, same as the stupid plaid on their stupid ties. The music in the chapel gets louder and louder, reaching a crescendo as I wrap my hand up in the sleeves of my shirt and my hoodie and punch through the glass. It goes down without a fight, clinking and shattering as it falls onto the floor near my shoes. The music gets even louder, and I clear away the last bits of glass from the bulletin board and rip down what's already there, photos from the March for Life and reminders about the PSAT and a flyer for tonight's chamber orchestra concert. Once everything's a torn, multicolored mess at my feet, I start taping up the posters in their place. If I'm leaving St. Clare's, if nothing

I do or say will convince my parents to let me stay, then I don't have anything to lose. This is what St. Clare's really is, this is what everyone should see.

I shake the can of spray paint, hoping there's something left in there. Above each poster, I write out the corresponding sin—LUST and GREED and ADULTERY—but it's messy and hard to read. I've never used spray paint outside middle school art class, and the fumes burn my eyes and throat more than I expected. I stand on my toes to reach above the bulletin board itself, on the dark wood wall, and write:

HYPOCRITES—WHO ELSE WILL YOU FIRE?

I underline the word "hypocrites." Twice.

There's applause from inside the chapel. I stare at the wall, marked over all with torn paper, tape, and red. It looks like I murdered it.

It doesn't look at all like I imagined, not that I had a plan, but I planned on it not looking like that. This was a bad idea. This was such a bad idea. What did I *do*?

The applause is still going, and I can't figure out why until I hear the scraping and shuffling of feet on wood. It's over—it can't be over, it's too early—but there are people coming my way, closer to me, to the disaster I am and the disaster I created. I scoop up the gutted folders in my arms and run on weak legs back down the hallways and dump what's left of the folders back into the big boxes at the top of the stairs. I don't know if

I got them all. I don't know if it matters. My hands won't stop shaking.

I sink down next to the boxes. I could walk out. I could walk out the front door with all the other people and maybe no one would know. Maybe no one has even noticed the massacred bulletin board and I can take everything down after they leave. Maybe I can stay here, at the top of the stairs, until Mom and Dad go to Belgium and all my friends graduate. I can be the Hunchback of St. Clare's.

No. The longer I stay inside this building, the worse it is. I'll go out by the back chapel entrance; it's closer and no one will be leaving that way.

The hallway's as quiet as it was before, but now every squeak of my shoes sounds like someone coming up behind me, every saint statue I pass is Father Peter or Sister Joseph Marie out to get me, and even Saint Francis of the Pigeons doesn't look smug anymore, but judgmental and pissed. I'm almost there. I turn into the hall that will lead me outside, and from where I'm standing, I can see all the way up the other hallway past the chapel to the front entrance, where a large group of people are gathered, staring at something on the wall.

I have to go. Now. I turn toward the back door, so close, so close, when I hear the creak of a door and a voice that says, "Michael?"

I turn around, and there is Lucy, peeking out from a doorway to the chapel I didn't even know existed. She's standing there wearing a white shirt and black skirt and carrying a water bottle and grinning at me because she doesn't know yet.

"What are you doing here?" she whispers. "What about dinner with your parents?"

A strangled, not-quite-human sound comes out of my throat. Lucy doesn't notice.

"I can't believe you came! Okay, so I know the Adagio, that second piece, was a total disaster, but the Haydn quartet went way better than I expected, except for Maura coming in two bars late—"

I want to let her keep going. I want to savor this moment where she's excited and she loves me, before the moment where she finds out what I did and skins me alive. But I can't, because I still have to get out of here.

She thrusts her water bottle at me. "I'm not supposed to leave during intermission, but I really need some water. Could you fill it up for me?"

"I—I can't," I say, and my hands are shaking again.

Lucy frowns. "What do you mean? The fountain's right—"

And then she looks up the hallway, toward the fountain. Toward the mass of people gathered around the bulletin board. Lucy looks back at me, her mouth slightly open, not knowing yet, but maybe starting to guess. She glances up the hallway again. Before she can turn back around, before she can ask or guess, I'm gone.

24

MAYBE IT'S BECAUSE I got two hours of sleep last night, or maybe it's because of the thick, cold mist that blanketed the whole town this morning, but St. Clare's looks even more sinister than usual. I'm standing by the front doors, hesitating to go inside, and the fact that the St. Clare's bell tower has disappeared into the fog isn't making it look more inviting. They should shoot a horror movie here.

I was never scared of horror movies. I always knew when a monster was about to pop out of a closet, always knew the blood and guts were really cornstarch and red food coloring. "Fear is healthy," Mom told me when I broke my arm climbing the tall, spindly tree in our old backyard. "It tells you when you shouldn't be doing something." Dad thought that was silly—you could be careful and brave at the same time.

I wasn't careful last night. And I don't feel brave, either.

If Mom is right, that fear is a giant orange DANGER sign

in your mind, I should leave right now. I should walk back home, crawl into bed, and pretend I'm sick. I should get on a bus to Santa Fe and change my name. I should do anything but walk under St. Clare's arched brick doorway, because there is nothing good waiting for me inside. At best, Lucy hates me now. At worst, I'm going to get shipped to a re-education camp deep in the Vatican City catacombs, and Lucy will *still* hate me.

Just as I'm about to go with Option A, faking a sudden and severe flu, a flash of red ribbon catches my eye. Lucy, wearing a wrinkled uniform skirt and an expression that would freeze fire, is making a beeline for me.

She called me three times on my walk home last night. Then she started texting. I didn't answer her, but I kept my phone on anyway, because every beep was a sign she still wanted to talk to me.

When I got home, I went straight upstairs to my room. No one stopped me or asked me where I'd been. "Not now," I heard Mom whisper to Dad as I went up the stairs. "He'll feel better in the morning."

I didn't, though, because I didn't sleep. Instead, I sat on my bed, staring at my phone as it vibrated with every new call and text from Lucy. I wanted to pick up. I did. I wanted to explain, or try to. But I didn't want to hear what she'd say back. At 12:18, she called twice in a row, and then everything went silent.

"Give me your phone." Lucy holds out her hand but looks straight ahead, through my chest and out the other side, like there's nothing in front of her.

"Wait, let me—"

"No." She taps her fingers against her outstretched palm. "Give me your phone. Now."

I hand it to her. She bends over it, seeming happy to have something to focus on that's not me.

"What are you doing?" I ask, and lean over her to see. She has our text conversation thread up on the screen, and her finger is hovering over the Delete All button.

I make a grab for the phone. "Don't!" I yell, and she jerks back. Two freshmen standing near us look over, startled. Lucy throws a nervous look in their direction.

"Do you want me to get expelled?" she hisses, looking right at me for the first time. "Is that what you want?"

I shake my head.

"Then shut up," she says, and taps on the Delete All button.

Everything Lucy and I have said to each other vanishes into the air like dust. If texts were made of paper, I'd have scraps to gather up. Something to salvage.

I wait for her to hand me back my phone so I can see the emptiness for myself, but Lucy isn't done. She finds my texts with Avi. Then Eden, then Max. She purges it all.

I get it, later than I should. She's deleting any evidence, making sure if I go down, the rest of them still stand a chance.

I should have done that myself, last night, but I didn't think of it. And Lucy knew I wouldn't.

Lucy brings up one final text conversation, and I know what it is without looking. It's our group text, where we planned our meetings and the party where I told Lucy I couldn't imagine not knowing her. Lucy presses Delete All one more time.

I don't stop her. I don't even try.

Lucy hands my phone back, then brushes her hands off on her skirt like they're contaminated.

"Find somewhere else for lunch," she says, speaking to my chest again. "We can't do anything about seat assignments in history, but otherwise, find somewhere else to be."

She turns to leave.

"I'm moving," I call after her. Lucy snaps her head around so fast I can hear the wind through her red ribbon. I look down at my shoes. "We're going to Belgium, in August. That's why this happened, I . . ." But then I can't say anything else.

I hear her breathe out, ragged and heavy. "Then we won't have to do this for very long, will we?"

I look up then, but she and her red ribbon have disappeared into the fog and the crowd.

"Told you you should have come," Connor says to his girlfriend as they sit down at our lab table.

"I had a soccer game, what do you want?" Jess mutters, taking out her notebook.

"Like soccer is more fun than learning Mr. Cartwright is a perv."

My blood freezes in my veins. "What are you talking about?" I ask.

He frowns. "You didn't hear?" I shake my head, and after checking to see if our teacher's watching, he pulls out his phone. "The Heretics people put this up during the orchestra concert last night," he says, scrolling through picture after picture of the red, massacred wall. "You can't really read any of it, but it's teachers' files, like personal stuff about them. Like Mr. Cartwright slept with students, which is super gross."

And also super not true. "You took a lot of photos."

"Oh no, my mom took these," Connor says. "That's why they suck. I was backstage; most of it was taken down by the time I got out." He puffs up a bit. "I play cymbals."

Jess leans in to look at the photos over his shoulder. "I mean, I guess what they did is useful, this time—I'm not going to take AP Lit with Cartwright next year—but, I don't know. This seems kind of . . . angry."

"Sociopathic," Theresa says, sliding into her seat next to Jess, her arms full of our lab equipment for the day. "I'd call it sociopathic."

"That's not what sociopaths do," Jess says. "Haven't you ever seen a serial killer show?"

"My family doesn't own a TV," Theresa says. She turns to Connor. "You're not supposed to be talking about what happened last night. Ms. Kerr and Father Peter told the whole orchestra not to, but no, you've got to send all these photos around, so now everybody knows—"

Connor gestures at me. "He didn't know! That's why we were talking about it. Not everyone in the world saw you tweeting on your recorder last night."

Theresa swivels her head to stare at me. "But you *were* at the concert."

My heart drops to my stomach. "What?"

"You were there. At intermission, I heard Lucy Peña ask you to get her water."

I busy myself with the beakers, trying to keep my hands from shaking. "It must've been someone else."

Theresa narrows her eyes. "She said your name."

Our chem teacher calls for order, so I shift my focus from the beakers to the instructions he's writing on the board, feeling the weight of Theresa's eyes on my back.

"By the way, Connor," I hear her say. "It's a flute, not a recorder."

In the end, Lucy didn't have to worry about seeing me in history class. During third period, we're herded into the chapel for mandatory Mass. At first, I'm terrified this has something to do with me and what I did, but it quickly becomes clear this was preplanned. The chapel is decked out in purple, and I hear Maura Kearney complaining that the ashes always make her break out. Ashes? What are they going to burn? Heretics?

I hang back as everyone files in, not sure where to go. I've always sat with Lucy and Avi, but I can't do that now.

As I scan the chapel for an empty pew or, even better, an emergency exit door, two eyes lock on mine. Max is sitting in a back pew, twisted around to watch people file in. Eden's by his side. Lucy must have told them everything, because Max is looking at me like I'm a ghost, and Eden visibly winces. I swallow hard.

Max puts his hand up like he's about to beckon me over but then hesitates. Eden shakes her head, eyes down. He steals one more look at me, his eyebrows knit together. Eden whispers something to him, and, hand on his arm, forces him to turn around and face the altar.

I feel like I've been kicked in the gut. I wouldn't have sat with them. Doesn't Eden know that? I wouldn't have done that to them, make them guilty by association. Not even if they'd let me.

Maybe I can stand at the back. There's a tap on my shoulder.

"Would you care to have a seat?" Sister Joseph Marie asks me with faux politeness.

"Um—"

"There's room up front," she says, and steers me to the very first pew, closest to the altar. She settles in next to me. Fantastic.

Mass starts, with bells and lethargic organ music, and I'm surprised by how much I remember about when to stand and when to sit. I recognize more and more of the call-and-response between Father Peter and the rest of us, too, but I keep quiet. It would be weird to say things I didn't believe, just because I know the words. We finally get to the sermon part, where everyone gets to sit for at least five minutes straight. My eyes are heavy and my concentration's shot, and all I want to do is sleep. But with Sister Joseph Marie on one side of me and Father Peter a couple feet away, I don't think I'd get away with it.

Father Peter surveys us from the altar. "Ash Wednesday marks the day Jesus went into the wilderness to fast, pray, and plan for the days ahead," he says. "And as Christ spent forty days in the desert preparing for His ministry, we spend the forty days of Lent reflecting on our sins, seeking forgiveness, and preparing for the joyful celebration of the Resurrection at Easter.

"People talk about 'Catholic guilt,'" he continues. "The idea that Catholics, with our many rules, feel more guilt than others, even in secular situations. In our society, we want freedom from guilt. Restaurants advertise 'guilt-free' chocolate cake. We've created a society where no one wants to feel guilty—they want to feel good. So the idea of guilt, the idea of Catholic guilt, is always framed negatively. But I disagree," Father Peter says. "Guilt is a gift."

Fear is healthy. Guilt is a gift. I'm scared and guilty, and I don't feel strong or grateful.

"Guilt is painful, that's undeniable. But when we acknowledge our wrongdoings, we begin to understand, for a moment, the pain Christ suffered on the cross. He died so that we might live, so that we might repent of our sins and be forgiven. The pain of our guilt is payment for the pains of his sacrifice."

I've never been this close to the altar before, and I've never been so close to the giant, bleeding Jesus-on-the-cross hanging on the back wall. There are gashes all over his body—on his torso, legs, arms. Blood trickles down from his crown of thorns and a cut on his side that trails from rib to pelvic bone. It's awful, up close. I can't believe people worship this, put a bloody, emaciated torture victim next to their stained glass and call it beauty. Pain isn't beautiful. Suffering isn't pretty. But maybe that's the point.

"Guilt allows us to acknowledge our faults and flaws—but guilt is not enough. It is only one half of the puzzle. We must then ask forgiveness from those we've wronged and from God, and resolve to do better in the future. Only then, after confession and penance, can the slate be wiped clean."

I can see, I guess, why that would be comforting. The idea that someone already paid for your mistakes and is waiting to absolve you and shower you with love. Even if the world won't forgive you, God will. But my friends aren't God. Lucy isn't God. She won't bleed for me and then open her arms in forgiveness. I hope she doesn't have to.

Someone jostles me. The homily is over, and everyone's shuffling into line. Is it for Communion? It seems too early. The girl next to me, a tiny freshman, jostles me again.

"Move," she says, nodding her head at the line forming at the end of our pew. I stand in line, still thinking about guilt and blood and Lucy, until I'm face-to-face with Father Peter, who is holding a bowl of something chalky and dark. Ashes.

"Remember you are dust," he says, drawing an ashy cross on my forehead with his thumb. "And to dust you shall return."

I stumble away. I don't go back to my pew. I walk to the back of the church, flakes of ashes falling from my forehead into my eyes. No one stops me as I push open the heavy door, run to the bathroom, and throw up my breakfast.

I spend lunch in the bathroom. I don't throw up again, but I still feel like shit, and besides, I don't have anywhere else to go for lunch. Lucy made that clear. I sit in the farthest stall to the left, knees drawn up to my chest, listening to people come and go. A lot of them talk about the incident at the concert. And even though I didn't sign it, everyone seems to think it was the work of Heretics Anonymous, anyway. Some people think it was awesome. Some people think it was confusing and weird.

I don't know what I wanted when I stuck all those files up and wrote on the bulletin board and walls. I don't know what I thought would happen. Did I think the school would rise up like it was the French Revolution and I'd be hailed as an anonymous hero before being exiled to Brussels? Or did I want to hurt someone, anyone?

There's no revolution. But I definitely hurt someone.

When I get to theology after lunch, Lucy and Avi have taken new seats on the far side of the room. My old seat is still open, an empty island in the middle of laughing, chattering classmates. Avi stiffens and starts to get up, but Lucy pulls him down, whispers something in his ear. They turn away.

In seventh-period Spanish, my last class of the day, I feel an odd sense of relief. Maybe, a desperate part of me hopes, maybe this is over. It's two p.m., and if they haven't figured out who put up the posters and spray-painted the wall, maybe they never will. Maybe they think acknowledging what happened will only fuel the fire. Maybe they'll let this go.

The classroom phone rings. My Spanish teacher looks up from her notes, surprised. She picks it up, listens for a moment, then turns back to us.

"Michael," she says, and has to actively search the room for me, I've sunk so low in my chair. "You need to go see Father Peter in his office. They're waiting for you."

They?

As I walk down the empty hallways, my mind's in a dozen places at once. How did they figure out it was me? Did they see me on their surveillance video? Did they find fingerprints? Do private schools have the resources to take fingerprints? Have I ever even been fingerprinted? I think when I was as a kid, as part of a stranger-danger program, but maybe your fingerprints change as you grow up. Maybe that's my best defense.

Maybe I'm in way over my head.

And what did my Spanish teacher mean by "they"? Who's waiting in Father Peter's office already, about to go down for something I did? Eden and Max? Avi? As I get closer to the office, I can hear someone crying—a girl. Oh no. Not Lucy. It can't be Lucy.

I round the corner and just about cry myself, I'm so relieved. The girl sobbing on the bench outside Father Peter's office isn't Lucy. It's Jenny Okoye.

Wait. Jenny?

"Hey," I say, and she looks up at me with wet, puffy eyes. "Are you okay?"

She shakes her head, glancing at the door to the admin offices. "They—they think I did that, what happened last night at the concert. Did you hear about it, the posters and stuff?"

"Yeah," I say, after a pause. "I heard about it."

"I didn't do it," she protests. "I wasn't even *there*. But first there was that thing with the fake paper last month, and now this, and everyone thinks I did it, and I didn't do *anything*!"

She collapses into a fresh batch of tears. I take a seat on the bench next to her.

"You're nice to stay," she says, her head in her hands. "You don't have to, though."

"I—" How do I tell her?

"I know why they think it," Jenny says, riding over me. "Because of Ms. Simon. Because I was upset about Ms. Simon and I tried to get things changed." She slumps back against the bench. "But I did everything the right way, I followed all the rules. I started a petition. I tried to write an article. Nothing worked and no one listened, and now they're blaming me for this?"

"It's not fair," I say. "This isn't your fault, it's—"

"I'm not sorry it happened," she says. "I wouldn't have done it like that, that's not me. But I'm not sorry it happened. What they did to Ms. Simon isn't fair, either."

We sit quietly for a moment. "Jenny," I say, but then I don't know how to finish the sentence. I'm sorry? This is all my fault? "Is this . . . is this personal, for you? What happened to Ms. Simon?"

She frowns. "Is that the only reason I could find this unfair? Because I like girls?"

Leave it to me to say the exact wrong thing. As always. "No, I didn't—"

"I don't really talk about it," she says. "Not because I'm ashamed or anything. I'm not. I just don't think it's anyone's business."

"I'm sorry," I say, feeling horrible for having asked. "You're right, it's not my business."

She looks at me for a moment. Then nods. "Yes. It is personal to me." She steals another nervous glance at the closed door next to us and swipes at her eyes with the back of her hand. "Ugh. I cry when I'm nervous, I cry when I'm angry, and all it does is make me look guilty."

"Don't tell them anything," I say, and she crinkles her brow. "No, seriously, when you go in there, don't say anything—"

"I'll be all right," she says, straightening her skirt, straightening her back. "My grandma used to say—I mean, she said it in Igbo, but—'You fall where God pushes you down.'"

"What does that mean?"

"It means I'm exactly where God wants me to be," she says, then pauses. "And exactly *who* God meant for me to be."

The door opens, and Ms. Edison steps out. Jenny closes her eyes. When I left Spanish class, all I was thinking about was how to get myself out of this, what I could say to get out of trouble. None of that matters now.

"Miss Okoye," Ms. Edison says, "can you follow me, please?"

Jenny shudders and starts to get up, but I'm faster.

"No, I'll go first."

Jenny whips around and stares at me, wide-eyed. Ms. Edison opens her mouth, but I'm through the door before she can object, turning the doorknob to Father Peter's before she can stop me. I push open the door to see Father Peter at his desk and Theresa in a plush, plaid chair, looking back at me.

25

FATHER PETER MOTIONS for me to take a seat next to Theresa. I glance at her, and she smiles back without teeth. No one who hand-embroidered crucifixes on their knee socks should look that smug.

Father Peter folds his hands. "Do you know why I've called you in here today?"

My head feels heavy and light at the same time, like I might faint. "Yes."

Theresa cocks her head like a confused spaniel. Maybe she wasn't expecting me to say that.

"I mean, I think this is about the chamber orchestra thing last night," I say. "Everyone's talking about it, so."

"Did you attend the concert last night?" he asks, so mildly I almost forget this is an interrogation.

"No," I say, and that's true.

"Liar," Theresa says, and Father Peter closes his eyes.

"Theresa," he sighs. "Please." He turns back to me. "Miss

Ambrose tells me she did see you in the hallway, during intermission."

"With Lucy Peña," Theresa adds. "He was with Lucy Peña and they were talking, and *I* think they were discussing the vandalism—"

"That's enough," Father Peter says.

"Leave her out of this," I snap at Theresa. "Lucy didn't do anything, and I'm not going to let you use her in your— Inquisition fantasy role play!"

Theresa whirls back to Father Peter, mouth open, but he cuts her off. "Is Miss Ambrose correct? Were you there?"

I swallow. "I was there. Not at the concert, just in the hallway. But Lucy didn't do anything; you can't—"

"Did you?" Father Peter interrupts me, with that same light touch. "Did you do something, Michael?"

I knew, the moment I got up from the bench outside, that I would do this. That I'd have to. Maybe I even knew before, when Lucy deleted all our texts in the courtyard this morning. But it's one thing to think about doing something that goes against every self-preservation instinct you have. It's another thing to bring the word up from your reeling stomach, suck enough air from your lungs, and force it through your clenched teeth. It's another thing to do it.

"Yes," I say, and I bet Theresa's swelling with glee, but I'm looking at my feet, not her. I say it again, so that I can't go back. "Yes."

"Were you responsible for putting up those posters? Damaging the wall?" I nod to both questions. "Did you have help?" he asks, and I snap my head up.

"No." I'm shaking my head so hard I'm surprised it's still attached. "No one helped me, it was all my idea."

"Please," Theresa says. "I saw you talking with her, you two were obviously plotting—"

Father Peter waves her off. "Were you responsible for anything else over the past few months?" I stare back at him. "The dress code, perhaps? Our Life Choices assembly? The unofficial school newspaper?"

"Yes," I say again. How many times will I have to say it before it gets easier?

"Really. All on your own?"

My breath catches.

"This group has been a disruption at St. Clare's," Father Peter says, "and I need you to tell me if there's anyone else involved."

I don't say anything.

"Because I have to say, I'm surprised these are the issues you'd choose. I thought, maybe a student with a real history of dress code violations . . ."

Eden. Max.

"Or someone who really knew Ms. Simon . . ."

Lucy. Avi. Jenny, still sitting on that bench outside.

"It was me," I say. "Heretics Anonymous is only me."

Theresa makes a noise of disbelief, but Father Peter keeps

his eyes on mine. "If you had help, you know," he says, "this would be a lesser offense. You're new to the school; it's a hard transition. If someone influenced you, if they pressured you—"

He's trying to open a side door, an emergency exit. He's giving me an out, steering me out of the burning wreckage I created and onto a fire ladder. And I want to take it. I want out. But I know who I'd be leaving behind.

I shake my head. "It was me. It wasn't Lucy, and it wasn't Jenny—I don't even *know* Jenny. She's sitting outside because she's a good person who cares about things, and you think that makes her suspicious, or guilty, or—she didn't do this. This is nobody's fault but mine."

Somewhere a million miles away, Theresa is squeaking her shoes on the floor. Somewhere a million miles away, Ms. Edison is telling Jenny Okoye to be patient, they'll get to her shortly. In my rapidly contracting world, the only inhabitants are me, Father Peter, and my crushing guilt.

Father Peter takes a breath in, but I get there first.

"No matter what happens next, that's what's true." I lock my eyes on his. "This is nobody's fault but mine."

Father Peter is still, even as Theresa shifts and fiddles with her braid. I wonder what he's thinking. Does he know I'm lying? Does he care? I can't read his mind, but I hope he can read mine: *I won't give them up.*

He presses the intercom button on his office phone. "Gloria," he says when Ms. Edison answers, "please write a hall pass for Miss Okoye and release her back to class."

Theresa's jaw drops. "You don't believe him, do you?"

"I appreciate all the help you've given me and the rest of the staff," he says to her, but she's already halfway out of her chair.

"It's not just him, it can't be!" she says. "He's covering for her, he's covering for Lucy—I have half a dozen serious suspects." She rummages through her bag, sitting by the chair. "If you look at the file I've put together—"

"Gloria," Father Peter says, his thumb on the intercom. "Please write Miss Ambrose a pass, as well."

Theresa's still thumbing through an overstuffed manila folder when Ms. Edison comes to escort her out. "But the name is Heretics Anonymous," she wails. *"It's plural!"*

After they leave, Father Peter and I sit in silence. I'm not sure whether to laugh or cry.

"Well," he says, and picks up his phone, "I think we'd better call your parents."

When they arrive a half hour later, Father Peter seats them on either side of me. Mom is trying not to look as anxious as she is. Dad isn't bothering to hide how pissed he is.

Father Peter gives them a rapid, CliffsNotes version of Heretics Anonymous, ending with my bulletin board massacre. When he's done, Mom and Dad look at each other, and I wait for them to unleash on me. But instead, Dad turns back to Father Peter.

"I don't buy it," he says. Father Peter raises his eyebrows. Mine rise, too.

"He couldn't possibly have done all of this by himself," Mom adds.

"Mr. and Mrs. Ausman," Father Peter says, "Michael confessed."

"And who is he protecting?" Dad counters. "Let's ask ourselves that. His girlfriend, for one—"

"Lucy had nothing to do with this," I cut in. "Just because she's my—" I choke on the word. "Just because she's my friend doesn't mean she did anything wrong."

"This just isn't Michael, it's not him," Mom says, and that sentence nearly slices my heart out of my chest. Because this is exactly who I am.

Father Peter pulls out a sleek black laptop. "We also have him on security camera footage."

He turns the laptop around to show us. It's bad quality, but there I am from a bird's-eye view, running down one hallway with papers in one arm, keeping my hood on my head with the other.

"That could be anybody," Dad says. And it could. My hood stayed up the whole time.

"I don't think Michael owns a jacket like that," Mom says, even though she washed it two days ago.

Father Peter brings up a new window. It's another video, of the hallway by the HA room, but from eye level, not high above like the security camera. Father Peter hits Play, and there I am again, throwing open the storage closet door and reappearing a minute later, arms full of folders and my face, what is unmistakably my face, turned directly toward the camera.

Everything's quiet. They are all watching me, but as I stare back at myself on the video, I'm almost relieved. I spent all day worrying and wondering how I was going to get myself out of this. And now I know. I'm not.

"Jesus H. *Christ*, Michael," Dad says, breaking the silence.

"Joe!" Mom says, her eyes darting to Father Peter's white collar.

"What the hell were you thinking?" Dad demands.

I shake my head, still staring at Past Me on the screen, envying that he doesn't know how badly he's fucked up. "I don't know."

Dad clears his throat. "Odd angle for a security camera," he says to Father Peter.

Father Peter looks embarrassed. "One of our staff members set it up in their classroom a couple of days ago; they discovered the footage during lunch."

"It's a teacher's?" Mom asks, sounding worried. "Why, have there been break-ins? Thefts?"

"No," Father Peter assures her. "It's—she was concerned about the water quality of the drinking fountains."

Ah. Ms. Poplawski. Mom only looks more worried at the possibility of substandard drinking water.

Mom touches my hand. "I don't understand why you'd do this."

I take a second. I don't know why I made it happen this way, but I know why I did it. "There's—there's really shitty stuff that goes on here, like sex ed that makes girls feel like unsticky tape and teachers who lose their jobs because they're happy."

I take a breath. Everyone's watching me, and Dad's fingers are on the back of my chair, curling and uncurling.

"Messed-up stuff happens and we don't get a say and no one cares how we feel. And they should, and that's why we did what we did." I turn so I'm looking at Dad and no one else. "That's why *I* did what I did."

Dad stares back at me, tightly expressionless. His hand drops from my chair.

"What you've done is serious," Father Peter says to me. "It's criminal."

"Hold on." Dad leans forward in his chair. "What laws did he break?"

"Those are confidential records. They have Social Security numbers on them."

Dad turns to me. "Did you use any of that information to impersonate someone? Did you steal anyone's identity?"

"Seriously?" He glares at me. I shake my head.

"Did you ever take the folders off school grounds?" he asks. I shake my head again.

"He shouldn't have looked at the records at all," Father Peter points out.

"Of course he shouldn't have. But I do wonder why such important, confidential information was in an unlocked storage closet."

"I think you're missing my point, Mr. Ausman."

"I think I'm missing the mention of a crime."

My eyes dart back and forth between them, like it's a tennis match. Dad might want to literally wring my neck right now, but he's standing up for me. Fighting for me. He won't throw me to the mercy of the criminal justice system.

"He's disrupted multiple school events," Father Peter says. "He's shown blatant disrespect for St. Clare's and encouraged his classmates to do the same."

Dad nods. "That *is* serious. And believe me," he says, staring down at me until I shrink in my chair, "I intend to deal with it seriously."

Then again, maybe I'm safer with the police.

"Look," Dad continues. "What Michael did was very disruptive, and very, *very* stupid. But he's not a criminal. He's a kid."

Mom jumps in there, holding out her hands. "The semester's nearly over," she says to Father Peter. "If Michael could finish out the year—"

"We would consider it a huge favor," Dad overlaps her. "And my friend Craig Collins, he's always liked Michael, I'm sure he would *also*—"

Father Peter waves them off. "I'd like to hear from Michael."

He turns to me. "Do you understand why what you did was wrong?"

"Yes." *It hurt Lucy.*

"And do you regret doing it?"

"Yes." *I regret hurting Lucy.*

"Do you want to stay here?" he asks. "Do you want to be at St. Clare's?"

If he had asked me that five months ago, I know what I would have said. I would have jumped at the chance to get away from theology, morning prayer, and a plaid tie noose. I don't know when it changed, whether it was my first HA meeting, or when our video popped up during the assembly, or whether it was an unmemorable lunch with Lucy and Avi or walking the track with Max or listening to Eden talk about Irish gods, but something did change. And even if none of them ever forgive me, I want to be with them. I want to stay and try to make things right. I want to be here.

"*Yes,*" I say, and a flood of tears rushes past all my barriers and blockades. "I'm—I'm so, so sorry."

"Good," Father Peter says, as if the sorry was meant for him. "I'm glad to hear it." Mom puts her hand on my back and rubs little circles.

"You'll serve four days of out-of-school suspension," he continues, and I try to get myself under control. "And you'll report to me every day after school until I decide otherwise. As for the damage to the bulletin board and the wall, that will need to be paid for."

Mom nudges Dad, and he digs in his back pocket, where he keeps his wallet. Father Peter holds up a hand to stop him.

"Thank you, but I don't think that's constructive," he says, and focuses back on me. "We'll be using funds that would otherwise go to end-of-year celebrations, and your classmates will know that."

He smiles, a little grimly, and stands. "I doubt you'll be very popular. But I'll see you on Wednesday."

26

AS SOON AS we trudge through the front door after a very silent car ride, Dad jabs his finger at me, then at the couch. "Sit," he orders, like I'm a dog. He hates dogs.

I sit on the couch and try to assess the situation. The worst has already happened, I think. I'm suspended from school and none of my friends ever want to speak to me again, so what else could my parents possibly do?

Mom sits next to me on the couch, her mouth set. "Obviously," she says, "you're grounded."

No shit, I think, but nod in response. When I look at Mom, her eyes look softer, and maybe a little surprised. Did she think I'd fight her on that?

"And obviously, we should discuss what's happened," Mom says.

"Father Peter already told you everything." I'm suddenly bone-tired, every muscle aching. I wish they'd get this lecture over with. I want to go upstairs. I want to go to sleep.

"So now you'll tell us," Dad snaps.

"We want to hear it from you," Mom says.

So I tell them. I tell them everything, from my first horrible morning at St. Clare's, to meeting Lucy and Avi and Eden and Max, to my first Mass and my first HA meeting, all the way through to smashing through the bulletin board's glass. I leave out a couple of things, like the coed slumber party and the alcohol I stole, but I tell them mostly everything.

Mom grabs my hand. "You shouldn't have done any of it," she says. "But I understand why you did."

"Marianne!" Dad sounds appalled. "There's no excuse for this. He got himself suspended, he *lied* to us, all because he met a pretty girl and didn't like following his school's rules."

"I didn't lie!" I protest, because I didn't. Much.

"You should have told us the second that girl asked you to join a—a cult, basically!"

"Don't be dramatic," Mom says.

I decide to ignore Dad calling Lucy *that girl*, when he obviously knows her name. "It wasn't about rules," I say. "Not all of it. They taught us things that aren't true, they made people feel bad for being different, they were hypocrites. Just because they have rules doesn't mean they're right."

"That's not the point."

"Are you saying all rules are good rules?"

"Of course not." He runs his hand down his face. "But if

you ignore whatever rules don't suit you, Michael, you're going to end up right where you are now, again and again."

"The living room?"

Mom digs her fingernails into my palm. Dad clenches his jaw.

"There will always be people you have to listen to," Dad says. "There will always be rules you think are wrong or unfair, and you know what? Too bad. You'll have to learn to make better choices."

"Oh, because you've made great choices," I grind out, feeling the molten lava again, knowing it's going to destroy everything in its path. "Dragging your family across the country, across like fifteen countries, wherever you want to go! Excellent choice." I wrench my hand from Mom's grip, because she's digging her fingernails in harder. "And then not even staying there with them. Getting on a plane and expecting them to deal with new houses and new schools and new everything—just because you want what you want!"

Dad pushes himself up from his chair. "You think that's what I want? I get on that plane, I sleep in a hotel bed instead of *my* bed, I eat dinner alone or with clients instead of my family, because those are the rules of my job. That is what I have been asked to do, by my boss, and by his boss, so I do it."

"You do all these things that don't make you happy," I say, "just because someone else told you to?"

"It's my job," he repeats.

"Well," I say, and look him square in the eyes. "I think that's pathetic."

His face goes slack, then hard and brittle. He steps toward me and I scramble to my feet, then Mom is between us lightning fast. She reaches out her hand toward Dad like a stop sign. He whips around and out of the living room, stomping up the stairs. I sink down on the couch, my heart fluttering in my chest, but Mom stays standing up.

"God, the two of you," she sighs, her voice shaky. "Honestly."

"I hate it when you say that. There's no *two of us*."

She sits down next to me. "Extremes, that's all I mean. All rules are good. No rules are good." Mom shakes her head. "Has it ever occurred to either of you there's a middle ground? On anything?"

She looks out the window at the rain that's started to come down hard and heavy.

"You should follow the rules when you can," she says. "Take a stand when you need to—" I open my mouth, because I *did* need to take a stand, and Mom holds up a finger. "But broken glass isn't the only way to change things, honey."

There's a thump upstairs. At first I think maybe Dad's dropped something, but then there's another. And another. It sounds like it's coming all the way from the top floor of the house. From my room.

"Stay here," Mom says, but I'm already off the couch. I run

up the stairs, past Sophia's room, then up the shorter, twisty stairs that lead to an attic that's not an attic. My door is wedged open by a big cardboard box, the kind that stores the printer paper in Dad's home office. It's not mine, so I can't figure out what it's doing in my doorway, until I see what's inside. What's inside *is* mine—my computer and its power cord, both gaming consoles, and half of my video games.

I step over the box and into my room to see Dad at my bookcase, shoveling the other half of my books in another box. What the hell? It's way too early to be packing for Belgium.

"What are you doing?" I say, panic rising. "Why's everything in boxes, put it back."

"No." He doesn't look at me, doesn't turn around.

"No?" He can't actually mean that, he can't actually be—

"Since you don't seem to appreciate all the things my job gives to this family, gives to you"—he plunks the old action figures from my desk into the box one by one—"I will hold on to those things, for now."

It's everything I own, practically, except for clothes and shoes. He's going to take away everything I own?

"You can't do that!" I shout, and I'm not going to cry again, not for the second time today. But, everything? "It's my stuff!"

"That I bought, using money I earned from being *pathetic*, apparently."

He ignores me, unplugging my phone charger. He sets the box down at his feet and strides over to me, hand outstretched.

"What?" I say, even though I know.

"Your phone." Two people have demanded my phone today, and I ache, suddenly, thinking of Lucy. He can't have this, it's my lifeline to the rest of the world. If one of my friends—if Lucy—decides they're willing to forgive me, this is the only way they can tell me.

"Michael." I shake my head, backing up so my back pocket, and by extension my phone, is protected. "You can hand it over now, or I can call the phone company and have them cancel service, and you won't ever get it back. Your choice."

That's not a choice. That's an ultimatum. I give him the phone, feeling every bit of my pride slip away as it leaves my hand.

"There are consequences to the things we do." He hoists one of the boxes on his hip and grips the doorknob, preparing to shut the door in my face. "And there are consequences to the things we say."

27

LUCY'S SITTING ON her porch when I arrive, but she's changed out of her uniform. She's got gardening gloves on, cleaning up what looks like a bunch of exploded houseplants. There's dirt everywhere.

"Go away," she says as I approach, not even bothering to look up.

I expected that. I planned this whole conversation out in my head last night. There wasn't much else I *could* do, alone in a stripped-down room, kept up late by the monster storm that raged all through the night, but think about what I was going to say to Lucy when I found a way to see her. Sneaking out was unexpectedly easy. I watched Dad's car peel out of the driveway this morning, then bided my time all day until I heard Mom grab her keys and leave to pick up Sophia from school. I hedged a bet that Lucy would go right home after school. She wasn't likely to be going to an HA meeting now.

I hold up my hands in a preemptive surrender. "I just came here to—"

"I don't want to talk," she says, shoving a broken flowerpot into a large plastic trash bag. "Did you get expelled?"

"No. I go back on Wednesday."

"Congratulations," she says. "Please go home now."

I thought she'd at least hear me out, at least let me apologize. That's how the conversation went in my head. New tactic. Change topics.

"What happened?" I ask, looking at the broken pottery, dirt, and wet flowers strewn across the porch.

"I had some hanging planters. The wind knocked them down last night." She turns away, like we're done.

"You have every right to be mad at me," I say.

"Yeah, I do, and I am."

"And I'm sorry. I'm so, so sorry. But you knew this could happen, we talked about it."

"No." She throws down the trash bag. "I knew we could get caught. I was prepared for that. But the way it happened—what were you *thinking*?"

"I wasn't," I say. "I was just so angry, about the move and my dad, and everything, so—"

"Right. Thanks for telling me, by the way."

Even trying to apologize for one thing brings up another shitty choice I made. I am a layer cake of failure.

"Why do you think I was at school?" I ask. "I was coming to

tell you, but I got distracted and did something stupid and I'm sorry, Lucy—I'm telling you I'm sorry!"

She shrugs. Picks up another clump of dirt. "So you're sorry. Okay. Good-bye now."

Lucy must know I won't give up that easily. She knows me. I sit down next to her, and she doesn't tell me to leave this time, so I don't. I start scooping up handfuls of dirt and placing them in the trash bag. I'm about to put a particularly heavy handful of dirt in when Lucy stops me.

"Don't!" she says, and swiftly plucks a soggy flower from the dirt in my hands. She blows the dirt off it, and then I notice the paper towel on her left side, covered in damp, half-broken purple flowers.

"They're hellebore blossoms," she says, fingering the flower with gloved hands. "My mom's favorite. I planted them last spring."

There's another hint of purple in my handful of dirt, and I carefully extricate the flower. Lucy must know these flowers are completely beyond repair, but I hand it over to her anyway, and she cleans it off.

"I did get in trouble, you know," I say. She looks doubtful. "My dad took my phone."

"You poor baby," she deadpans. "Someone should alert The Hague."

"I don't know what that is."

"Then you clearly haven't done this week's history home-work."

Amazing. Even when she's ready to excommunicate me from her life, Lucy still finds a way to guilt me about school.

"He wanted to blame it on you." I don't know why I'm telling her this. I shouldn't. "When we were in Father Peter's office, even though I already said it was me, my dad wouldn't listen. He tried to pin it on you."

This doesn't faze her at all. "What am I supposed to say? Thanks for not throwing me under the bus?"

I shake my head. "Just my shitty luck this happens the one day my dad's actually on this continent. So here he comes, barging in and almost screwing everything up, trying to get you in trouble, because—I don't know, he's embarrassed of me, or—"

Lucy whirls around suddenly and flings a handful of slimy wet dirt at my chest.

"What the hell, Lucy?" I say, trying to wipe it off my hoodie.

"You are so fucking *clueless* sometimes," Lucy explodes, hurling another clump of dirt at me. I've never, ever heard her swear. "He was trying to protect you, Michael. He was trying to keep you from ruining your stupid life, because he *loves* you. He loves you. He stuck by your side, probably lied for you, because you're his kid and that means something to him. Why don't you get it? Why don't you get how *lucky* you are?"

There's dirt in my mouth, and I spit it out. Her fists are clenched, and so are mine.

"You don't have a monopoly on suffering, okay?" I say, my voice rising. "Other people get to be mad about their lives. Your broken leg doesn't make my sprained ankle hurt any less."

289

"Sprained ankle," she says. "Your life is barely a toothache. And you don't even know."

I came over to apologize. I tried to help her clean up the mess, I tried to make her feel better, and she yelled at me and called me ungrateful, just like Dad. I am so sick of being yelled at, so sick of people picking at my flaws. I can do that, too.

"You know what I think?" I tell her. "I think there's a part of you that *needs* to be the one suffering the most."

"What?" she says, suddenly quieter.

"See, because I have been my doing my theology homework, and there's this section about 'redemptive suffering' and basically how pain on earth brings you closer to God."

"I know what redemptive suffering is."

"Which, aside from being massively fucked up and weird, is also why all those saints you like so much were okay with being tortured to death. They thought it made them stronger and holier, and I think *you* feel like your suffering makes you stronger and holier too, but it doesn't."

Lucy's big brown eyes have narrowed into slits, but she's not telling me to stop, not with words and not with a dirt snowball to the face, so I keep going.

"You let yourself get hurt. You let it happen and you think it'll bring you closer to being, I don't even know. Saintly? Perfect? You get hurt and you keep getting hurt because you put your trust in people who don't deserve it."

"Yeah, like who?" Lucy bursts out. "Like who, Michael?"

"Like *God*," I say, and press on even though she throws her hands up in the air. "No, I'm serious, because if God does exist, if He listens to your prayers and still sticks you in this shitty situation, in a church that doesn't even want you, then He doesn't deserve your faith. You put all this faith in a God who clearly doesn't listen to you, and a mom who took off without you and who *isn't coming back*, Lucy, she isn't coming back, and she doesn't deserve your faith, either!"

The way Lucy looks at me then, I think she might stab me with one of the broken planter shards, or maybe suffocate me with the trash bag full of dirt. But she doesn't. Without a word, she gets up, goes inside her house, and locks the front door with a sharp, definitive click. I sit on her porch, surrounded by broken pottery and twisted purple flowers.

Lucy also trusted me, and I didn't deserve that trust either.

Some people drink when they get nervous. Some people pace. My mom cleans. When Great-Aunt Carol got in a car accident, Mom washed every single dish, bowl, and piece of cutlery we owned by hand, did eight loads of laundry in three days, and reorganized the garage. What happened yesterday isn't nearly as bad as a car accident, but from the smell of lemon Pledge wafting through the open window by the back door, it's bad enough.

I push open the door and the kitchen floor is sparkling, but there's no sign of Mom. Her usual routine is living room, then kitchen, then laundry, so I hedge my bets on her being in the basement. If I can make it up the stairs, she'll never know I was gone.

I take the stairs two at a time, replaying the scene with Lucy in my mind. Why did I say that? I don't know that her mom isn't coming back, and even if I did, saying it wouldn't do anything but hurt her. It was useless, and selfish, and now Lucy will never forgive me. She'll never split sweet potato fries with me again, or let me copy her theology homework, or kiss me, or run her hands through my hair, or—

"And where exactly have *you* been?"

But it's not Mom standing at the top of the stairs, looking down at me. It's Dad.

This doesn't make any sense. I saw his car leave this morning; he should be on a plane right now, not at home, wearing jeans and a sweater and glaring at me.

"Well?" he says, and I'm still too surprised to say anything back. "Where were you?"

"I went for a walk."

Dad exhales heavily. "You went for a walk. Without telling anyone. While you were grounded."

None of those sentences are questions, but Dad stares at me like he's expecting an answer.

"Yes?" I say.

"Did you think your mother wouldn't know?" he asks. "Did you think she wouldn't notice you were gone?"

"Uh—" I try to think of something else to say besides the truth, which is that it wouldn't have mattered if Mom caught me. She'd probably have attempted some half-hearted talking-to, but discipline isn't her strong suit. Her lectures end with hugs. And often snacks.

"Come on." Dad gestures for me to continue up the stairs. "Let's have a talk."

We go into my room, and it doesn't look the way I left it. The bed's still unmade, but the bookshelves aren't bare anymore. I don't see my gaming consoles or my computer, but otherwise, the room looks like it did yesterday morning, messy and mine. I look at Dad, not sure whether to thank him—was it even his idea? Then I notice my astronaut figurine, the one Dad used to hide around the house, positioned so it looks like he's reading through a book on my desk. I pick it up.

"I can't believe you still have that," Dad says.

I set the astronaut back down. "Of course I still have it."

Dad motions for me to sit on the bed. He takes my desk chair.

"Where did you go?" he says.

Where did I go? Where did *he* go, besides Brussels and London and a thousand other places, probably, where did he go, besides everywhere but his own home?

Oh. On my walk.

"I went to talk to Lucy." I might be imagining it, but his face softens.

"How did that go?"

"Badly," I admit, twisting my comforter in my hands.

"I bet."

"She hates me," I say, and my eyes are stinging. "I just want her not to hate me."

Dad opens his mouth, then closes it. "When you hurt people," he says, "even if you didn't mean to, you don't get to choose where they go from there. When you hurt someone, it stops being about you, or what you want."

I don't know if this is a pep talk, but if it is, it's a terrible one. Just another one of Dad's lovely platitudes that somehow never seem to apply to—

"I hurt you," he says. My head snaps up. "I know I did."

Dad is not an apologizer. Mom said once it was because he always had to be so sure, so confident at work, that he couldn't turn it off at home. This is the closest I've heard him come since he accidentally closed the car door on Sophia's finger.

"Is that why—" I gesture around at my wonderfully cluttered room. He nods.

"I was angry," he admits. "What you said, it really dug at me, and on top of everything else yesterday, I overreacted. But it's more than that. Moving here hurt you. You rallied, and made friends—questionable friends—but it still hurt you. And I hurt you by not acknowledging it. By not making more of an effort to be home. By not listening to you. And I'm sorry."

Holy shit. A real, full-blown apology.

"Me too," I say, because I am, and even if I wasn't, it would be the right thing to say.

"Your mom doesn't work, and I do, so choices get made based on that," Dad says. "But it doesn't mean I'm more important than her, or you, or Sophia. That's not how I feel." He pauses. "Is that how you feel?"

"Sometimes. Like with the sandwiches."

Dad's forehead creases, like he has no idea what I'm talking about. "What sandwiches?"

How does he not remember this? "Whenever we'd go to the beach or on a car trip, Mom would make everyone PB and J. Except you. You always got a way better, way fancier sandwich. Like the whole thing was about you."

Dad is still for a moment. Then he says, "Do you know why I won't eat peanut butter sandwiches?"

I shrug. "Because you don't like them."

"Yes," Dad says. "But do you know *why* I don't like them?"

I always assumed it was one of Dad's things, like everyone has. Sophia can't have any of her food touch on her plate. I like olive oil but hate olives. Mom gets visibly nauseous whenever we pass a fried chicken place. I shake my head.

Dad sighs, and I notice he's started picking at the threads in the chair cushion, which isn't like him at all. He hates people picking at stuff, like water bottle labels. It's another one of his things.

"Do you remember meeting your grandfather, before he died?" he asks.

I don't see what this has to do with peanut butter. "Yeah, all his furniture was covered in plastic and he asked me what my name was, over and over. His nurse was nice, though. She gave me candy."

Dad keeps picking at the cushion. He opens his mouth to say something, then stops. Like the words are there, but he can't figure out whether I should hear them.

"My dad," he begins, and I realize I've never heard him say those words: my dad. "My dad had a hard time holding down a job when I was a kid." He shakes his head. "He liked hanging out with his buddies more, or watching TV, or sitting around the house. There was never a lot of money going around, and he didn't want government help, so my mom stretched everything the best she could, for me and my brothers."

A mom who died before I was born. Brothers I've never even met. Dad clears his throat.

"You know one of the easiest, cheapest meals you can make? A peanut butter sandwich. It sticks to your ribs. And food pantries always have a loaf of Wonder Bread and some Skippy. So I ate peanut butter sandwiches practically every day of my life, for at least one meal, until I left home." His mouth twists. "I can't stand to eat it now. It's too hard to get the taste out of my mouth."

He looks at me, and I don't know what to say. He never talks about his family, about his childhood, and now I know why. Because it was painful, and sad, and hard in ways I can't imagine. Our two-door fridge, constantly stocked with whatever I could want, never seemed important until now.

"Dad. I'm sorry. I didn't—"

"That's not what I wanted for you and Sophia," Dad says. "And I thought, if I could do what my dad didn't, have a stable job and raise you in a clean house in a good neighborhood with good schools, you wouldn't need anything else. I thought if you were fed, and clothed, and safe, that would be enough." Dad shuts his eyes. "Obviously, it's not."

"We need you," I say, not trying to rub it in, only show I understand. "Mom needs another adult around. Sophia wants to Skype with you every night, and she started sleeping with one of your sweaters." I pause, and I can feel Dad waiting. "And me. I need you here, too."

I drop my eyes to the comforter, suddenly embarrassed for some reason.

"I know," Dad says. "I need to be here. And you need to stay here." I look up. Did he say *stay here*? "We all do," he continues. "For now. It's not fair to move you or Sophia so soon. When she's out of elementary school and you're at college, we'll reconsider."

My heart is pounding and maybe I'm dreaming, because— *stay here*? "But your job, and Belgium, and—"

He holds a hand up to stop me. "I sat down with Craig this

morning and we've reworked my position slightly. I'm going to be taking on more responsibilities at our local branch, traveling less, and taking a small pay cut." He smiles. "So *you* are going to do everything in your power not to get kicked out of your very expensive private school. No more stealing from nuns, no more drive-by vandalism, no more worrying the hell out of your mom. Do we have a deal?"

If he can negotiate with his boss, maybe I can, too. "Can I have my phone back?"

He laughs. "Nice try. Not yet."

And I know this isn't going to end with us hugging it out, or declaring how much we love each other, because that's not us and might never be. But something has changed, small and quiet. I know things about him I didn't before, things he doesn't share with people, parts of him that hurt. He wants me to understand him. He wants to understand me. And even if he won't give me my phone back, he wants us to start to become equals. He's asking me to agree.

I nod. "Deal."

28

OVERALL, BEING SUSPENDED is not the worst thing that's happened to me. I don't have access to my phone, and the TV is also off-limits, but I have books and homework and SAT prep to do, anyway. Mom keeps treating me like some kind of wronged political prisoner, bringing me sandwiches and apple slices with peanut butter. But by Monday, I'm bored of my books and can't look another Spanish conjugation worksheet in the face.

On Wednesday, I'll be back at school, where my one, singular goal will be to convince Lucy I'm not a horrible person. I don't know how to fix this. If I could just understand what was going on in her head—

I yank open the bottom drawer of my desk. How could I have forgotten? I do have a window into Lucy's head and heart, bound and annotated and titled *The New Revised Standard Version, Catholic Edition*. I have her Bible. I curl up on my bed with a bowl of chips and start to read.

Genesis is straightforward enough, and I know the story of Moses and the ten plagues of Egypt, but the further along I go, the weirder things get. David kills Goliath and also his mistress's husband, then David's son rapes his own sister, and it only goes morally downhill from there. By the time I reach Judges, I've got to talk to someone about all this.

"So there's this guy, and he's traveling around ancient Judea with his concubine," I explain to Mom as she does dishes and Sophia does Punnett squares for fun at the kitchen table. "And he decides to spend the night at this other man's house. So then, for *no reason*, this perverted mob of townspeople show up and are like, 'We want to have sex with your guest, hand him over.' So then the concubine—"

"Michael, this is a wildly inappropriate story," Mom says, nodding her head at Sophia.

"It's in the Bible!" I say.

"I know what a concubine is," Sophia protests.

"You do?" Mom says, probably regretting buying Sophia a subscription to a research database for Christmas.

"Yes," Sophia says. "It's a purple flower."

Mom looks relieved. "That's a columbine."

Here's how the story ends: The man who owns the house won't give up his guest, but he *will* give up his daughter or the traveler's concubine. So they shove the concubine out, the sex mob rapes and murders her, and then the traveler takes her body, cuts it up, and sends a piece to each of the tribes of Israel.

Lucy's annotations say it's a pro-hospitality message. I say it's sick.

I don't understand how the St. Clare's library can ban so many books for being "inappropriate" when they have a whole row of Bibles. Harry Potter might be a wizard, but I'm sure he never hacked a woman to pieces.

I decide to skip ahead to the New Testament. In the Gospel of Luke, I find the Magnificat, Mary's song of joy and revolution, and I hear Lucy's voice as I read it, remembering the way she whispered it on the Day of the Little Candles. As I move through the other Gospels, I find myself liking Jesus, in spite of myself. He's a good guy, healing the sick, raging against hypocrites, and giving solid life lessons. Be kind, be generous, be forgiving. I like this one, too:

Be careful not to practice your righteousness in front of people in order to be noticed by them. (Matthew 6:1)

Lucy doesn't have a note for that, but I think it means you should do what's right because it's right, not because you want people to see and praise you for it.

In that same Gospel, Peter, Jesus's disciple, asks Jesus how many times he must forgive someone who's wronged him. Seven? Peter suggests. No, Jesus says, better make it seventy-seven. All men must forgive others, he tells his followers, to be forgiven by God.

When I get back to school, I hope Lucy keeps that chapter and verse in mind.

✦ ✦ ✦

At home over the last few days, I wondered what going back to school would be like. Would I be greeted with applause and flower garlands as I walked through the hallways? Probably not, given the money redirected toward a new bulletin board. Would the St. Clare's Crusaders bludgeon me with Bibles? Maybe, but I could take them.

In the end, all I get are stares. Stares in the hallway from people I don't know, stares from teachers, and stares from Connor and Jess across our chemistry lab table. The only one who isn't staring is Theresa.

"Can you pass me the iodine?" she asks Connor, even though it's sitting right in front of me. I hand it to her. She looks straight ahead. "Connor," she repeats. "Can *you* pass me the iodine?"

I don't know if Theresa thinks she's hurting my feelings or if she can't bear to touch my sinful, vandalizing hands. I put the iodine down and let Connor pass it to her.

By lunch, I'm exhausted by the weight of people's eyes on me, and all I want to do is sit with Lucy and Avi and tell them everything that's happened since last Wednesday, like it's normal again. But Lucy told me to get lost, and I doubt our last conversation sweetened her on my lunchtime presence.

I catch Max at his locker, stuffing his forbidden cloak under some textbooks. He jumps when I say his name, then relaxes.

"I thought you were Father Peter," he says, and I try not to be offended. His eyes dart to his cloak. "You won't tell, right?"

"Never."

He smiles, but only for a split second. "I'm not really supposed to be talking to . . ." He trails off, making a quick sweep of the hallway with his eyes. I don't think he's watching out for Father Peter.

"I know," I say. "I'm so sorry, Max."

He shrugs. "It's okay. I mean, it sucks you got in trouble and it sucks *more* that we can't ever go down to the room again. But I figure you didn't mean for that to happen."

A flood of relief washes over me, because if Max understands, Max whose idea of a hot date is a dead Polish physicist, then Eden and Avi and Lucy will come around. If Max understands, maybe I'm not lost.

"It's lunch," I say hesitantly. "Do you want to—?"

Max's face drops. He busies himself with concealing his cloak in his locker. "I want to be a good friend," he declares. "It's important to be good to your friends." He pauses, to make sure I get it. "But I have to be a good friend to Lucy, too. And she was here first."

He closes his locker, and I swallow down the hard lump in my throat. *Forgive before you can be forgiven.*

"It's okay," I say. "I understand."

I find a table by myself in the corner of the dining hall. This is the first time I've ever sat alone at lunch, not counting the time in second grade I tormented Emma Kaprow with a puppet made out of bologna and the lunch aide made me sit by myself.

I should have sat alone my first day at St. Clare's. I should have been alone, but I didn't make it that far. Lucy made sure I didn't. I scan the cafeteria for her red ribbon, and find her standing by a trash can, busing her tray, her back to me. Suddenly, Theresa's beside her, and I can't hear what she's saying, but she looks pissed. Is this about Heretics Anonymous? Theresa jabs an accusatory finger in Lucy's shoulder, and then I'm up before I can think better of it. I march across the dining hall and wedge myself between Theresa and Lucy, facing Theresa so Lucy doesn't have to acknowledge me.

"What's your problem?" I say to Theresa, and she glares back at me.

"Is that a serious question?" she snaps. "You and your girlfriend are practically terrorists."

People need to be stingier with the word "terrorist." And "girlfriend."

"What happened was my fault," I say, and Theresa folds her arms across her chest. "If you're going to lose your shit on someone, it should be me, not her."

"You?" Theresa sweeps her braid back, looking at me like I'm a bug she'd rather crush than talk to. "I don't care about you."

"You cared enough to turn me in," I point out.

"You were guilty," she says. "It was the right thing to do." She takes a step closer. "But you don't care about my faith. You don't *know* anything about my faith, or this school—you did all this stuff for *fun*. Not because you cared, not because it mattered to you. So you aren't worth my time."

Theresa turns on her heel and goes, and I find Lucy has disappeared and been replaced by an unsmiling Avi.

"Don't come near her," he says.

"I was trying to help."

"Your chivalry knows no bounds," he says. "Leave her alone, or I'll—"

"What?" This is none of Avi's business; he's not Lucy's bodyguard, and she doesn't need one, anyway. "You'll kill me?"

"Hell no," he says. "I'm not going to prison for you."

And then he's gone too, and I'm left standing by the trash. Alone, again. A hundred eyes staring, again. I head back to my table. My fries are cold. My friends hate me and my enemies can't even be bothered with that.

"Hello," a voice above me says. Jenny has sidled up to my table, lunch tray in her hands. "May I sit down?"

I nod warily. I nearly got her kicked out of school, so I can't imagine this conversation going well. She sits. "Jenny," I say, because I can guess why she's here. "I am so, so sorry."

She scoffs. "Sorry for yourself."

"Sorry for everything." She shrugs and picks at the cinnamon roll on her tray. "You didn't end up getting in trouble, did you? I heard them send you back to class."

"No, I didn't get in trouble," she says, and relief washes over

305

me. She notices. "And before you start thinking you did me some big favor, maybe consider that telling the truth was the *least* you could do. Absolute bare minimum of human decency."

Ouch. Fair, but ouch. "I know."

"You're not a hero. Don't think you're a hero."

I've never thought that before, and I'm not starting now. "I know."

"As long as that's clear," Jenny says. "Has anyone told you about the news report?"

"No one's really talking to me at all."

"One of the local stations ran a segment last night," she says, tearing off a piece of cinnamon roll. "About Ms. Simon, and the concert, and all those posters you made."

Oh, good. Now the whole tri-county area knows I'm a massive fuckup.

"They didn't say your name or anything. And it was really just a hook to get to the issue of firing teachers under morality clauses. The reporter also contacted a bunch of St. Clare's kids, and they talked about Ms. Simon and why she had to leave. They mentioned my petition, and I got to say something on camera."

Is this the same girl who stumbled through her history report last fall? It's hard to believe. But it is.

Jenny shakes her head. "I know my petition might not do anything. I know Ms. Simon probably won't get her job back. But now people know what happened to her, they know what

St. Clare's did. Maybe they'll think twice before sending their kids here. Maybe they'll ask questions. Maybe St. Clare's will want to change."

That's all I wanted. But is that true? I don't know. If Jenny maybe-believes it, I can, too.

"I hope they do," I say.

"You know what's messed up, though?" Jenny says. "If you hadn't made those posters, this probably wouldn't have made the news. I worked for months and got nowhere. What you did got all the attention, and it wasn't even your fight." She pauses. "But something good did come of it. Despite your best efforts."

"There's a metaphor in there, somewhere," I say.

"Straight white boy destroys everything, world stops to listen?" She pops a piece of cinnamon roll in her mouth. "That's the history of the Western world."

It makes me feel like shit, but she's not wrong.

Jenny gestures at the textbooks I have on the table. "What are you working on?"

"History homework."

"Oh." She pushes her lunch tray aside. "Want me to help you get caught up?"

At least one person at this school doesn't want me dead. Things are going better than expected.

29

BY THE NEXT week, people stop staring. I've comman-
deered the two-person table in the dining hall and bring books
and homework. Occasionally, Jenny joins me. With all the
extra study time, I might pass precalculus. If I get an A, I will
consider the possibility of earthly miracles.

Even my hours helping Father Peter aren't as bad as I
thought. Boring, yes. Monotonous, yes. And if I never have to
fold another program for Sunday Mass, I will die happy. But he
leaves me alone, doesn't lecture me or force me to relive what
I did.

One day, as I'm doing battle with a rusty paper cutter from
1965 and Father Peter is ignoring the fact that I'm losing, Max
walks into the office.

"Hello, Mr. Kim," Father Peter says. "Are you here to pick
up your costume?"

Max's face darkens. "I'm here to pick up my *cloak*, Father."

Father Peter lets that go, pulling the cloak out of his desk's bottom drawer. "I've tried to be lenient," he says, and Max's hands twitch. "But next time, your parents will have to pick it up. Please, leave it at home, like we discussed."

Max nods and accepts the cloak, holding it close to him. "Bye, Michael," he says as he leaves.

"Bye."

I turn back to the paper cutter, but I can feel Father Peter watching me. "Are you two friends?" he asks.

"Sort of." Once fellow secret society members, now just sort-of friends. A sort-of friend can still stand up for another, though. I turn to face Father Peter. "He calls it a cloak. Not a costume."

I expect him to ignore that, or to tell me to focus on the paper cutter that's so close to claiming one of my thumbs. He tilts his head. "Do you think I'm being unfair?"

The correct answer is "no." The correct answer is "I just got off suspension for things I did because I thought you were unfair, so maybe I don't have the best judgment."

"The cloak's important to him," I say.

Father Peter nods. "But the dress code doesn't include cloaks. If I let him wear it, wouldn't I be treating him differently than the rest of you? And wouldn't that be unfair?"

I want to say no, out of principle, but I stop. I think. I feel a spark, deep in the pit of my stomach. A spark of an idea, an argument. Not a smashing-glass rage of an argument, but something better, a reason. "I think you're already treating him differently than the rest of us."

And again, I expect him to stop the discussion. "How so?" he asks.

I pause and let the words become clearer and crisper in my head. "A cloak is an article of outerwear. Right?"

Father Peter nods.

"And in the dress code, outerwear like coats and jackets don't have to be from the uniform company, right?"

"No," Father Peter concedes. "But coats aren't worn in classrooms, or during PE—"

"But they *can* be worn in the hallways, during passing period; they can be worn before and after school on school grounds, which is basically what Max is already doing."

He stares at me, his pale eyes boring into me like they did on Ash Wednesday, but what's behind them is different. He goes back to his computer. "I'll think about it."

The next day, Max struts down the hall in his cloak, a canary-colored note on Father Peter's personal stationery held tightly in his fist.

When I get to the dining hall, Max and Eden are waiting for me outside. Max has safety-pinned the note to his cloak.

"Was it you?" Eden asks. "Did you convince Father Peter to let him wear the cloak?"

I'd thought about telling them, right after the conversation in Father Peter's office. I thought about texting Max, letting him know what I'd said. But then I thought, who would that be for? Max, or me? I didn't want him to think I had an agenda or I'd done it to get back in the group's good graces. *Be careful not to practice your righteousness in front of others, in order to be seen by them.*

"I don't know," I say truthfully, because who knows why Father Peter did what he did?

"Come on," Eden says. "Max sees you in the office and the next day he changes his mind?"

"Also Father Peter told me it was you," Max says, bundled in his cloak like baby Jesus in the manger.

"I'm glad he's letting you wear it," I tell Max, and start to walk past them, trying so hard not to hope they'll forgive me, because that's not why I did it.

"Wait, Michael," Eden calls. I stop. So does my heart. I turn around. "We saved you a seat."

I eat lunch with Eden and Max every day that week, and they fill me in on everything I missed while I was suspended. Before I even got to school on Ash Wednesday, Lucy went down to the HA room and spirited away the club charter—the one we all signed. This horrifies me. She could so easily have been caught. No one's been down to the HA room since.

"I don't think we can ever go back," Eden tells me, sending fresh ripples of self-loathing through my veins. She's right. Nothing will ever be the way it was before.

"How's Lucy doing?" I ask them. Eden and Max share a look.

"We haven't really been talking all that much," Eden says carefully.

"Because you didn't want to look suspicious?" I ask.

"Yeah," Max says. "But also—I don't think Avi wants to. Especially since we started talking to you again."

Ouch. Understandable, but ouch.

"This has been hard for Lucy," Eden says. "When she's hurt, she hides. Honestly, I think she wishes Avi would leave her alone, too."

The first day I was on suspension, Father Peter held an all-school assembly and announced that the person behind HA had been caught and had apologized for what he'd done. I think this is a very liberal interpretation of what I actually said, but whatever.

"Father Peter said this was an 'opportunity to heal,'" Max says. "Like we cut everyone open, or something."

In some way, I think we did. What I did—what Heretics Anonymous did, ever since the video—opened people up. It wasn't a clean cut, but we saw what was inside everyone. I get why Father Peter thinks that was bad, but there was good there, too. Just like Jenny said.

Nothing can be the way it was before. But that doesn't mean it can't be repaired.

With Eden and Max back in my corner, I turn my focus to Lucy. I think Avi will follow Lucy's lead, but Eden is skeptical.

"He's a grudge holder," Eden says. "Lucy—she's not, but

what you said at her house . . . I don't know."

For the next couple weeks, I give Lucy space. Even after Dad gives me back my phone, I don't text her, though she probably blocked my number. I don't approach her in history, though she jumps out of her desk the second the bell rings and is out the door before I even think the words "I'm sorry."

She seems determined to avoid me, and I've let her, but on a cold day in March, I decide to break that streak, because I have to. It's her birthday.

"I want it on record I don't think this will work," Eden says as we eat lunch that day. She jabs at her roasted carrots as Max and I share pork dumplings he brought from home. "And if she asks, I had nothing to do with this. Nothing. Got it?"

I nod, nudging my backpack with my foot to make sure it's still there. Inside is Lucy's present, wrapped up carefully and tied with a bright red ribbon. Eden, who knows Lucy's locker combo, will secretly place the present in the locker, where Lucy will find it, and forgive me, and stirring music will play as the credits roll.

I hand the package over to Eden, trying to block it from Lucy's view on the other side of the dining hall. Not that she's looking.

"It's a weird shape," Eden says, examining it.

"You have to keep it upright," I tell her. "Or it's going to be a huge mess."

"Is it ice cream?" Max asks. "Because Lucy is lactose

intolerant, so I don't think you should get her ice cream."

Eden tucks the package carefully into her bag. "No, she's not. She just didn't want to eat those cheese curds you brought from Minnesota."

Max looks stricken. "But they're so good! Did you know if you feed cheese curds to rats they gain the ability to digest beer?"

I check my watch for the eighth time in two minutes. Lunch is nearly over, and Lucy hasn't stopped by her locker yet. She always makes a stop before theology, because that textbook's a monster, so where is she?

She appears in a flash of skirt and ribbon, thankfully without Avi by her side. She undoes the combination lock, and my heart pounds with every click and turn, and then it drops into my guts as she yanks the lock down and off. She stares inside the locker. Pulls out the package. She looks left and right, and I dive back behind the hallway corner. I count to five, slowly, and by the time I look around the corner again, she's got it unwrapped. In her arms, she cradles a small pot of flowers in full bloom. Hellebore.

"Lenten roses!" the woman at the flower nursery said as she rang them up yesterday. "Don't they bloom so nicely this time of year?"

A couple of the flowers are dented from the wrapping paper, but they're vibrant and bright, and look brighter in her arms.

It's not enough to replace all the flowers she lost, not enough to make up for the storm and her mom and the things I said, but it's a start.

Lucy stares down at them and gently fingers a petal. She snaps her head up more quickly than I can react, and then she's staring at me, holding the flowers, trying not to cry. I stare back. She shoves the flowers in her locker and walks off, forgetting her theology book and leaving me and an open locker in her wake.

30

LUCY SKIPS THEOLOGY. I catch Avi glaring at me, like he knows I'm responsible for this, like I'm responsible for everything else. I try to focus on Sister Helen and her lesson, but my notebook stays blank and my mind stays stuck on Lucy at her locker, Lucy who hasn't forgiven me, Lucy who rejected the flowers.

Eden was right, this never had a chance. I thought it was the perfect gift—something to replace what she lost, something to show I was still thinking of that day, something she couldn't get herself, not without a car. And it still wasn't enough.

The topic of Sister Helen's lecture is the change between the covenants of the Old Testament and those of the New. I admit, the whole thing's more interesting now that I've skimmed Leviticus and read all the hyper-specific laws for myself, but the intricacies of animal sacrifice are starting to make me feel sick.

"As you can see," Sister Helen says, "much of ancient Israelite worship revolved around the idea of sacrifice, from food to animals, a holdover from older practices. During Christ's life, Jewish people still made 'burnt offerings' of goats and sheep at their temples." She turns to the board and writes HOSEA 6:6. "But even before Christ, a shift was being made. In Hosea, God says, 'I desire mercy, not sacrifice,' and Christ himself repeats this scripture in the Gospels."

I desire mercy, not sacrifice.

I remember this line, and I remember Lucy wrote that for mercy, you could also read loyalty or love. I desire mercy, not sacrifice. What I gave to Lucy was a sacrifice, not burnt and bloodied like a slaughtered cow, but a sacrifice. I said, "Here, take a gift in exchange for the pain I've caused you, take a bought thing in exchange for the hurt in your heart." Lucy, like her God, desires mercy, loyalty, love. She doesn't want my burnt offering.

There are tears threatening the corners of my eyes, frustration curling my fingers, and a touch of anger hunching my shoulders, because there is nothing I can do. I can't make Lucy talk to me again, can't make her see me the way she once did. The anger's growing stronger, because why not? Why can't my offering, my sacrifice be enough? Why won't she forgive me, why won't she plant the flowers or say my name? I've done all I can do, apologized and paid for what I did. Her Bible, the book she lives her life by, says you're supposed to forgive someone who has wronged you seventy-seven times over. So why won't she?

But then—it also says no person can be forgiven until they first forgive. I forgave Dad for dragging me here. I'm starting to forgive Father Peter and everyone at St. Clare's for the things they've done. But maybe I'm still not done, maybe it's easier to forgive some people than others. Maybe I haven't forgiven Lucy.

I have to forgive Lucy for not forgiving me. I have to let her go.

The chapel is different when it's empty. During Mass, with a hundred kids and teachers shifting and rustling their hymnals and the terrible organ bleating, it feels awake and alive.

Empty, it feels more like a museum, silent and cavernous, light reflecting off stained-glass windows and onto the altar, bare and warm. The world outside might as well not even exist. There is nothing but silence and space.

I sit in the front pew, the same one I sat in on Ash Wednesday, and can still feel the slick coldness of the ashes on my forehead. I don't know why I'm here, other than school's over and I don't want to go home yet. At home, there's Mom and Sophia and Dad now too, but there's no silence. I want silence, for a minute.

"Are you all right?"

Sister Helen stands a few pews back, some books in her arms.

"Yeah," I say, but it comes out as a whisper. I clear my throat. "Yes. Sorry, Sister, I can go."

"No, no, stay as long as you like. I was putting some hymnals away." She deposits them in a pew and makes her way down the aisle, lowering herself into the pew next to me. "It's nice like this, isn't it? Quiet."

I nod, but then feel like I should explain, like I have to be clear. "I'm not a—I mean, I don't believe in any of this, or—"

Sister Helen waves her hand. "I've been in Egyptian mosques, in Buddhist temples, in beautiful synagogues in Warsaw and Jerusalem. I don't need to believe in Buddha or wear a Star of David to find peace there."

Peace. I want that, but I don't know if I'll find it here.

"Believe in what you like," she says. "But there is a place for you, here."

That's what Lucy said, the first day I met her. *There's room for people like us.*

"You know, there's a long tradition of challenging authority within Catholic history," Sister Helen continues. "Rebels and revolutionaries have always been part of the church."

"Yeah," I say. "But don't they usually get burned at the stake?"

She laughs. "Thankfully, the church has evolved on that front. And it will keep evolving."

"Not fast enough," I say, thinking of Ms. Simon and her wife. Of Lucy, who will never be a priest.

"Very slowly," Sister Helen agrees. "Just like real evolution. It took millions of years for *Homo habilis* to become *Homo sapiens*, but I don't think it will take quite that long for the church."

I stare at her. "You believe in evolution?"

"I have a degree in human genetics, so I think I'd better."

I don't know why I assumed she wouldn't, just like I assumed she didn't have a degree in anything but Jesus. What else don't I know about her, about Father Peter, about Sister Joseph Marie? About everyone?

I focus back on the altar, decked in dark, somber purple for Lent, and listen as Sister Helen shuffles slowly back up the aisle to the chapel doors. I expect to hear the heavy wooden doors shut but instead hear someone coming back down the aisle. Did Sister Helen forget something? No, it's not her labored, heavy walk, but footsteps crisp and quick.

Lucy.

I feel her before she's there, before she does her half bow and crosses herself in front of the altar, before she takes a seat in the pew across the aisle. We sit in silence. She's come for a reason, and I'll let her take her time. She stares at the altar, at the hemorrhaging Jesus in front of us, anywhere but at me.

"Max told me he saw you come in here," she says. "I thought he was kidding. I looked everywhere for you—literally, everywhere—before I came here."

The thought of Lucy searching for me swells my heart and brightens the fluttering, fragile bit of hope I have left.

"Is this, like, a *ploy*?" she asks. "Did you come here so I'd think you were sorry, you were different? Do you want me to believe you're religious now?"

"I'm still me," I say. This is the closest she's been to me in days, weeks. I don't even care that she thinks I'm playing her. "But I *am* sorry. So, so ungodly sorry."

She gives me a quick glance, then focuses on the altar. "And the flowers? That's because you're sorry, too?"

"Yes."

"And you chose to apologize by breaking into my locker?"

"I didn't know when else you'd get more."

"What?"

"The closest flower nursery's a half hour away. You'd need a car."

Lucy looks at me then, full on, her brown eyes battling something. "That was . . . nice of you." She shuts her eyes. "God, I don't want to be mad at you anymore!"

I didn't know there was a fifty-pound anvil on my chest. I didn't even know until this second, when it lifted.

"Well," I say, and my voice sounds squeaky. "I don't want you to be mad at me, either?"

"But I am," she says. "I am and I'm not sure if I ever won't be. Avi says I should never talk to you again, but I don't want that, but I don't know what I do want, and I *don't know why you're in this chapel!*"

I get up and slowly move across the aisle to sit next to her, leaving space between us. She doesn't ask me to leave. I wait for a moment, then say what I've wanted to for weeks, possibly forever.

"I do not believe in God," I start off.

"I had no idea."

"Hear me out. I do not believe in God, I do not believe in heaven or hell or in aliens, honestly, but I can believe in what I see and feel on earth, and I've felt . . ."

What have I felt, in the last six months? Joy, and despair, and rage, and love, I think. And more, threads in my veins and surges in my blood that can't be described.

"I don't have a God," I continue, "and I don't have a religion. But I do have a church. I do have a place that makes me safe and protected and known, like you said about Easter Mass when you were a kid. I have a place I feel known."

Her lips part a little, and I think she knows what I'm about to say.

"It's you," I finish. "You're my church."

Lucy stares at me. She shakes her head like a dog clearing water out of its ears. "No. You can't do that to me; I can't *be* that. I'm a person, I need to make mistakes, too. I can't be God."

"I didn't say God," I remind her, "I said church. God is perfect and infallible, right?"

She nods.

"The church does its best to interpret, to pass down what's

good, to shine a light and be a safe haven, right? But the church can make mistakes, and it has, yours especially. You can make mistakes, you can be human, but—you're still the greatest good I've ever known."

I grab her hand then, because it feels right. She puts her other hand on top of mine, and we're layered, skin on skin on skin, until Lucy says: "Let me guess. Your new religion encourages forgiveness?"

"It's a major tenet."

She chews on her lip. "That's the thing about brand-new religions. They need structure. For Catholics, confessing your sins and doing penance to receive forgiveness is a sacrament. It *means* something."

"Okay," I say. "So let's do it."

"What?"

"Let's do it. I'll do it, right now."

She looks confused. "The priests do confession on Saturdays; you'd have to come back."

"I'm not Catholic. I don't care about priests, or God. I don't need their forgiveness. I need yours."

I grab her hand and pull her up. She squeaks in surprise but doesn't protest as I lead her to the back-right corner of the chapel.

"You've got to be kidding," she says, looking at the empty confessional.

"Never been more serious. Which side is for the priest?" She points, and I open the door to the opposite side and climb in. She stands there, unmoving.

"Come on," I say. "Every future priest needs practice."

Lucy cracks a smile but still stares at the door. I know this will be the only time Lucy sits on that side of a confession booth. She knows it, too. She opens the priest-side door and climbs inside.

It's stuffy and dark with both sides shut, tiny beams of light shining through the crosshatching in the doors and the grate that separates us.

"I've never done this before," I remind her. "You have to tell me what to say."

She clears her throat. "You say, 'Forgive me, Father, for I have sinned.'"

"Forgive me, Lucy," I say. "For I have sinned."

"Then, you talk about what you did. Who it hurt. Why it was wrong."

So I do. I start from the moment Lucy left my house with her viola. I tell her about dinner, about going to find her, about hanging the posters and regretting it instantly. I tell her about what I said to my dad, what he told me about his life, even though they aren't sins against her. I tell her about how it felt to eat lunch alone, how it felt to watch her hurt and know it was no one's fault but mine.

When I'm done, we're both quiet. In a small, forceful voice, Lucy gives her next instructions. "This is the part where the priest gives penance. Like saying so many Our Fathers or Rosaries."

"Please, no Rosaries. Have mercy."

"No Rosaries," she agrees. "I want you to apologize to Eden and Max and Avi, like you apologized to me. Same level of detail, everything. I want you to drive me to the nursery and help me plant new flowers. And I want you to come with me to Easter Mass."

"Is that all?" I say, not quite believing I got off so easy.

"No," she says. "I want you to promise you'll never, *ever* do something like that to me again."

"I promise."

"Then go and sin no more."

"The woman caught in adultery!" I say, because I know that line.

"I—what?" Lucy says.

"Go and sin no more, Jesus says that to the woman caught in adultery, and *you* said it was a doubly important passage because Jesus didn't explicitly reject the Old Testament laws that condemned her to death, but he still convinced her accusers to let her live, and some translations—"

"Oh my God," she interrupts, sounding breathless through the grate, sounding like she's smiling. "You read my Bible."

"Yep," I say. "So I know there's a commandment about taking the Lord's name in vain."

But she never even hears me, because she leaps out of the

priest's booth, flings open the penitent door, and kisses me, longer and harder than she ever has. And when she kisses me, there is no confessional, there is no altar or chapel, no fear or hurt, sins or forgiveness. There is only us, wrapped up in a moment and in each other.

I don't believe in God, but that doesn't mean I believe in nothing.

I believe in love. I believe in the love Lucy shows me, the kind I'll try hard to give back to her in full. I believe in things I can't put into words, but things I know to be true.

I believe in us. I believe in this.

Amen.

ACKNOWLEDGMENTS

Saint Ambrose once said, "No duty is more urgent than that of returning thanks." And while he had some unfortunate opinions on heretics, I think he was right about gratitude. So let me start by returning thanks to my childhood church, Newman Hall–Holy Spirit Parish of Berkeley, California. Thank you for showing me the best of what religion can be. Sorry about the cannibalism joke in chapter five.

All the gratitude in the world to my agent, Sarah LaPolla, who first encountered this book in its infancy and expertly guided it through its awkward, adjective-heavy adolescence. Thank you for seeing what this book could become, even when I couldn't.

Thank you to my amazing editor, Ben Rosenthal, for championing this book from the beginning. Your enthusiasm was infectious and your insights were invaluable. I'm forever in your debt. Thank you to Mabel Hsu, David Curtis, and the entire

Katherine Tegen Books team for all your hard work—and of course, to Katherine Tegen herself. Thank you for believing in this book.

To my writers group—Brian, Emily, Michelle, Siena—thank you for all the snacks, book recs, and endlessly helpful notes. Thank you also to the Electric 18s and the Class of 2k18. I feel so lucky to have shared my debut year with such talented people.

Thank you to all my writing teachers over the years, especially Doug Zesiger, Myla Churchill, Kate McKean, Deloss Brown, and Matt Carton. Eternal thanks and gratitude to Chris Malcomb, the first person who made me believe I could be a *real* writer. I wish you could have seen this.

All my love to Rob. Thank you for every single conversation about medieval history, depressing cartoons, and weird hagiographies. Most of all, thank you for sharing your life with me. On our first date, you admitted to not really liking young adult fiction. Four years later, you've celebrated every little victory by my side, talked me through my toughest moments, and even read a YA book or two. So I guess the joke's on you, buddy.

Thank you to my large, loud, loving family, new and old, biological and chosen. If I named every one of you, this would go on for pages, but I hope you know who you are. Special thanks to Carrie, for bursting into tears when she heard this book would be published. A lifetime of hugs to Leah, my brilliant, precious sibling and the bravest person I've ever met.

And finally, thank you to my parents, for supporting my writing career every step of the way and without any hesitation. This book would not exist without you, and not just because you literally gave me life. This book would not exist without you because without your unwavering love and encouragement, I never would have been brave enough to write it. Mom and Dad, I can't thank you enough, but I'll try anyway.

Thank you. Thank you. Thank you.

Turn the page for a sneak peek at Katie Henry's

LET'S CALL IT A DOOMSDAY

An engrossing contemporary tale tackling faith, friendship,

family, and the impending apocalypse (maybe).

ONE

HERE IS ONE way the world could end:

In a peaceful corner of northwest Wyoming, under the feet of park rangers, herds of deer, and thousands of tourists to Yellowstone National Park, lies a giant reservoir of burning, deadly magma called the Yellowstone Caldera. First, there would be earthquakes, the kind you can't sleep through. Then would come the supereruption, a rare seismic event. Rare, but possible. Rare, but overdue. The park would be a lake of lava, but the real problem would be the ash, which would blanket the entire United States, coast to coast. In the Rockies, the ash would crush buildings, devastate crops, suffocate animals and people. Even a few inches would make national highways impassable, ruin farms, shut down air travel. Life as we know it would be over. The entire planet would grow colder.

Here is another way the world could end: I could fail my driving test for a third time.

"Twice isn't even that many times to fail. Two times, that's all, and my parents look at me like I've murdered something. Something cute. And fuzzy." I take a breath. "There are bigger problems in the world than me not being able to drive my sister to ballet. Millions of people don't have clean drinking water. Two-thirds of the animals on Earth might be dead in five years, did you know that? And at any time—*any time*—a gamma-ray burst could destroy the ozone layer and kill us all."

"Could we bring this conversation back to you?" Martha asks.

We're not actually having a conversation. She's a therapist and I'm a client, and even though her office is made to look like someone's living room, we're not doing this for fun.

"Sure," I say. "Forget the world, *I* could have bigger problems than not being able to drive. I could be an alcoholic. I could be a shoplifter. I could be selling my dad's muscle relaxants in the park across from school, did they think about that?"

"Do you think there are some fears wrapped up in this experience?"

"It's not irrational to be scared of driving. It's the most dangerous everyday activity."

"It's good to take safety seriously," Martha concedes. "And I know I've said this before, but fear can be a very useful tool. Everyone experiences fear, and there's a good reason for that. It helps us identify danger. It helps us survive."

"Yeah, exactly, we should all be *more* scared."

"But sometimes, people experience fear that's constant, or very intense, or out of proportion to the situation," Martha adds gently. "And when fear keeps you from living your life freely, that's when it has to be addressed. Not eliminated completely. Just managed."

"My mom says I can't go to college if I don't know how to drive," I say. "Like it's the equivalent of a high school diploma. And I'm not getting that for almost two more years, so what's her rush?"

"It sounds like you're feeling a lot of pressure."

"For no good reason! I can take the bus to school, I can walk to church and your office and the library, I can get on BART if I want to go to San Francisco. I'm fine." I pause. "People are too dependent on cars. Like, sure, if a geomagnetic storm destroyed the electricity grid and society collapsed, you could use a car to get somewhere safer—"

Martha clears her throat. I keep going.

"—but we live in a city; the freeways would pile up. And gas expires, it oxidizes, so all the cars would be rusted from the inside out, anyway. You can't count on cars."

"Do you think this is a worthwhile thought pattern, Ellis?"

Is anything you do worthwhile, Ellis?

I shake my head.

"Let's talk about what happened during the driving test."

"Nothing happened."

"What do you mean?"

3

"I sat in the DMV parking lot with the . . . driving evaluator, or whatever—and *nothing happened*." I pause. "Because I couldn't turn the car on."

Martha tilts her head. "Couldn't?"

I've only been seeing her for a few weeks, but I know what it means when she repeats a word I've said. It's like when you insert your card at the train station and the turnstile spits it back out. Try again. She's looking for me to say *wouldn't* or *didn't want to* in place of *couldn't*. But I really couldn't. I had my finger on the button and my foot on the brake but my brain was already out of the parking lot and on Claremont Avenue, calculating exactly what would go wrong.

> *You could hit a pedestrian.*
>
> *You could hit an elderly pedestrian.*
>
> *You could hit a child pedestrian.*
>
> *You could hit an elderly pedestrian carrying a child pedestrian and get arrested for manslaughter and your parents will have to pay restitution to the elderly/child victims and you'll never go to college because of your horrible guilt and will instead live in the basement for the rest of your life and befriend the rats.*

Alternatively, I could humiliate myself in front of a DMV employee. At least I've got a road map for that.

"What feelings are coming up, right now?"

I shrug. "I'm fine."

"'Fine' is not a feeling."

"Is 'annoyed' a feeling?"

She smiles. "Yes. Is that what you're feeling about your driving test?"

"It's not a big deal to me. So I guess I'm annoyed it's such a big deal to other people."

"That's understandable." Martha pushes a dark, springy ringlet back from her face. "Is this something you've experienced before? Or is this a new feeling?"

For someone so serene and unflappable, she talks about feelings a lot. Never hers, though. Only mine.

"It's not new." I hesitate. "It's actually kind of constant."

"Tell me about that."

I slump back on the couch. The more information you dredge up and vomit out to someone, the more they seem to want.

> *Is it really that horrible to have someone listen to you? Your parents are paying for this. You're wasting their money.*

"Everything my mom and dad think is important, I don't want anything to do with. They want me to get my license. They want me to be in AP classes. They want me to hang out with girls from church more. I don't care about the things they care about. I just don't."

> *Not only are you wasting your parents' money, you're using it to talk crap about them.*

"It goes the other way, too," I say, trying to seem like less of a jerk. "They don't care about what I care about, either." I pause. "They don't *want* me to care about the things I care about."

"Can you give me an example?"

I give her a look like, *Come on*. She smiles. She waits.

"Like disaster preparedness," I say. "Like the end of the world as we know it."

"Where do you think your interest in survivalism comes from?" she asks.

I shake my head. "I'm not a survivalist."

"Oh?"

"Survivalists have skill sets. Hunting and fishing and living off the land, and I can't do any of that. I'm a prepper. I have supplies, not skills. Or, I would have supplies, except my mom told all my relatives they can't give me gift cards anymore because I'll spend them on 'bizarre internet stuff,' as if she won't appreciate properly filtered water you don't even have to boil first."

"Okay," Martha says. "Prepping. Where do you think your interest in prepping comes from?"

My palms itch. I try to put my hands in the pockets of my cardigan, but they don't fit. I take them out.

"Do you know," I ask Martha, "where the word *interest* comes from?"

"Where it comes from?"

"The history of the word. Its etymology." She shakes her head. "It's Latin, if you go back far enough. The noun form of *interesse*, which means, literally, 'to be between.' It was more a legal term, though, not like we think of it now."

"It's impressive you remember all that."

"Well, I wrote it down," I say. "I can remember anything if I write it down."

Absentmindedly, I touch the front pocket of my backpack. That's where my notebook is. Kenny #14. The first Kenny was an eggshell-blue diary from Deseret Books, a gift from my aunt on my ninth birthday. My mom suggested I name it. I chose Kenny. She hated that so much I stuck with it for thirteen more notebooks.

Martha shifts in her chair. "How much progress have you made in your workbook?"

I've made exactly no progress in *Stress Free and Happy to Be Me* because I buried it in my sock drawer the first day I got it.

"The workbook is one tool," she says. "It's designed to give you strategies for situations like your driving test. When you feel overwhelmed, or anxious."

Hearing that word always makes my throat tight. I'm not in denial, I know it's what I am. Martha was the first person to say it like a diagnosis, not just as an adjective. All the diplomas on Martha's office walls—Howard University, Smith College, UC Berkeley—only make it feel more official. Generalized anxiety disorder. It's not the word itself, it's what people mean when they use it.

"But maybe it's not the right tool for you," she admits. "I'd like to give you an assignment for this week."

"Okay."

"You've probably written down some facts about how the world could end. Or change drastically. Yes?"

I nod again.

"Have you looked up any of the times people thought the world would end, and then it didn't?"

No. Those people were wrong, whoever they were, whenever they were. Why would I care about things that didn't happen? I shake my head.

"This week, I'd like you to look up some end-of-the-world predictions that didn't come true. They can be from last year, they can be from a thousand years ago."

I can do research in my sleep. "So you want a list, or—?"

"Go deeper than that. Look at what happened to those people afterward. When the world kept going, what did they do? What changed in their lives, and what didn't? How did they move on?" She looks at her watch. "And then next session, we can talk about it. Sound good?"

If it means the workbook can stay buried in my sock drawer, it sounds great. I nod.

"Wonderful." She glances at her watch. "Our time's about up for today."

I grab my backpack. Martha opens the door for me.

"Have a good week," she says. "And try not to focus too much on the driving test, okay?"

But as I walk past the other offices and the eternally wilted potted plant at the end of the hallway, that's all I can think about. Me at the wheel of a car, and all the things that could go wrong. Martha calls this "catastrophizing."

> *You could hit the gas instead of the brake. You could run over a kindergarten teacher or a volunteer firefighter or the Dalai Lama.*

Never mind that the Dalai Lama doesn't even live here.

> *What if he was giving a lecture at UC Berkeley and you murdered him, what then? It's possible. Anything terrible is possible.*

When I walk into the waiting room, I expect to see the little redheaded boy who sees Martha right after me. He's usually here when I get out, destroying a *Highlights* magazine and demanding more Goldfish from his exhausted mom. I've taken to calling him the Red Demon.

> *You're a horrible person. He's a child.*

He did whip a Tonka truck at my face once.

> *And everyone still likes him better than they like you.*

But the only person in the waiting room today is a teenage girl, sitting cross-legged in one of the armless wooden chairs, her eyes closed.

I shouldn't stare. Emily Post may not have written about therapy, but some things are unspoken. You ignore the other people in the waiting room. You do not make small talk. You keep walking when a maladjusted third grader hurls a toy at you, though it is permissible to step on his bag of Goldfish in revenge.

I shouldn't stare at this girl and her loose, long, wavy hair, the color of an old penny. And scraggly at the tips, like it hasn't been cut in a while. She's in faded jeans and a navy hoodie that's way too big for her. It engulfs her torso and hides her hands. Her feet are tucked under her legs. I wonder if she's even wearing shoes.

And as I'm standing there, staring, the girl in blue opens her eyes.

I squeak and stumble back.

She smiles, big and broad, like we're best friends reunited. "Hi," she says, and the way she says it, it's clear she remembers me, even if I can't remember her.

"I'm sorry," I say, and don't even know for what. For staring at her? For forgetting her name? "Do we—how do I know you?"

She tilts her head. "You don't know me," she says. "Not yet."

This is how serial-killer shows start. In five network-TV minutes, a grizzled detective is going to find my corpse by a drainage pipe, strangled with a navy blue sweatshirt.

The girl's still smiling. It's like she doesn't even know I'm internally debating whether she's a criminal mastermind. I have to say something. Anything. Anything not about murder.

I clear my throat. "Um. What?"

She opens her mouth, but closes it fast as we hear high heels clipping down the hallway. Martha appears in the waiting door almost inhumanly fast. She looks at the girl in blue, then at me. Her serene mask, the nonjudgmental face she wears in our sessions, vanishes. Only for a second.

Martha looks back at the girl in blue. "You're very early." She pauses, awkwardly, like she swallowed a word.

The girl gets to her feet. She is, in fact, wearing shoes. "I walked, and it didn't take as long as I thought it would."

"We'll start now," she says to the girl. She flicks her eyes to me. "See you next week."

Martha starts to usher the girl through the door. The girl glances back at me as she goes. "See you sooner than that."

She grins. Martha shuts the door behind them. I stand in the empty waiting room alone.

If we were in a session, Martha would ask me to name what I'm feeling right now. It's easier to do inside my head than out loud.

Confused. Intrigued. Nervous, as always.

I can name Martha's feelings, too, the ones on her face when the mask dropped. Surprised. Wary. Maybe even scared.

I can't do that for the girl in blue, because I don't know her.

I don't know her, but I think I will.

Thoughtful and witty contemporary novels from

KATIE HENRY

Don't miss these entertaining tales!